PALAWAN PASSAGE

a novel

LAMBERT BLOCK

Library of Congress Registration Number: TXu000805660

Paperback ISBN #: 978-1-7325328-0-9
Kindle eBook ISBN #: 978-1-7325328-1-6
ePub eBook ISBN #: 978-1-7325328-2-3

Printed in the United States of America

Interior Design: CreativePublishingBookDesign.com
Cover Design: Kit Foster Design

PALAWAN PASSAGE

To Lucy

May our voyage together never end

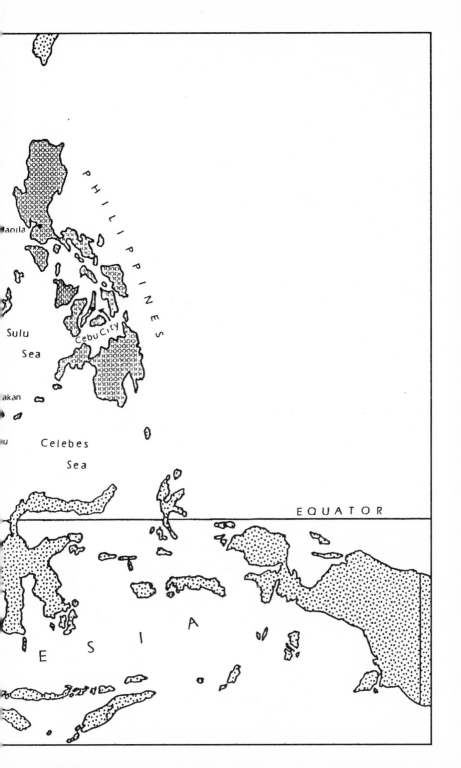

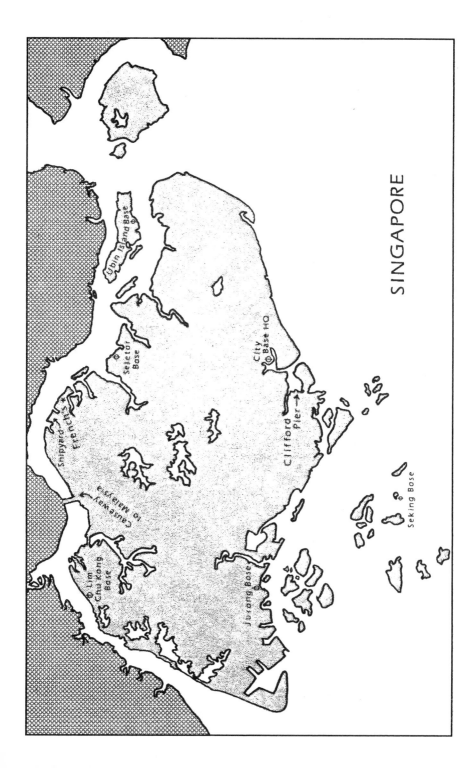

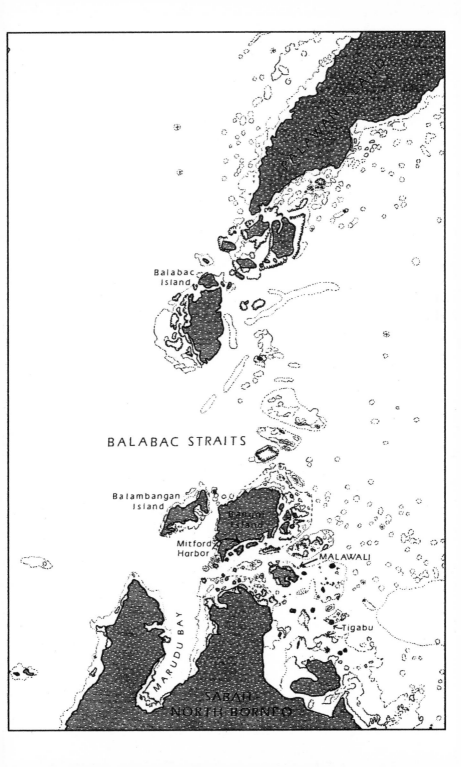

CHAPTER ONE

My descent into Singapore began somewhere out in the South China Sea. I can't say exactly where it began because the airline pilot chose to fly the entire Manila to Singapore route just above the stratus layer, and the cloud cover wrecked everything. I'm no complainer, don't get me wrong, but to me this flight is a reconnaissance run whenever I'm aboard — six times so far in '79, not counting my return flights. I carry aerial maps and even some photos to help me with my view. So you see I suffer when I can't look down; that's just the way it is.

The South China Sea is a battleground unlike any other. There are typhoons in the north, rebels in the south, a raft of shipwrecked refugees to the west, and a civil war in the east. Add to this the conflict in the Spratley Islands, where four different countries claim simultaneous sovereignty on an almost submerged chain of sandbars, and you've just been introduced. I am Kim Barnaby, the man with his nose to the window.

I felt cheated. It would be another two months before I would be back here, and the clouds just kept on coming. I was slumped in my seat, having long since lost patience with the pilot and the clouds when the whining sound of lowering flaps suddenly brought me to. Up ahead I could see the Malaysian mainland coming on and down below the shipping lanes that lead to Singapore.

I began to strain the limits of my vision now, hoping to pick up on a landmark that would tell me which approach path we had been assigned. The summer months have always put my flight's downwind leg exactly where I want it, but come October, the winds back down to nothing, and the tower can put us anywhere. I would like to see us enter our downwind approach above the north shore, following the river-like strip of water that separates the island of Singapore from the Malaysian Peninsula. At a point just above the Johor Causeway, the landing gear would begin to growl and the left wing would lower. If I got the approach I wanted, the entire left side of the plane would get a perfect view of the Sembawang Shipyard and just beyond it my floating home, the forty-three-foot sloop I call *Windigo*.

"Well, I've missed it again," I whispered to myself while making the seat belt tight. I could feel the anxiety build within me, knowing my month away might have brought any number of calamities into my life. Was *Windigo* still afloat? Had she broken her moorings and simply drifted away? Had she been stolen? I had no way of knowing until I could see her. And since the left wing dipped just as we came over land, and well before the causeway, I knew it would be hours before I could lay my worries to rest.

The pilot had swung down to the south above the huge ship anchorage that lies along the southern shore. Beneath us were hundreds of anchored freighters and tankers all riding to the tide in perfect formation. Along the edges, transiting ships sent "v" shaped wakes over a glassy calm sea. Island sailing schooners sat motionless in the tide, their sails stretching for wind that wasn't there. The business of high-seas transportation was everywhere the eye could see. The right side wing dipped, and we turned onto our final approach.

The sound of screeching rubber ended the fifth work cycle in my year's contract with the Placid Oil Co., and I had the coming month at home in Singapore to make up my mind about renewing my contract for another year's work aboard their flagship, the *Penrod 76*. As always, I would choose a life aboard *Windigo* above all else, but at this point nobody was asking me to choose between my two homes. Placid Oil simply wanted me to let them know if I'd be back for another year's work after the Christmas break. It seemed simple enough at the time, but then, that's what this story is all about.

The *Penrod 76* is nothing like any of the ships we had just flown over. In fact, it's debatable if she is a ship at all. She wears her name on the stern like a proper ship, and she has red and green running lights, but that's where the similarities end. The *Penrod* was designed to move up and down above the water's surface, not to travel across it. Stripped to its essentials, it's nothing but a huge work platform built to stand high above two very primitive submarines. You could call it a type of catamaran because it does have two separate hulls, but in reality it defies a traditional nautical description. The Ship's Registry had to make up a new category for vessels like the *Penrod*. They call them semi-submersibles, and they are a marine engineering marvel for the offshore oil exploration business. The new ones, like the *Penrod,* can hold position almost indefinitely while drilling in depths 1500 feet above the sea floor. They are the biggest and most expensive treasure hunting ships ever built.

I work aboard the *Penrod* for a month at a time. When the second shift comes aboard, I return to my boat. In the beginning this meant nothing more than riding the service boat into town and boarding *Windigo*. A year ago the town was Cebu City on the island of Cebu in the central Philippines.

Long before the *Penrod*'s arrival, I had become part of Cebu City's waterfront scene with *Windigo* riding at anchor just off the San Miguel Brewery's wharf. My 43-foot sloop was way out of her element sitting in a fleet of tired island freighters and local fishing boats, but in time my comings and goings drew less and less attention. Apart from tending to my boat, I spent my days exchanging correspondence with a handful of shell collectors who are scattered across the U.S. and Canada. Cebu and her close island neighbor, Mactan Island, are the current world headquarters for specimen quality seashell harvesting and exports. I run a one-man mail order business exporting specimen quality seashells to collectors throughout North America. My clients are generally quite dedicated collectors with specialized interests. As their collections become redundant with easily collected species they find they need a personal representative at the wholesale marketplace. I am their representative, and they are my clients. It's that simple. My specialty is in the dwarf and juvenile varieties. Not only are they the hardest to come by, but also their size allows me to stock a good inventory aboard *Windigo*. I always send out more than what is requested, and I seldom get returns. It's a sleek business.

I could have continued this trade for quite a while had my life not been so continuously interrupted by a constant parade of life-threatening natural disasters. The Philippines attract typhoons like a magnet, and with the exception of the months of January and February, there always seems to be at least one brewing. There are about twenty typhoons recorded in the western portion of the North Pacific each year, and almost all of them threaten the Philippines at one point in their lives. Maybe half of the twenty actually enter the Philippines, and of those there are usually two that totally devastate the place. I've watched a couple of big ones pass just north of here and learned that Cebu's so-called harbor is much too large to shelter my sailboat from anything like a direct hit. But what's really demoralizing is my being left behind to watch the entire commercial fishing fleet leave the harbor and head into shallow estuaries right before the storm hits. *Windigo*'s deep keel makes joining their exodus impossible. Even if I could get over the sandbar that blocks the river's mouth, I couldn't get close enough to the mangroves to tie off like they do. So, my only tactic has been to leave the harbor and find shelter somewhere else. My trips to Bonbonon on Southern Negros were tedious and nerve wracking. It's the best shelter a small boat like mine could ask for, but it takes all day to get there, and there is no reliable way to return to

Cebu without sailing the boat back. How often had I run to Bonbonon for shelter, only to see the typhoon veer away at the last moment. I've lost weeks at a time hiding from storms that never arrived. Disruptions like these were infuriating, but you only need to sit through one good blow at anchor in Cebu Harbor to realize how crazy it is to call Cebu City your homeport.

It was a year ago, last December in fact, that I sat aboard *Windigo* and vowed to work out a better way to handle the storms. I had gone so far as to consider relocating further south, below the storm track's southern limits. I was even considering a move to Zamboanga in the Sulu Islands. A lot of the shells I select come from that area, and if it were any place but the Sulu, I might have overridden my friends' advice and tried it, but I had been too long in Cebu not to know how serious the civil war had become down there. When I found out that there was a government prohibition on foreign tourism to that area, that ended it. I was left with no better option than to make storm moorings for myself and try to go it alone in Cebu Harbor.

It was the business of manufacturing just such a mooring that caused me to start coming ashore via the pier ahead of the brewery. My friends at L'Nor Shipyard had become involved in my project, and my walk to their facilities took me through a part of the port I had only known from the street. It was a deserted area that was exposed to the long fetch of the southeast breeze. The choppy conditions along the pier made it untenable for anything except the larger ships, but the shallow water along the pier could not accommodate their deep draft, so it lay empty in all but the calmest weather. I thought perhaps the brewery would someday expand its bottling plant in that direction and use the pier to tie off its big barges. They were big enough to take the chop and could easily float at the pier.

I was surprised to see the entire scene at the pier change in one short morning. It began when a big rig tractor entered the grounds and deposited a brand new aluminum sided office trailer midway down the pier. You don't see this type of thing in the Philippines, ever. It's so much easier and cheaper to slap up a structure paying third world wages that the idea of prefab housing is unheard of around this part of the world. Viewed from where I was anchored, it looked like a cargo ship had abandoned one of its containers on the pier. When I came ashore that morning and read the sign on its door, I knew I was wrong about the brewery and the barges. The Placid Oil Co. out of Houston, Texas laid claim to the trailer, and they no doubt had plans for the pier. That was the morning the oil industry arrived in Cebu City.

Placid Oil was not the first company to come to the Philippines looking for oil. A couple of years earlier oil deposits were tapped in Philippine waters off the China Sea side of Palawan Island. They were being developed by ICI, the big multinational company, in partnership with the Marcos government. The find was not big, but at OPEC prices there was money being made. Cebu City never saw much of that enterprise because it used Puerto Princessa on Palawan as its dockside headquarters. But, with the arrival of that little piece of Texas property, everything was soon to change.

In the days that followed I became friendly with some of the advance men Placid Oil had sent out to set up the preliminary operations. Like good hard-working Americans, they moved into the trailer the same day it arrived and began work the moment the electrical connections were hooked up. They told me the trailer had come by ship from the States and that there would soon be two ocean-going supply tugs docking at the pier. They said the supply tugs were escorting their semi-submersible up from New Zealand, and that they would stay throughout the contract. I told them I didn't know where they intended to drill, but that they were going to have a hell of a time bringing deep draft tugs up to the pier. They reacted in a way that told me I had brought up a problem they had not considered. So, while one of the men picked up the phone to call their leasing agent, the other asked if they could charter my boat for the day.

We spent the rest of that day sounding the depths around the pier using both *Windigo* and my dingy. It was simple work, but the backwash of waves bounding off the pier flooded the dingy more than a couple times when we measured close in. By the end of the day we looked like drowned rats, and I volunteered *Windigo's* shower to put things right. Of course fresh clothes went with the shower, so it was natural that we went together back to their hotel for dinner and an exchange of clothes. The day's work turned into an evening of great conversation and sea stories. I was as curious about their work as they were about mine, and the more we talked about theirs, the more local knowledge I supplied. In the end, when talk turned to payment for the day's charter, I made a joke that changed my life. I said, "Just put me on the payroll, and we'll call it even." To my surprise they agreed without hesitation. I taxied back to *Windigo*, wondering how that day would change my life. By the time I climbed aboard I knew I would never have to use the storm mooring I was making. My new job would let me hold on to my export business and take my boat out of typhoon alley once and for all.

The oil companies staff their rigs with two totally separate crews. For each job aboard the vessel there are two teams. While one team is on leave, the other is at work. This approach keeps stateside family ties closer, and there are fewer accidents aboard the rig. Placid Oil pays all travel expenses between the rig and its workers' homes as part of the work contract. My decision to base out of Singapore did not give anybody a problem. In fact, 95 percent of the crew commutes to Texas or Louisiana, making my hop across the South China Sea look like nothing. For me, one month on, one month off is perfect. Before I leave for Singapore I spend a couple of days canvassing the shell stalls on Mactan Island to see what's been taken in. The shopkeepers always hold on to their best shells, knowing I will pay the premium if it's one I need. The bargaining can sometimes take a couple days, but usually I'm out in one.

CHAPTER TWO

The northeast monsoon creeps into Singapore in the late fall. A careful observer will notice the change around the last week in October, though he will not find it by looking at synoptic charts or by calling the weatherman. He will see it first out in the ship anchorage, out where the Buginese fishermen anchor their engine-less sailing prahus. In the late summer months, they gather in Singapore as they have been doing since the 18th century, riding the southeast breeze between Indonesian trading ports, trading and picking up everything a thief can lay his hands on. They are called sea gypsies by the local officials who police their activities from the moment the first boat arrives on the summer wind. They are themselves a timeless reminder of an era of savage history that predates the British arrival in Singapore. For them, time has stood still; their boats have not changed, they still navigate without charts, and they still pull a knife to settle even the smallest argument. The immigration office in Singapore would like to keep them aboard their prahus and never let them come ashore. They are throwbacks in every sense of the word. They are also some of the world's most skilled coastal sailors, and when they finally raise sail to leave, the city of Singapore breathes a sigh of relief, and a handful of weather-watchers know the northeast monsoon has drifted into the area.

On land the change is so subtle it goes unnoticed until sometime in early December. It is marked not so much by the change to a northeast breeze as by the formation of huge thunderheads down along the shores of the big island of Sumatra. The clouds usually begin to form in the heat of the midday sun and build throughout the afternoon. The northeast breeze that is almost unnoticed on Singapore slowly moves the scattered sea clouds down to the shores of the big island where updrafts carry them up above the island's jungle interior. They collect and become taller and darker as the afternoon goes on. By sundown the western skies around Singapore are as black as smoke, and an ominous twilight envelops the island. Then, what little breeze there was gives way to an eerie stillness that lies over the island until the black curtain that brought an early sundown makes its approach. It comes on with a blast of chilling air, and in moments there is nothing but rain and the sound of more rain behind it.

In town, the traffic slows to a standstill until the first wave of rain subsides and a little visibility returns. The roadside gutters, then swollen with water, offer the city's bus drivers their chance to clean the sidewalks with a wave of their own. They run as if on rails, undeterred by the lack of visibility, throwing six-foot cascades out onto the sidewalks. They are the last to stop driving and the first to start up again at the earliest sign or let up. When it is at its wettest, the buses own the streets and the sidewalks too. But theirs is a short-lived game at best and confined always to the commercial districts where Singapore resembles many other international capitals. Once the wave of rain abates, Singapore's network of open topped concrete drainage canals begin to take over, and, as if by decree, the city's streets and sidewalks are cleaned. Even the drainage canals that collect a good deal of trash get washed clean. In the time it takes the black curtain to run the twenty-six-mile length of the island, the sun usually drops away completely, and the downtown streets are left wet to sparkle and glisten in the city's night lights.

Out along the island's northern shores, out where urban development has not made its mark, the passing curtain of rain leaves behind a much different scene. Out beyond the old rubber plantations, scattered stilt houses and fisherman's shanties lie along a densely wooded shoreline. Out here, thick jungle foliage lines the rain soaked rutted roads, and equatorial ooze rules. The already slow pace of rural life beyond the kampong hardly misses a beat in the driving rain. Malay pig farmers and small time gardeners huddle beneath galvanized roofs, content to let time pass while the rain turns their small plots into a swamp of wet pools and little streams.

The Chinese taxi driver I had picked up at the airport made the usual protest when I directed him off the paved road. We had already gone well beyond the fringes of his first-hand knowledge by the time we turned into the town of Sembawang. I was hoping his sense of adventure would take me the rest of the way into French's Marina.

I had remained quiet throughout the ride from the airport, not wanting to rattle his confidence with my halting Mandarin, nor prejudice him against me when the last muddy quarter mile challenged him. We were stopped, the rear wheels still on the pavement with our headlights aimed low, lighting a wet and threatening morass of soupy mud holes that lead back into a black canopy of thick jungle vegetation. I knew this moment would come. Even in dry weather the taxis balk at this spot. Experience had taught me to expect a fifty-fifty probability between riding and trekking the last leg if I handled this moment wrong. I was weary from my flight in from Manila and not in the mood to forfeit my travel clothes to the quagmire that lay between me and the shoreline.

"Just a little further," I said, feigning the voice of an aroused sleeper. "Not much more." I leaned forward and by laying my arms across his seat back, I moved into the position of an enthusiastic coach. "Go a little bit to the right side. Okay, okay. It's not far now."

Whether aware of my charade or not, the driver rolled off the pavement and began to smash and splash his way into the pitch-black jungle. I had no way of knowing if he could understand my words, and I didn't care. He had obviously conceded to the idea that left standing in the darkness, I would likely not pay the fare. And a muddied taxi at this hour was much less a problem than a lost fare all the way to Sembawang. He had a good sense of adventure, and I got lucky. We dodged and lurched past Ghee Seng's Sari-Sari and eventually wound up at the wire gate that innocuously guards the perimeter of Mr. French's property. The road is forked at this point, and with some further coaching the taxi driver turned around and disappeared into the night, leaving me in total darkness.

Mr. French's wire gate serves only one purpose, and it is not security. It stops the progress of cars and allows all others to pass. There is almost nothing of value at French's Marina; in fact, to call it a marina is to stretch the truth beyond recognition. It is in reality nothing more than a four-room concrete block house and a few slapped-together utility sheds set back a few yards from the shores of the Johor Straits. There is nothing to steal here except possibly the quiet of the night.

Slipping past the gatepost with my duffel bag on my shoulder, I entirely forgot the slop of wet mud at my feet. I was gripped with an anxiety that had compounded itself with every day I had been away. Groping past the familiar row of wooden seats that bracket the open-air courtyard, I made for the closest shore side to try to get the first glimpse of my boat and put to rest a month of accumulated worries.

Probably the least analyzed navigation aid known to man is his ability to look into darkness and superimpose an accurate image. The physical eye has very little to do with night vision. It is mostly instinct and a good track record. My time at sea had taught me to trust the voice of my subconscious when roaming in the night, and as I stood scanning the tree top silhouette of the Malay coast, I let my eyes dream into the darkness. I paused to savor the night sounds, convinced that my unattended floating home lay untouched a hundred yards out in the darkness.

A familiar sense of relief came over me as I turned to fetch the rowing skiff that had lain upside down during my month away. I kicked it off its blocks with a shoe so full of mud that it took three slippery blows to flip it onto its flat bottom. Once upright, it slid down the wet bank with ease, but getting afloat is never that easy at French's. The bottom slopes away from the shore very gradually around here, and depending on the height of the tide, there can be as much as twenty yards of soft muddy seabed lying between the firm land at the bank and the water's edge offshore. If the tide is high, simply removing shoes will handle the problem of getting afloat. But if it is anywhere below half tide, I have to be prepared to deal with another good dose of equatorial ooze, because there will be mud up to my kneecaps before I find water enough to float my skiff.

French's Marina makes no provision to assist in this maneuver, though I have found this to be part of the place's charm. There is no dock. It's little consolation, but there is in its place some evidence that an attempt was once made to build some kind of elevated walkway out to a would-be pier. But, whether due to the strength of the current, or simple lack of conviction, the attempted walkway never progressed beyond its earliest substructure. It takes a good imagination to visualize the scheme they had in mind because all that got accomplished was the driving of four wooden pilings. They run at ten-foot intervals out into the current and look more like derelict remains than simply a blown attempt at dock construction.

Mr. French, to his credit, managed to find the perfect rationale for the failed enterprise when he began to call the posts "the grid" and represent them as Singapore's only free marine service. In a classic British tongue in cheek way, "the grid" has become a landmark of sorts, used to direct newcomers in from the Straits and at the same time promise free tidal dry docking to those bold enough to use it. In other parts of the world this array of pilings might be called a careening station, where boats come to tie off at high tide and wait for falling water to expose their boat's underbody. At French's it is more like a quicksand pit. The sailboats that have attempted to lean against the posts have found no firm bottom to support their keels. They slowly descend into the mud, burying their keels until buoyed by the bilge, they literally float on the muddy bottom.

Low tide at "the grid" has become something of an initiation rite at French's. While nobody actually recommends its use, it is still called "the grid," and inevitably some newly arrived sailor will take advantage of the free service. All the boats in the anchorage conspire in silence to let the activity take place, knowing fully well how it will turn out. It's a harmless joke that builds and builds as the incoming tide fails to lift the dried boat from the suction of the muddy bottom. About the time the boat's waterline stripe is a foot below the rising water, just when panic has set in her owner's mind, the wake of a passing ship usually comes through to rock the hull enough to break the suction and let the boat rise to float again. It is the extraordinary look of relief that comes to her owner's face when his boat lurches back to the surface that fuels weeks of good-natured kidding. In the end, no one has ever lost more than a little pride on "the grid," learning there are no free marine services in Singapore.

With my gear aboard, and my shoes, socks, and pants removed, I buckled on a pair of plastic sandals and pushed off into the ooze. When finally afloat, I sat on the gunwales, kicking my feet clean while coasting in the current. In the darkness of the damp night air I could make out familiar shapes streaming alongside a closely packed grouping of newly arrived cruising boats. The anchorage had grown while I was away, and the Frenches were obviously enjoying a popularity only December could bring them.

December puts the Indian Ocean bound circum-navigator in one of three places. They are either at sea approaching South Africa via Mauritius — making for the Red Sea via Colombo or the Seychelles — or dawdling into Singapore to wait out the cyclones that rage in the Bay of Bengal. Those who go to South Africa are the fast track sailors. Those who make the Red Sea early are the masochists, and those who come to Singapore for Christmas are looking for a good party. I was ready for one myself.

I must have rowed past five new boats by the time I came abreast of *Windigo*, her dark blue hull barely mirroring the distant lighting of the shipyard. Rising above her faint rippled reflection, she appeared more neglected than I wanted to admit to myself. My hand gripped her peeling varnished toe rail as I steadied the skiff alongside, and I tried to think of the last time I had crawled backwards down the decks laying varnish while dripping sweat in the tropic sun. The fact was that I had not done this job for years. Back in Cebu, I would hire a couple of the painters from the casket company to come by on Sundays. I took great pride in their work and vowed to keep up with their varnish after I left for Singapore, but once here, I found nobody interested in the task, not even myself. I was too tired to let it get me down, so I dumped my gear into the cockpit, climbed aboard, and called it a night.

CHAPTER THREE

The following morning came early for me when I woke to the sounds of slapping lines and clinking bottles. *Windigo* was in the midst of a series of jerking snap rolls that had me clinging to the berth as I tried to regain an awareness of where I was and what was going on around me. I took longer than I should have to put it together. My month on the drilling platform had numbed my senses, and for one short delirious moment I had no explanation for the chaos going on around me. Bottles clinked, plates rattled, and everything I had brought aboard the boat slid and crashed within the lockers and drawers that surrounded me. I was desperate to run forward the moment I could find safe footing, as I had no recollection of how I had left the foreword cabin the night before. I expected nothing less than shattered glass and a room full of spilled lockers as I bounced my way through the narrow passage that leads to the main cabin.

The passing ship's wake had caught *Windigo* directly on her beam ends, and we were still recovering when I stood somewhat bleary-eyed looking into the main cabin. I could hardly recognize the scene. There were no signs of projects left half finished: no typed pages scattered about the dining area or seashells left to roll around the pilot berths. There were no pots and pans left swinging on the gimbaled stove. The woven baskets that I use to hold fruits and vegetables had remained where I had left them. My month's absence was easily the most recognizable thing in the cabin. It was as I had left it a month earlier, and except for the near empty bottle of red wine I found tipped over, draining in the galley sink, there was no evidence of my return last night.

The smell of damp earth and the incessant calls of Gee Seng's tireless roosters swarmed about me as reality returned to my waking mind. Through the galley window morning light showed a fleet of steady masts riding none the worse for wear in the current of a rising tide. I stood dazed in thought, staring out the porthole above the swing stove, more interested in checking out the new arrivals than in igniting the gas beneath my kettle of water. I'm not sure how many clicks I fired at the burner, but by the time I gave it my full attention, I had counted six foreign flags in the anchorage. Apart from the boats I knew, there were a couple of French boats with windsurfers strapped to the cabin sides, a hard chine ketch from Australia, a tiny Dutch sloop, and a converted racer from New Zealand. Christmas was less than twenty-four hours away, and I was easing into the holiday mood. When the radio played "The Holly and The Ivy," I knew my morning was made.

I had joined the choir in earnest and was headed back to the galley for a second blast of Nescafe when I noticed Frank's inflatable dingy approaching along the starboard side. His little two-horse outboard blared into the cabin as he circled in the current and passed beneath the galley porthole. I could have guessed I would see him first upon my return. In the short time he and his wife had been at French's, they had extended themselves into every social layer there was around here. For me they were *Windigo*'s guardians while I was away. Never mind that there was virtually nothing they could do should disaster strike. It was the offer that mattered, and I could not deny their best intentions when they asked if they could look after my boat. I let the choir master carry on without me as I set aside an extra cup and quickly headed up the companionway steps to greet my visitor from the cockpit.

"Let me have your line," I shouted. "How is everything?"

Without looking up he shut down his motor and scrambled to ship the oars that were lashed atop the gunnels of his rubber inflatable.

"You don't have to do that," I said, trying to end a procedure that would inevitably lead to a formalized request to board. "Leave them where they are and come on up. I've got coffee going, would you like some?"

Frank stayed crouched down, shifting the oars while the current carried him further down toward *Windigo's* stern. At the last moment his hand reached up to grab my boat's toe rail, and he stood up to hand me his line. "You never know when one of those big ships will send us another tidal wave," he said. "I'd hate to mess up your paint job with these oars slamming around."

While he climbed the lifelines I looped his line through one of the stern chocks and took it to the cleat. "What about that coffee?" I said while ducking back beneath the cockpit awning. "Can I get you some?"

As he nodded his reply I headed below, leaving him to settle in the cockpit. He found shade by sitting high up on the coaming with his bare feet resting on the cushioned seating. From his shaded perch we went through the sugar and cream formalities in a clipped cadence. When I had the preparation in hand and moved to the cockpit entry, Frank shifted to meet me and took the cup. He settled back onto the cushioned seat and with his elbows stretched wide, lying across the coaming, he looked more the part of *Windigo's* master than I.

"How was it in the Philippines, Kim? Anything exciting happening up there? "

"I'd be the last to know," I said. "They never tell the crew anything about what's going on down in the well. But tell me, when did all the new boats get in? I've never seen it so crowded around here."

"Gees, you should have been here three days ago. We had a real crowd then, but quite a few went around to Clifford Pier after the shoot-out the other night."

"Don't tell me those French guys had another blowout," I laughed. "You know those guys attract some real bizarros."

"No, no. It was nothing like that, Kim. This was more like military action," he said. "I mean we're talking gunboats and machine guns, man!"

"Oh really?" I chuckled. "What happened?"

"Well it must have been four in the morning, the other night, when a couple of those high-speed patrol boats came flying through the anchorage doing about forty. Man, their lights were moving all around the place. We heard some Malays shouting and then heard shots ... real close by. Nobody was sure what happened.

We still don't know, but it scared the hell out of the group of boats that had just come in that day. The Frenches figure it was some Malaysians running tin ore across the Straits. I had no idea there was anything like contraband around here. Anyway, that morning a whole group upped anchor and went around to Clifford Pier."

"Were any of the boats hit?"

"No, not that I know of. Barb and I came aboard your boat that morning to check it over, and from what I could see, you're okay. I mean I'm sure we were not the targets. But the funny part was that later in the morning, everybody noticed the Dutchman on the thirty footer going up his stick and staying up there for what seemed like hours. When he came ashore somebody asked what he was doing up there so long. He said his boat had been shot at a few times before, and he always inspected the rig after a shooting. Within a half an hour every mast in the place had somebody hanging on it looking for bullet holes."

"Sounds like a hot time in the old town," I joked. "Why didn't you take off with the others?"

"We talked about it. I was ready to leave, but you know Barb and Teresa have such big plans for tomorrow night's Christmas party; she wasn't about to let me do it. Besides, we ran into Rob Stevenson. You know, the guy off that little black ferro-cement boat. He said the shooting had nothing to do with the sailboats in the anchorage. He figures the Singapore patrol boats were giving chase to a smuggler, and they fired a few rounds to let everybody in the kampong know they meant business."

"Oh, they mean business, I can tell you that," I said. "Didn't you get boarded by the patrol boats out in the roadstead?"

"Well sure, everybody does, but well ... To be perfectly honest about it, we stayed below through all but the end of it. I mean we heard the shooting, and we saw the lights through the windows, but we weren't about to go on deck to get closer. I don't know ... What do you think, Kim? We've heard so much about pirates since we got here. The guys on the ham radio figure the entire China Sea is crawling with them. They think I'm taking a big risk just to be sailing on the outskirts of this area. I don't know what to think. Have you read the newspapers? The *Straits Times* is full of awful stories about what's happening out in the South China Sea. The Vietnamese boat people are being slaughtered, yachts have gone missing, and nobody knows what's happening out there."

"If you are asking me what I think about the other night, I don't know what to say. It sounds strange though. We've never had anything like that happen since I've been here."

Frank took a long time sipping at his cup of coffee. It made for one of those conversational pauses that let my words hang in the air. I knew he was looking for a much broader reply to the subject, and if I followed the path the conversation was taking I knew where it would lead. Frank was looking for a second opinion. One that he could use to balance the view Rob Stevenson had given him. I knew Rob never held back when the subject came up. He had seventeen years of China Sea stories to tell, and most all of them involved his shooting his way out of danger with the cache of weapons he has hidden in a cave over on Tioman Island. I knew enough not to directly challenge the mythology he had cultivated. Rob's status in Southeast Asian sailing circles was legendary. And for all I knew, his stories were true.

"Look, Frank," I said in a calming voice. "Those incidents you're thinking about all happen way up in the Gulf of Thailand. That's hundreds of miles from here, and those Thai pirates are only pirates when they are not fishing. I mean the South China Sea is full of fishing boats; they are not all pirates. The Vietnamese refugees who leave Vietnam during the Northeast Monsoon have to run with the wind, and that takes them right through the Thai fishing grounds in the Gulf. That's when the fishermen become pirates. Once the monsoon changes, the refugees head north for

Hong Kong, and if their motors run long enough to get them there, they have a pretty good chance of staying alive. Nobody I know has sailed into the Gulf since Rob tried it last year. You'll have to ask him about the trip the next time you see him. It's really quite a tale. Anyway, you're not headed up there and neither am I, so what's to worry about?"

"Well, you tell me. I remember sitting in Bali talking with some other cruisers about all this. One of the guys said he heard reports about merchant ships being attacked by high-speed chase boats. He said those attacks happened on the Western side of Malaysia, right on our route to Sri Lanka. A lot of the cruisers in Bali felt the threat of attack up here was a lot more frightening than crossing the Indian Ocean in one blue-water shot. They figured they'd rather take their chances on the high seas."

I wished I had not become involved in this talk of pirates. Every time it comes up, and it comes up all the time, I go through my "Don't sweat it" routine. It's almost become a reflex action for me. I always come off as the guy with all the answers: "It hasn't happened for years. It doesn't happen in those waters. It never happened that way." I interpret rumors, pass on half-truths, and even bring in my own version of geopolitics to ease people's worries. If it were not such blatant self-deception, I'd believe it myself and relax.

"Listen Frank, you're talking about the '60s. That business in the Malaccan Straits was all political. The Indonesians were trying to break up the formation of Malaysia. Those attacks were provocations designed to make the armed forces look bad. Good God, man, look at the military around here now. I bet you can't get around to Clifford Pier without getting boarded. The Straits are no problem. The military will escort you out of town just like they escorted you in. As long as you wait till after Christmas before crossing the Bay of Bengal, you've got no worries. Nobody I have talked to has had a problem in the Straits. Don't sweat it."

By this time Frank had finished the coffee and was pushing the cup to the threshold of the companionway. "I'm relieved to hear you say that," he said. "That thing the other night has left us a little shaken. I don't want to think we'll be heading into more of that kind of action when we leave this place. I'd like the winds and the seas to be my only worry. To hell with the pirates, man!"

He stood and turned to grab the loop I used to tie off his dingy. Untying it, he fed the line through the chock and began walking forward, towing his dingy to a point amidships.

"We've got to run down to the immigration office for another stamp," he said. "Can I get you anything in town?"

"I'll be going in myself," I said while taking his line.

As he climbed over the lifelines to step down to the dingy, I thanked him for keeping an eye on *Windigo*. He raised his smiling face, and with a squint-eyed wink, he said, "Don't sweat it."

He was still smiling when I threw his line onto the undulating bottom of his rubber boat. I watched him kick the two-horse into action while he drifted aft in the current. He seemed a happier man as he turned and moved off into the anchored fleet.

I went below decks wondering if I had eased Frank's anxieties as much as I had added to my own. It takes no great insight to see that my "expertise" belies my own fears, and every time I catch myself recoiling to this subject in such a predictable manner, I end up debating my own backlog of close calls and run-ins. There are real threats and imagined threats out in the China Sea. In the years I've sailed these waters I have learned to run from both and ask questions later. It's curious, but it's not the running that is hard to get used to; I'll change my course on a whim. It's the questions that come up after I'm out of harm's way that bother me. Without a direct confrontation, I'm never sure what I've left behind.

I moved to the chart table and flipped on the ham radio, hoping to catch the end of the morning's "Breakfast Show" and eavesdrop my way out of my spell of self-analysis. Moving the dial just slightly, I listened for the familiar voices and call signs I have come to know. In some cases, the voices I hear raise the familiar faces of sailors and friends I've met over the years. The other voices are those of the more transient cruisers, talking among themselves as they move westward through the area. Their talk is usually cruising "shop talk," the backbone of which is the endless exchange of information concerning immigration clearance procedures in the neighboring countries. They become easily bored with the gossip and small talk of the more permanent members of the net and usually sign off early.

I caught the very end of the net, a period where call signs are dropped and conversations become chaotic unless you know the voices that are doing the talking. Not much had changed since I had left for my month aboard the rig. Victoria Sugar 5 Juliet Bravo, a land based Hong Kong station was droning on about his life's career in the British Civil Service, and only a few of the hard core were left to indulge him. Judging by the intense volume and the pegging of my "S" meter, I could tell my good friend Bert Lange was still hooked up across the island at Clifford Pier. If ever there were a kind heart that could go the distance on the radio it is KH7DQ-MM3. Put a microphone in his hand, and Bert will talk your ears off.

Over the years the "Breakfast Show" has attracted only two land-based stations. One in Hong Kong and the other in Brunei. Both these stations operate throughout the day, moving up and down the ham bands looking for opportunities to talk. Neither have any direct contact with the sailing world, but in time they both have become fixtures in the "Breakfast Show." They bring a different operating style with them due to the fact that they have specialized antennas and unlimited power sources. They talk louder and much longer, and once they get going, there's no telling when they'll stop.

When I heard 73s being passed between the stations I knew things were winding down. All that was left was for the individual stations to say their call signs and sign off.

I called "Break" into the microphone and waited for a response.

Only after the formalities of the shutdown were complete did Bert return with "Come back, breaker."

Turning my transmission power way down, I said his call sign, then mine before saying, "How's that coming through, Bert?"

"Hey, you sound great, Kim. I knew you'd be back in town one of these days. How's everything up at French's? You know, I was just talking about you the other day ..."

It was easily five minutes before his finger came off the transmit button. Bert was a kindred spirit, a fellow single-hander with a lot of miles under his keel. We had shared anchorages all over the Pacific before I landed in the Philippines and he went on to Singapore. I put my mic on the chart table, knowing by habit the form our conversation would take and was wandering about sorting shells when he gave me my first opening. My reply simply coaxed more of his banter and sent him into another jag that filled the main cabin with another raft of rambling boat talk and gossipy tidbits. It was just the kind of welcome back spiel I wanted to hear. The inauspicious mood Frank had left with me was gone and I could see a great day shaping up.

My eye was caught by the sheen coming off the shells I had been laying out in the cabin, and in a moment of cheerful inspiration I picked up the mic at the chart table. "Listen," I said at the break, "suppose I drop by later this morning. I've got a little gift I want you to have. You'll be aboard, won't you? Over."

"Look, Kim," he said. "You don't have to wear your Santa Claus suit just to make a social call on me. Of course I'll be here. Today's the day I put the gearbox back on my motor. It's been repaired for the third time this year you know. The third time's a charm, right?"

I put the mic down and walked away from the chart table smiling. Bert was off and running.

CHAPTER FOUR

Once away from the northern coastal area, the road to downtown Singapore runs through some remarkably tranquil countryside. Between tightly packed roadside villages there are stretches of level farmland where the scattered remnants of untended rubber plantations bracket carefully manicured fields of green leafed crops. Low-lying orchid nurseries draped in stretched black mesh lay in the distant fields looking like dark barges on a shimmering river of green foliage. Hillsides dense with towering mahogany trees throw cooling shade across steep roadside embankments where dark skinned Malay field workers walk in a single file, indifferent to the parade of cars and buses that fly past them. The hush of rural life in the interior is short-lived though, as more and more villages line up in quick succession and eventually blend into the sprawl that surrounds the central city.

Somewhere south of the reservoirs, about where Upper Thompson Road becomes simply Thompson Road, and with the last panorama behind me, traffic lights took control, and I rumbled into position behind a line of smoking buses and green checked taxis. My run across the island had taken about thirty minutes, and though I had covered about fifteen miles in that time, my motorcycle gave me no advantages in downtown traffic. It would take another thirty minutes to make the next few miles down to the financial district and Clifford Pier. I leaned back on the split-level saddle and let the twin cylinders of my Norton Commando shake the soles of my sandals on the hot pavement. Above me, strung high between the streetlights, red banners trumpeted the coming Chinese New Year. As I twisted to take in the scale of the decorations, I could feel the hard bulge in my pack roll across by backbone. I stood tall and lifted the pack's shoulder straps, trying to reposition the awkward shape into the contours of my back, but try as I might, the big Pacific triton I carried seemed to fight my every shrug. Twitching for one last adjustment, I jerked my bike through a cloud of blaring exhaust and followed the flow all the way down to Shenton Way.

It was nice being back, riding the streets of a town that had become so pleasantly predictable in the past year, and what a change had come over me since last Christmas. My freelance days chasing shells and dodging typhoons in the Philippines seemed so strenuous from where I was now that I wondered if I could ever go back to it. With another Placid Oil check stuck in my shirt, ready for deposit, and the festooned monuments of downtown Singapore flying past, I could easily see the way the coming year would pass. "Kung Hei Fat Choy" the red banners proclaimed: "Rejoice and Grow Rich in the New Year." Who was I to argue with that? If Placid Oil wanted another year, I couldn't imagine turning them down.

I dumped the Norton in a slot three stories above the pavement and walked the ramps down to street level, wondering how it would feel to spend another year up at French's watching the cruisers come and go. Maybe in a year I would feel the paralysis that sets in on live-aboard sailors, but for the moment I had none of it. Singapore had been good for me. As I walked beneath the clock tower that looks down on the Clifford Pier concourse, I was in that frame of mind that delights in taking stock of things while they are the most manageable. Even the Indian merchants raving at me from their stalls could not disturb me. I passed through their gauntlet unscathed and began to make my way to the pier that lies immediately behind the concourse building.

The scene at the pier is easily the most international in all of Southeast Asia. At any one time there might be three hundred merchant ships lying at anchor out in the roads: waiting to off-load or take on cargo, waiting for clearances, waiting for sailing orders, or simply waiting for a change in the weather. Whatever their reason, they all have crew members who come ashore and return to their ships via the service boats that enter the inner harbor and come to Clifford Pier. Every day hundreds of people from every maritime nation in the world clamber up the concrete steps that lead up to the concourse level. They leave behind a jostling fleet of massively overbuilt water taxis queuing for position to approach the staircases. The sounds of roaring diesel engines and the smell of exhaust sweeps up from the water into huge queues of waiting crewmen who stand mesmerized by the frantic boat handling going on below them. Above the thunder, high-pitched chopping sounds and a rush of white water bring each docking to a dramatic conclusion. When the inevitable collision with the pier comes, the concrete always seems to take the worst of the damage. The boats simply bounce off the walls until the lines are made fast and the passengers begin to climb ashore.

I moved against the flow of human traffic until I finally reached a position where I could look out into the inner harbor and spot the small fleet of yachts. No ships or large vessels are allowed to enter this sheltered water. In fact, within a few months even the handful of cruising sailboats that drop anchor here would be denied access. Nothing stops a sailboat as well as a low fixed bridge, and I have no doubts that mast heights were carefully analyzed during the planning of the causeway and bridge that were being built on top of the breakwater. The inner harbor was built to service the shipping industry, not to offer free shelter to cruising yachts. However, for the time being, it was obvious that the cruising sailors anchored here had the best free anchorage ever offered in a major international capital.

I spotted Bert Lange's little thirty-four footer anchored with the other boats and began my search for one of the motorized sampans that sometimes lay off the sea walls. Amidst the bedlam that rules at the concrete staircases, there is no place for these small throwaway boats. The aged drivers of these flimsy craft know where they don't belong, and they will not go near the steps until the rush hour has passed. I spotted one bobbing up and down in the backwash a few yards off the pier head and gave him a whistle. He motioned me over to the steel railings that form handholds for a metal ladder that hangs down off the pier. If I wanted a ride out to the sailboats, I would use the ladder or not go at all.

Once I was standing on the lower rung, hanging over the surging water, he produced a little rope and wrapped it around the grooved flywheel of his vintage outboard motor. He kicked it over with a flop of his bony wrist and shot off in my direction, only to shut it off again. As the sampan drifted beneath the ladder I timed my jump to land on the small platform that covered the bow. With a parting shove the bow came around just as the Chinese boatman pulled his rope again and set us off into the inner harbor. It was a tricky maneuver, and I was relieved to have earned the boatman's nod and not a swim in the harbor.

I sat amidships with my back to the driver and motioned with my arm toward the rear of the sailboat fleet. Whether he was looking or not, I couldn't tell. I had my eyes fixed on a huge wake that a passing water taxi had sent us. I assumed he did as well because he stopped the motor and we coasted into the wall of water and avoided taking the wave into the boat. We proceeded in this on and off fashion until we had left the corridor that leads to the breakwater entrance. When we had left the worst of the standing waves and wakes behind us, we got back to speed and I turned to straddle the seat, giving the boatman a "thumbs up" to show my appreciation for his courtesy. He waved his acknowledgment, and in his delight he showed a smile that would turn a dentist's stomach.

We passed through the fleet of cruising boats, picking up two whistled calls along the way. The boatman raised his hand to signal his intention to come back for a pick-up while I continued to direct our progress to the sloop at the end of the row. When we rounded up to make our final approach on Bert's boat, I noticed two dinghies tied to the stern cleat. It meant that I would be interrupting somebody's visit, but I figured the engine work that was going on below decks could do with another bystander.

I passed a Singapore dollar into the boatman's hand and moved to the bow platform, showing him I was ready for and exit "on the fly." As we swept by the yacht's stern quarter, I grabbed its lifeline and lifted myself over the rail while giving the sampan a parting shove with my trailing foot. I caught the boatman's eye as he moved off, and I gestured to my wristwatch. Pointing one finger above it, I mouthed "One hour ... One hour." He nodded his head while motoring away.

The sailboat was still rolling to the weight of my boarding when the racket of the departing sampan finally calmed. I stood at the rail in that moment, bobbing up and down, expecting some kind of reception or acknowledgment from below decks. What I heard was a muffled shout coming up through the deck below my feet.

"Get that son of a bitch before it rolls into the bilge. Awww, shit."

I leaned my head into the companionway and looked down on two bent bodies covered in grease and sweat. They had their heads hung, trying to peer beneath the three-hundred-pound diesel engine that sat between them.

"We'll get it later," Bert said, raising his sweat-covered face from beneath the engine. "I've got a whole bag full of those nuts up in the cockpit. Can you get me one, Kim? They're just over there."

I moved with the motion of his hand and found the bag where he had pointed. There were only two nuts left in it, so I lifted the bag down to his waiting hand.

"Only two left?" he smiled. "We're almost finished! Give me just a minute, Kim." He groaned while wedging his body back into the space behind the engine. "All I've got to do is tweak these two, and I think we've got it."

As he went about the task I tried to think if I had met the guy who was helping with the alignment. He had not said a word, but I was fairly sure he was from the States, figuring beards were the rage among Americans that season, and who but an image-conscious American would suffer the discomfort of a beard in these latitudes. I could easily place this guy aboard the staysail schooner I had passed while coming out to the anchorage. The beard, the boat, it all fit together. I was just about to ask him what part of The States he was from when Bert announced the end of his work and pulled himself out of the engine room.

"Kim Barnaby," he said. "Meet the best bloody sailing mechanic this side of the breakwater. By God, this guy knows all the tricks of the trade. We just did a full day's work in one hour. By golly, that went fast."

As my hand slid into his oily grasp he said, "Howdy, I'm Bill Nichols off *Gypsy Cowboy*, the little ol' schooner out there. How you goin', Bucko?"

"Bloody great, mate," I countered. "How the hell did you let this old boy talk you into all this dirty work anyway?" I said, slipping into a *Penrod* voice.

"I was the one who told him to dump them old flex mounts and get a new set. How was I to know he'd up and do it? Next thing I know he's showing me the new mounts. What can I say? I had to make sure he put 'em in right."

"Yeah," I said looking over to see how Bert was taking it. "We wouldn't want to see another clutch pack go up in smoke just cause those old rusty mounts were misaligned."

"All right, Barnaby, now you've gone too far," Bert laughed. He turned to Bill and said, "You'll have to excuse my friend. He's been at sea for the past month. You know how it is."

Bill sensed that he was in the middle of a private joke and reacted with a somewhat strained smile.

He began wiping his hands with the tee shirt he had brought along. Turning to me he said, "You say you been sailing for a month? Where you been, mate?"

"Oh, I'm not sailing much these days," I said. "I do a month out on an oil rig in the Philippines, then I fly back down here for a month off; one on, one off, that sort of thing."

"Kim keeps his boat up at French's while he's away," Bert interjected. "Maybe you saw his blue sloop while you were up there last week. It sits way out nearest the channel."

"No, I don't pay much attention to other people's boats and hell, I was only up there that one night," he said. "I like it down here much better. I ain't been shot at once down here."

Bert was on his knees gathering the wrenches that lay scattered about the rear of the cabin. His efforts at a quick clean up were aimed at clearing the space where the entry ladder belonged. Once in place he could move Bill into the cockpit and take his mind off the engine repairs that had dragged on for the past month. He looked up at Bill and said, "Yeah, I feel kind of responsible for that."

Turning to me he continued, "I was the guy who sent him up there. Kim, what the hell's going on up there at French's? Bill and the others came back saying all hell was breaking loose up there. What's going on?"

I slid aft along the cockpit seating as the stairs were fitted beneath the companionway. "I wish I could tell you, Bert," I said. "I only heard about it this morning. I'm guessing it was some kind of warning to the Malays. You know, the ones running tin ore across the Straits."

"It was SOME KIND OF WARNING, Jack. I was THERE!" Bill grimaced as he climbed the steps and sat across the cockpit from me. "You ever seen machine gun fire at close range in the middle of the night? It's not fun, mate. Took me right back to the Mekong, man. I mean, we used to run like that: lookin' down night scopes, shooting the shit out of anything that moved." He paused. "Now, I might be a little new around here," he went on, "but I've been shot at before—a lot, you know. And I just don't like being on the receiving end of that kind of shit."

"What makes you think you were a target?" I countered.

"Oh, I know who the target was, but that kind of shootin' off a boat makes everything a target. I just figured, fuck 'em. I'll get the hell out of here as soon as the sun comes up and let the gooks go ahead and waste each other. Why should I have my butt on the line? I just got here."

"Okay, I get it," I said. "But, you say you saw it. What was it? What were they aiming at?

"Well, just give me a minute, Jack. This shit still pisses me off! I mean I went up there for a Christmas party and got my ass shot at by a bunch of ..."

"Hold on there, Bill!" Bert broke in. "Can you kick it back a notch? Kim just wants to know what went on up there. We live here you know? We both want to hear what you saw."

"Okay. I'll take you through it," he sighed. "Ya see, I'm kind of a light sleeper, ya know, and it was late, maybe three thirty or somethin' like that. Anyway, I was up on deck fixin' to take a pee over the rail when I spotted a couple of guys paddling some kind of gook runabout into shore. They weren't making very good time 'cause they were trying to be real quiet, and I could tell the boat was heavy, like it was too big to be paddled. Well, I stayed on deck till they reached shore, somewhere right close to the marina. I couldn't see all that much, but I'm pretty sure I seen them talking with friends or somethin'. Whatever, I guess it took 'em about five minutes to do whatever it was they were doing. Anyway, they left, being even quieter than when they came, 'cause this time they rode the current downstream, not making a sound. They went a long way before they started up their motors and finally took off. I figured it was nothing and went below. 'Bout an hour later, I heard a couple big engines start up, maybe big Cats or somethin'. Sounded like it was somewhere up by the lights, ya know, up a ways from the boats. Well, I came up on deck to look around and I'll be damned if that same runabout was drifting into shore again. That's when all hell broke loose. I mean, that's when the big boat with the lights opened fire on the gooks. Man, those little bastards got their motors goin' and flew right by me. I mean there were flames jumpin' out of those guns — real shit was flying, mate. And those little fuckers got out of there so fast you wouldn't believe it, Jack. So, if that's what you call a warning, I'd hate to be around when it got serious."

"Could you tell if it was a government patrol boat doing all the shooting?" I asked. "Did you see any uniforms or markings on the boat?"

By this time Bert was standing on the steps of the ladder in the companionway wiping the sweat from his oil streaked face. "Christ, Kim! Who else goes around shooting a machine gun in Singapore? You know they give you the death sentence around here just for having a gun at the scene of a crime. You don't even have to shoot it!"

I ignored Bert's comments and asked again, "Did you see a number or anything like that on the patrol boat, Bill?"

"No way, man. Their searchlights caught me right in the eyes. After the shooting, man, I wasn't worth shit. Hell, I was hiding in the cockpit!"

"You're right," I said. "I was just hoping I could make some inquiries with the authorities. With the patrol boat's ID number, I might get some answers; otherwise I don't think I'd get to first base. The last thing they want is some nosy outsider poking around in their military affairs."

"Yeah, you better skip it, Kim," Bert replied. "They make it hard enough to stay here with all the immigration and visa red tape they throw at us. You sure don't need to get singled out as a troublemaker, meddling in their dealings with the Malays. You could end up right back in the Philippines dodging typhoons again."

"Roger on that," I said, slipping into radio jargon. "They *do* like to use a heavy hand to get what they want around here."

"You better believe it, Bucko!" And with that, Bill rose to his feet and began scrambling for the rope that held his dingy to the stern of Bert's boat. "I gotta run," he growled. "Bert, when you get the exhaust back on and everything's ready, you let me know. I want to be around when you fire her up."

He pulled the little lapstraked dory up alongside the cockpit and turned to face me. "Nice talking to you, Barnaby. We'll catch you later, Bert."

As Bert heaped on the "thank-yous," Bill stepped down, tossing the line on the bow seat of the dory.

We watched him shove off into the current and begin rowing before we spoke.

"He seems pretty freaked," I began. "And yet you'd think he'd feel protected. I mean, the marine police ran off the bad guys. Nobody was hurt, scared maybe, but not hurt. Really, it sounds to me like what Rob Stevenson called it 'just a warning to knock off the contraband.' Why I'll bet French's doesn't see action like that again for years."

Bert returned to the cockpit and said, "So you think it's safe for me to come up tomorrow then?"

"Listen, Bert. Teresa's already got you on the list. I spoke to her this morning. Hey, this is nothing but a local matter. My guess is the Malays were using the anchorage for the drop because they figured the gun boats wouldn't dare use that kind of force with a lot of yachts around."

"Well, they figured wrong. Didn't they?"

"Sure," I said. "And they won't be using the marina for that kind of venture again. If anything the place is better off now. The cavalry just chased the bad guys away. They won't come back, I'm certain of that. Hey look, I wouldn't sweat it."

I looked out into the anchorage and noticed the Chinese boatman making deliveries again. He had his eye on Bert's boat as though he was worried I'd hail his competition. As I raised my hand in his direction, a proprietary grin flashed across his face.

"Bert, I'm going to let you get back to your motor," I continued. "You've got a lot to do before this thing's ready to go anywhere. I'll look for you sometime tomorrow. Okay?"

As I gathered together my stuff sack, I remembered the big triton that had been sticking me in the back all morning. "I think you're going to like this one," I said. "They don't come much bigger than this, you know."

I untied the drawstrings at the top of the stuff sack and eased the seventeen-inch specimen shell out into the daylight. It lit up the cockpit, grabbing Bert's unfocused attention with its full-blown brilliance. His expression seemed to freeze. "Yeah, it's a knock out," I said, while handing the two-pound shell across the cockpit. "Now you're going to have to find a place to put it."

I enjoyed every second of his stunned silence. In those moments the brilliance of nature's form left him dumbfounded, unable to measure the beauty he held in his hands. He sat motionless, lost in the perfect beauty of a shell species that so captures the imagination that it shares its name with the son of the Greek god of the sea.

"Jeesus," he finally said, twisting the spiraling form as if to read its inscription. "I've never seen one as nice as this one before. I never knew they had this kind of coloring or luster. How does anybody put a price on something like this? It's out of this world, Kim."

"That one never rolled up a beach or dried out in the sunlight. It's been harvested. You know, plucked from the depths by divers. Keep it out of the direct sunlight and it'll look like that forever."

By this time the sampan had rounded up into the current off our stern, signaling the end of my visit. We exchanged parting words up until the noise of the sampan's raucous motor cut us off. I rose to stand at the rail and waited for the tire that wraps its bow to kiss the stern quarter beneath my feet. Judging the moment of impact, I climbed over the lifelines and eased onto the moving bow platform, pushing away just enough to prevent contact between the two boats. With a final wave I was away.

The boatman wandered through the fleet of anchored sailboats, trying to make eye contact with anybody who would give him their attention. He was obligated to my return to Clifford Pier, but not before he had canvassed the entire anchorage. I was happy to be along for the tour. It gave me a chance to look for familiar faces among the new arrivals. We passed Bill boarding his schooner and I gave him a wave. He nodded his reply then swung a pointed finger across the fleet toward the big cargo schooner that sat closest to the breakwater. The boatman reacted immediately, turning the sampan toward the calls and waves of a group of crewmen who stood together at the stern of the big three-masted boat. I could see his mind counting heads and chalking up a bonanza as we made a beeline toward the hulking hundred footer.

Minutes later we were bobbing around beneath the stern of the *SV Nighthawk*, a fairly well kept hundred-foot steel cargo schooner out of Sydney, Australia. In the time it took to make our approach, the waiting crewmen had scattered, so the boatman shut down his motor. He fitted his oars into their locks and prepared to kill some time rowing while his party made ready to board. I ran my eye up and down the boat's hull, trying to judge the amount of work a boat like this one could demand. Obviously this boat had been kept too long at commercial wharves and had paid the price. Close up she showed warped plates and punched in areas at the bow and stern. Her dark blue paint was an attempt to conceal her injuries, though it only worked where the paint had oxidized and gone super flat.

We moved in on the boarding ladder when the group of crewmen re-formed at the railing above us. There was no clamoring for position or last minute hustling going on. They seemed content to stand at the rail and look down at us without any haste at all. Apparently their immediate job was complete and they, like us, were waiting for a disembarking passenger. She finally arrived to a flurry of helping hands, and in seconds the nicest looking tourist I had seen in SE Asia was climbing down the ladder. Without hesitation she reached for my shoulder to brace for her jump. I stood steady in her grip, feeling much more than a simple grasping hand at my shoulder. In fact, I was reading more into her grasp than her wildest imagination could know. My not so subtle mind was telling me things I had not heard for months.

She landed on the flooring between the bench-type seats, and with my elbow to steady her, she sat down looking aft, directly in front of me. She wore loose-fitting clothes: a simple white blouse with pockets that never get used and pleated khaki walking shorts, exactly the same as the Chinese rickshaw drivers wear. I figured she was too caught up in the sendoff the crewmen were giving her to notice the attention I was giving her. When the oars were shipped and the motor began, she turned to face aft and returned my approving stare. Her look triggered a kind of lecherous smile I reserve for only the most attractive females, and knowing my pent-up state of mind, I probably overdid it because she turned away in a flash. I debated trying to shout over the motor noise but dropped the idea. The circumstances dictated silent patience and that was all there was to it. I spent the rest of the trip to shore hoping we would run out of gas so I could have a word with her. It didn't happen.

We arrived at the concrete stairs without incident; the queues were gone, and the rush hour was over. Mid-morning traffic was flying by the concourse building, and Clifford Pier was back to normal. I passed a Singapore dollar to the boatman and waited for the girl to do the same. She dug into a big double handled carry bag and produced an Italian leather purse half its size. I stood by waiting to use the opening line I had so carefully crafted on the trip in. It would go something like "Have you just come up from Indonesia? I bet you loved Bali," or something like that. Her fumbling around with her purse was ruining my timing. The more I ran the line through my mind, the less I liked it. I finally broke in saying, "Maybe I could help."

"Yeah!" she said still looking into the purse, "If you can break a twenty. I mean I've never taken one of these little boats. I mean I just cashed some traveler's checks, and I don't have anything but twenties. You don't suppose he has change, do you?"

"Let's not complicate his life by asking," I said while slipping another bill into his waiting hand. "Have you got everything?"

"Yes, but ..."

"Don't give it another thought," I said, trying to make the most of the moment. "It's nothing."

I gave her my arm to hold while she climbed to the lower threshold on the wet staircase. Her light brown hair swept across my face as she bent to brace on the railing that ran up the length of the stairs. She paused to see me gather up my gear, then headed up the steps. I stepped to the threshold, looked up and let my imagination run. When she reached the top of the stairs I looked back to the boatman who was still fending off. His smile was back. I was sure he had looked into my mind.

I let her go on and on as we walked through the concourse. "You've just got to let me pay you back," she began. "I feel so foolish taking money from a perfect stranger. Come on, let me get some change, will you?"

By the time I spoke we had passed through the entire building and were out in the sunlight amidst the throng of pedestrians waiting to cross Shenton Way.

"Okay," I said. "We'll call it even if you will cross the street with me and let me buy us lunch. Have you been to Telok Ayer? It's right over there. Really, it's a perfect place."

"Oh, cut it out," she said. "I'm the one trying to get back to even. Quit fooling around and let me off the hook."

The light had changed and I moved with the crowd out onto the pavement. She had no choice and stayed with me. I figured I had played this scene for all it was worth, and I was ready to let her go if she really wanted to. But I had nothing to lose in forcing the issue. I stepped up onto the sidewalk and headed off toward the food stalls saying, "No, I insist."

She could simply take the other direction and be done with me. A Singapore dollar amounted to little more than fifty U.S. cents, and despite the good time I was having, half a dollar was really not worth the debate. I fully expected her to stop at the curb and lose me in the crowd.

"Look," she called after me, "if you'll stop walking so fast, I'll be happy to eat with you."

I turned and for the first time noticed the blue color in her eyes: a china blue, like the blue you see in Wedgwood china. She moved to walk beside me, sizing me up with eyes that never blinked.

"Did you say it was close by? This won't take long, will it?" she said nervously. "Really, I've got so much to do today."

"This can be as brief as you want it," I said. "They've got the world's best fresh pineapple juice in this place. They grind it up with ice and give it to you in a plastic baggy. Sounds great doesn't it? Stick with me, and you won't be sorry. I'm Kim Barnaby."

I led the way into the wrought iron Victorian market building that gives cover to a hundred tiny kitchens. A few years earlier the government had decided to concentrate the roving food vendors who worked the financial district into one area. The old market building became a beehive of cinder block stalls and flaming propane stoves. Customers simply walk in and take a seat at any of the metal card tables that are scattered beneath the peaked ceiling. The walls of the building are the kitchens, and within, a hundred signs hang, offering fast food for every ethnic pallet.

We grabbed a couple of red metal chairs at a table that sat within the breeze of an oscillating pedestal fan. The place was buzzing with the voices of hundreds of white-shirted office workers and well-dressed secretaries. Young boys and girls in rubber sandals ran among the tables with their trays held high. Old men in baggy suits read papers, oblivious to the company at their table, and giggling office girls hid their laughing behind raised hands.

She was quiet, her china blue eyes looking around the place, feeling the press of activity that surrounded our table.

"What do you think?" I said. "Have you been here before?"

I waited for a response that never came. She seemed lost in thought until the fan's breeze caught her hair and pushed it across her cheek. She flicked her head and swept the back of her hand across the side of her face. Then she smiled and said, "Did you say something, Kim?"

"So, what would you like?" I said raising my voice. "You point and I'll translate. They'll have it here before you can say Big Mac."

She liked that and laughed, "Let's get some of that juice you were talking about and we'll talk awhile. My name is Jill, Jill Schaefer. My brother is the skipper of *Nighthawk*."

She gave me about ten minutes: about twice the time it takes to down a big glass of iced pineapple juice when sitting less than eighty miles from the equator. She seemed to know how far to go with my questions, giving replies then turning the same question on me. I learned that she knew the sailing life—her brother had pursued it ever since she could remember. At least once a year she would leave her job at a San Francisco art gallery and fly to visit with him. He had run charter boats out of the Med, the Caribbean, French Polynesia, and on and on, eventually ending up on *Nighthawk*. She had joined the boat in Malaysia and had sailed into Singapore with him. They were very close.

I wanted to carry on right into lunch but when the juice vendor's pick-up boy came for our empty glasses, Jill took advantage of the moment and pushed her twenty-dollar bill into his hand. As he went for change, she smiled brightly. "Now I've got you, Kim Barnaby," she laughed, "and I'll make you work real hard to get back to even, you watch."

"I look forward to it," I laughed, unable to hold back the same lecherous smile I had used earlier. "When can I get started?"

"It won't be easy for you. I've got to fly up to Thailand as soon as I can get a ticket. It's art business, you know, but I'll be back, and you'll get your chance. I promise."

"Okay, I'll hold you to it," I said rising to my feet. "Can I drop you off in town? My motorcycle is just across the street in the Citibank lot."

She took her change in front of the juice vendor's stall, and we walked out into the sunlight. She led me back up Shenton Way to the covered taxi stand that we had passed earlier.

"I'm afraid of bikes," she said. "Really, they are too dangerous, and I'll be much better off in a taxi."

She moved into the queue of people at the stand. "Besides," she said, "I'll need him all afternoon. Just tell me that you'll stop by the boat next week. I'd love to see you again."

I gave her the longest look I had put on anybody in years. "You can count on it," I whispered while turning to the traffic.

I didn't look back 'til long after I had crossed the street and headed down toward the bank. She waved and I smiled. Maybe I was too easy.

CHAPTER FIVE

I had time to think later in the day. Time I spent silently standing in the queue at Citibank and later in the market over on Orchard Road. Last minute shoppers and holidaymakers crowded the banking and shopping districts to a near standstill. Inside, a pre-holiday blitz filled the aisles and ran bent queues beyond all limits. I stood my ground, all afternoon, waiting and watching, half stepping to the press of a hundred nudging elbows and shuffling feet. Early on it was easy, buoyed by holiday anticipation and the sparkling notion a pair of china blue eyes had left behind. But as the afternoon dragged on, my expectations withered, and my morning's infatuation seemed to run out of substance. In its absence I wore a blank face and regressed into the mundane.

I didn't want to believe any of what Bill had said. In fact, I had felt an instant dislike for him the moment we met. Who in his right mind would call Malaysians "gooks"? I'd like to forget that name ever existed. And what the hell was a "gook boat" anyway? I knew too much about his brand of bullshit to let it roll over me. I see it all too often aboard the rig back in the Philippines, and it always gets me going. Who are these guys? What makes them do it? Is white supremacy back in fashion? Whatever, I've been around SE Asia too long to let it pass. Bill was a write-off, and God knows he was no "mate" of mine. And who the hell is Jack?

I would have been happy to let it go at that, but I couldn't. The thought that French's had been shot up just wouldn't let me put it to rest. The scene Bill described was stuck in my mind like a bad dream, and regardless of what I thought about him, his version brought the incident right to my doorstep. It crowded my thoughts and turned the afternoon sour. It was a reality I couldn't fight off with a casual denial.

I rode back to French's under a cloud. Late afternoon showers were breaking out along the western skyline, and long shadows were fading in the pale light. I gunned the Norton along, pressing every opening for a breeze that might clear my head and take my suspicions with it. I just couldn't imagine the Malays doing anything so bold as unloading cargo right in the anchorage. It simply couldn't be, not with so many better places just minutes away. Bill must have dreamed it. I supposed he needed an excuse to leave. It just didn't make sense any other way.

My suspicions finally gave way to the open road, and in the end I rolled into the compound standing high on the pegs, stretching like a jockey. Across the rutted courtyard, under the galvanized pavilion, a few couples sat thumbing magazines and sipping beer. Beneath the low roof I could see towels and loose sacks of clothing spread out on a pair of long tables that ran parallel to the shoreline. A couple of ladies with wet hair fidgeted at the edge of the covered concrete slab, waiting for their men to make their dinghies ready for departure. It was late afternoon happy hour at French's, and the showers were running non-stop.

I had no intention of joining another queue, not after the day I had put in. I parked beneath the over-hangs of Mr. French's empty garage and pulled a tarp over the Norton. Sometime later in the evening Teresa would return to serve dinner in the pavilion, and I might feel a lot more social. For now, it was all I could do to manage a pleasant nod as I made my way past the building over to where I had left my skiff.

It lay behind the pavilion, in the work area at the far end of the French's property. A pair of weather-beaten tool sheds split this space into two separate work zones, one being for paint and varnish, the other for woodworking. Between the sheds, a wide path led down to a place on the shoreline where the guests tied off to the columns that formed "the grid." As was my habit, I had pulled my flat-bottomed skiff up high-and-dry, setting it to rest at the edge of the path, well above the high water mark. I walked to its side and stood for a while, looking out into the anchorage and beyond to the Malaysian mainland.

In the dark flowing water, a never-ending parade of man-made debris drifted before me. Bits of Styrofoam that never break down swirled with leaves in the backwash of a tree limb that stumbled along in the shallows. It cartwheeled and brought two impaled plastic bags to the oily surface and then twisted in the soft bottom. I let it draw my eyes down along the shore, past the makeshift railway lift the Frenchmen had slapped together, and beyond to the casuarina roots that marked the far edge of the French's property.

They had let this part of the compound go to seed since the Frenchmen had moved in. Nobody picked up the debris that got hung up in the roots anymore, and the underbrush had been let go to grow to the height of my knee. The trees that had been pruned for overhead clearance shed branches that cluttered the area and hid hundreds of rusting tins and sun bleached plastic waste. I walked the tide line down to the roots, kicking at bits of garbage as I went along.

There's no garbage like kampong garbage. I've watched it float by *Windigo* for years, and I know more about it than I ever wanted. The bulk of it rolls around unnoticed below the surface, out of sight and forgotten. Some of it ends up on dirty beaches like this one or becomes lodged in mangrove roots, never to move again. The part that floats is the part I know about. I've gone so far as to tell people I could navigate the passage to Hong Kong without charts or a compass, simply by reading the advertising on the plastic bags that float in the China Sea. You find them everywhere. The closer to port you get, the more floating bags there are, and eventually you will see them everywhere you look. I tell them, that's when you need to know what kampong garbage looks like. Kampong garbage never goes far from home; it rides out of town, then turns back with the tide, so it never gets lost. If you know what it looks like, you can follow it to its source and make port in the worst weather. The trick is to follow the trail of broken rubber thongs. It's not kampong garbage until the rubber shoes start to outnumber the plastic bags. Once the balance tips to the shoes, you're home free.

Distant thunder rumbled, and I turned to retreat. I moved up off the wet foreshore looking for firmer footing in the underbrush, but found it worse there. December's rain had made this area fully saturated, and it surprised me to find it turned to soft marsh. I stopped in my tracks, wondering whether to continue or leap back to the tide line where it was firmer. Scanning the underbrush, I was looking for a graceful way to make my exit when I found the very thing I had hoped to miss.

Beneath the brush, almost hidden by the ground cover, a cluster of small pools dotted the soggy marsh. They each held a measure of black water that made them appear more conspicuous as I came forward to look down on them. They were soft at the edges, and some had collapsed into others, making them appear larger as they ran down toward the shoreline. In some of the smaller pools the trampled stalks had already righted themselves and the trail was all but gone. Behind me my own footprints were filling with black water and by tomorrow the grass would hide them as well. I looked to the water's edge, half expecting to find the final confirmation my suspicions demanded, but of course, there was nothing. Relentless tides had swept away whatever trail a laden boat's keel would have made in the banks.

There was nothing in the shoreline that really confirmed Bill's story. The cluster of pools I took for smugglers' footprints may have been nothing more than somebody's wayward trip to the outhouse. I wanted something more significant. Something a beachcomber of my caliber could hang his hat on. For a moment I thought I had found it in the leather sandal I found jammed in the mud alongside the pools. Judging by its size, it looked right, being small and fairly narrow, but beneath the caked mud it carried an Italian stamp in the sole, and that seemed to discount any connection it had to the smugglers. To a connoisseur of kampong garbage, shoes are a dime a dozen, and my leather specimen had probably been tossed out into the brush, judging by the way it lay in the mud. It made more sense to see it that way. Otherwise, I would have to believe that Malaysian smugglers were wearing Italian sandals to work, and that just didn't wash.

I walked further inland following the pools until they faded to mere impressions in the dryer high ground. Eventually they disappeared altogether, leaving me close to the property line in the area behind the dry-docked boat. The Frenchmen had turned the space into a no man's land with their rubbish. It was spread out among the trees and underbrush in a pattern that radiated away from their high perch. Standing on deck, ten feet up in the trees, they managed to pollute a considerable distance, tossing paint buckets and wood scraps far into the trees. Closer in there were mounds of old newsprint and magazines that sat like targets waiting their next aerial bombardment. I waded through their misses, quietly passing beneath the boat's overhanging transom on my way out, and in a weary gesture of resignation I tossed the muddy sandal to the ground.

Out in the anchorage a gust of chilled air swept a carpet of flickering ripples across the water. It rolled through the fleet, twisting the boats out of their tidal set, sending them veering and charging about like a team of startled horses. Behind the wind's shadow, up by the causeway, a curtain of rain splashed a sprawling white line on the dark water. I rowed for all I was worth, turning every now and then to judge the distances and estimate the point of convergence. We arrived together, the white line spitting a thousand rippling rings in the water around *Windigo* while I gathered up my gear and scrambled for cover under the whiffing cockpit awning.

I stood breathless in the noisy downpour. The thunder rumbled around me while a sudden darkness of night swept away the silhouettes of the other sailboats. For a moment I felt isolated and free. My mind swarmed with images I had found while sailing far offshore in the night, and for the first time in a year I felt the urge to get away. It came over me like a squall, first as a sprinkling of memories, vigorous and exhilarating ones, then as a burst of inspiration. I fought it, knowing it would derail everything I had going, knowing it had more to do with the onslaught of a holiday depression than anything real. I went below to unwind with a bottle of Yugoslavian red wine and didn't show myself on deck until well into the next day.

CHAPTER SIX

The Christmas party turned out to be much bigger than anyone expected. For a lot of the old-guard British residents who showed up early on, it was a sort of holiday fanfare for Mr. French who had just rebounded from a bad bout with dengue fever. He met the early arrivals at the steps in front of his house and ushered them up to the porch for gin and tonics. From there they sat in the evening light looking across to the brightly decorated pavilion that was still being made ready for the evening's affair. Teresa had given the last minute details to Barb and some of the other sailing ladies who hurried about fussing with the buffet arrangement while a couple of husbands whacked up the last few strings of lights.

With the final preparations intact and with the pavilion lacking nothing but food, we were waved off into the anchorage to make ourselves ready and await the appointed hour. I rowed out to *Windigo* in time to watch Bert's sloop turn out of the channel and set a bead on my bow. He circled behind my stern and came up alongside bellowing "Merrrrrry Christmas" loud enough to echo into every cockpit in the anchorage. Horns and whistles blasted back a response that shook the trees and sent Gee Seng's roosters into a frenzy. From that moment on into the night, horns blasted and a spontaneous chain reaction of sound echoed Christmas cheer all the way down to the kampong.

It was late twilight when I rowed ashore. A fading patch of blue-black light hung in the western sky, back lighting the tree-topped horizon in a jagged silhouette. It was the time just before total darkness when lights glow their warmest, and the stars take over the sky. The pavilion was fully lit, shooting rays of warm vibrant colors over the dark waters that rippled in my skiff's wake. It was the first clear night I'd seen in so long I had forgotten what colored lights could do on rippling water. It set a dream-like stage beneath the pavilion. Wild colors shimmered and danced beneath the feet of a hundred nameless players who spoke an unrecognized language that floated out on the night air. I picked up my pace, straining to stay in the mainstream of colors while rowing for a front and center position just below the stage.

It wasn't long before I could recognize the language and identify some of the players. Even at a distance, it was easy to distinguish between the groups of guests. The sailing crowd, being true to Pacific traditions, had come decked out luau style, sporting enough Hawaiian prints and Balinese batiks to inundate the place in tropical colors. They swamped the resident expats who came up from the suburbs in tasteful white guayaberas and fresh pressed linens, looking like a group of wealthy plantation owners. As always, everybody was busy interviewing one another, and as always, regardless of the language being spoken, the subject was sailing and travel. Far away names and faraway places rang out above a din of heavily accented chatter and raucous laughter.

I skidded my bow into the soft muddy bank and stood to make my leap ashore. A dark umbra masked the water's edge, leaving me standing atop the bow seat, half bathed in blinding colored light, searching for firm ground somewhere out in the shadows. I stood there, preoccupied with the lack of light, lost in the technique of my upcoming leap. A hard push would drive the skiff back into the water and leave me ankle deep in mud with no trajectory whatever. A soft push might not cover the distance. In my moment of indecision, I must have lost track of my surroundings because when I finally landed on shore, I received something of an ovation from the pavilion. I had no idea how long I had been on stage, and in that moment I was the actor who walked on having forgotten all his lines. My only course was to bow gracefully and head for the bar where Bert's big hairy forearm waited to wrap across my neck in a consoling welcome that made me feel all the more conspicuous.

"That was quite an arrival," he said, laughing as he led me the last few steps to the bar. "You looked just like Washington crossing the Delaware," he said, giving my back a thump. "By God, if I had a flag, I'd have to wrap you up in it."

"I wouldn't like that, Bert," I shot back. "They only wrap the dead in flags, and I'm not ready to be dumped over the side just yet. But you can check on me tomorrow. When this party is over, I think I may be ready."

"If you are," he blurted back, "I'll know what did you in. Take a look over there," he said, pointing across the pavilion. "I'll bet you'd die for that one."

"You know," he went on, "she's been asking about you."

I took the bait and wheeled around saying, "That's a cheap trick, my friend. You should know better than to fool with somebody who just returned from a month at ..."

My voice fell the instant my eyes met her smile. She slowly raised her hand to shoulder level and gave me the identical wave she'd used on Shenton Way. It was a tentative gesture, really little more than a raised hand, but it stopped me cold and begged a reply.

Without my saying a word, Bert ripped the cap off an Anchor beer and pushed it into my side saying, "Opportunity knocks only once, old buddy, and this one looks like yours." He slipped the bottle into my hand and with another whack on my back, he sent me off. "I'll stand by with the flag," he chuckled.

I waded into the crowd, all smiles, nodding greetings and exchanging quips as I made my way to where Jill was standing, but by the time I reached her, she had rejoined a conversation with the guys off the dry-docked boat and was speaking French at a mile a minute clip. She moved back a step as I joined her, flashing me a quick smile that held me by her side while she continued. I stood and watched as she spoke, unable to follow at the pace she kept up, but, just like the Frenchmen, hanging on her every word. She was the image of sell-confident beauty: underdone and unadorned by modern affectations.

She caught me with the bottle way up to my mouth when she suddenly broke into English. "Kim," she laughed with a gleam in her eye, "You know Jacques and Dominique. Could you please tell them what you see on the table over there? They're calling it a Chinese fondue. I know they can't be right. Could you tell them what it's called?"

"I thought you were on your way to Thailand," I spluttered. "Did your trip fall through?"

"No, no," she said turning to face me. "I'm still going. I just don't leave 'till tomorrow." She paused to watch the effect her words had on me. Then, with her hand pointing toward the long tables she continued, "What is that thing, Kim? I know I've seen those before. I just can't remember what they're called."

As much as I enjoyed her sense of familiarity, I couldn't help but react in surprise to the way she was putting me on the spot. "They're called Mongolian fire pots," I said sharply. "I think they slipped over the Great Wall with Genghis Khan. When are you coming back? From Thailand I mean. How many days will you be up there?"

"You see?" she beamed, spinning to address the Frenchmen. "It's a Mongolian fire pot! Another Marco Polo export! *Que dire de plus!*"

They seemed to understand what she was talking about better than I because they both reacted with shrugged shoulders and uplifted palms, as if to grant her a moment's triumph. She turned back to face me with a smile that melted my reserve. "Maybe we could go somewhere and talk," she cooed. "We've got so little time before I have to leave."

She laid a final burst of French on Jacques and Dominique while I guided her out of the pavilion.

Whatever it was she said, it seemed to have no effect on them. They weren't even watching. I suspected they were hard losers.

I took her across the courtyard, down to the row of wooden seats that face out into the anchorage. It was dark and much quieter down by the water, and for a while nothing was said as we both fell under the spell of the night air and the rippling reflections.

When she broke the silence it was in a soft voice, almost apologetic in tone. "I'll be away about three days," she whispered, "though it could be a bit more. It really depends on what they've got set up. Does that answer your question?"

"I just wanted to know when we could get together," I said. "You know, we left it pretty loose the other day. I thought maybe I could run you around the island when you get back; the bird park, the zoo, that sort of thing. Maybe dinner, a moonlit sail, a weekend up at Tioman; whatever makes sense."

"It all makes sense, and there'll be time for almost everything after my trip. It's just that there's a lot riding on this trip; it's art business you know, more middlemen than you can count. I really hope it doesn't take too long. Anyway, I'm sure you'll understand. You solo sailors are supposed to be famous for your patience."

"Who told you that?"

"My brother tells me patience is the most important lesson sailing teaches a man. Don't tell me you haven't learned patience, Mr. Barnaby."

"When you put it that way, how can I argue?" I laughed. "You're too much, Jill. I only hope the people in Thailand are ready for you. Though even if they are not, I'm sure you'll find a way to get what you want, just the way you want it."

"What I want is a quick trip and your promise to take me sailing when I get back. Could we do that, Kim? I'd love to go out on your boat."

"We can do better than that!" I said standing up. "Let me run you out to *Windigo* now, for a quick tour. Who knows? Maybe we'll get a sail in tonight!"

"You're not the least bit patient!" she laughed. "Somehow that doesn't surprise me."

I wasted no time getting us launched and away from the lights that had compromised my landing. Jill didn't slow the process at all, she had her shoes off before I had untied the line, and she knew when to get in and where to sit. "You've been here before," I said, fitting the oars into the forward oar locks.

"Oh, no," she said shaking her head. "I've never been here before tonight."

"No, no," I laughed. "I mean the dingy. You get aboard like you've been here before. You know, it's unusual to find someone who does it as casually as you did. I meant it as a compliment."

"My brother and I grew up sailing prams in the Bay area," she said with a smile. "That's cold water sailing. You flip over and you're in for some real chills. The first thing they taught us was to step to the middle and stay low. I guess it's something I never forgot."

The conversation ended the moment we reached the strength of the current. The oar locks came alive and a rhythm of laboring squeaks and rattles took over in the skiff. Jill knew the signal and quietly observed the action while we slowly hitched our way into the fleet. She watched the hulls pass in the darkness, then set her gaze to the far shoreline. When I finally got the angle I needed, I let up and things got quiet except for my breathing.

"It's so peaceful up here," she began. "Peaceful and yet so exciting. Do you ever feel it, Kim? I mean when you look way over there, across the water, beyond Malaysia. Do you feel the mystery? Do you ever see Buddha's smile?"

I stood up to grab the rail as we came down on *Windigo's* dark form. Jill stayed seated and did not speak. When we stopped, I stood there holding the rail with both hands, steadying the skiff, waiting for her first move. Still, she did not move. I waited. When she finally rose, she used one motion to scale the lifelines and disappear into the cockpit. I slid aft, hand over hand, down the rail to the stern cleat. Her silence had me puzzled.

I slipped past her without saying a word, moving through the darkness as if it were light. Throwing the hatch open I swung below deck like a trained animal, landing at the chart table with my hand on the light switch. It came on and soft red light filled the cabin. I looked up into the cockpit to see if I had her attention.

"You've been here before!" she laughed. "Do I have to do it that way?"

"No, no," I chuckled. "You can save the acrobatics for later, my dear. Come on down and let me show you the place."

She came below laughing as I walked about flipping light switches and gathering up loose files. "It kind of takes you by surprise, I guess. Since I don't think I ever told you what it is I do." I held up a pair of big triton shells, one in each hand. "You might even call it art business," I said smiling. "Chalk up one more middle man."

"You see," I said, pulling drawer after drawer of specimen shells into the light, "it's something like an art gallery down here. Do you see any you like?"

I left her to wander through the drawers while I went to the galley to mix up the house specialty. It became a production I vowed never to try again. I don't know what possessed me. It's hard enough to serve a glass of beer on a sailboat; a Singapore Sling is pure fantasy. By the time the drinks were complete and the cherry brandy was floating at the top of both glasses, I had so cluttered the galley counter with bottles and squeezers and shakers and strainers, there wasn't room for the box of little paper parasols. Through the whole enterprise Jill stayed forward, moving the drawers in and out, pausing only to read the Latin names before going on to the next layer. She was in her element, studying in close, with the intensity and thoroughness of an experienced appraiser.

"So, you know shells!" I volunteered.

"I know art," she said, reaching for the drink I offered. "And I know a good collection when I see it. Yours is unbelievable, Kim. The way it shows the growth development of each species, I mean there are so many different sizes in such a controlled progression. And, they're all so perfect. They're like miniature sculptures. I've never seen anything like it. It's so ... ontogenetic."

"I hope that means what I think it means," I laughed.

"It means you've got something you can be very proud of, Kim. I know at least five museums that would pay whatever you ask for this. It's extraordinary. How did you ever manage to find them?"

"It's not hard. You only need to know what you are looking at and be willing to pay the price."

"Oh, come on, Kim! You're not telling me you went out and bought all these shells. It can't be that easy."

"Well, with some it is. The ones that live below a couple hundred feet are beyond my capabilities. So, I buy and trade for them. I know a few of the Filipino skippers who tow the deep-water trawls and sometimes they'll let me look over their haul when they're cleaning the catch. I get some good ones that way. Then of course, there are the shell shops."

"Okay, but what about the others, the shallower ones. How do you get them?"

"Again, sometimes I'll trade for what I need, but usually they're not available, and the really hard to find specimens get hoarded just like fine art. You never see them in the shops."

"I see them here, Kim," she said, pointing to the drawers. "I counted three Glory-of-the-Sea cones, and that tray of Golden Cowries! They must have come from somewhere."

"I used to hunt shells in the Southern Philippines. Live ones, you know, with SCUBA gear and all that. *Windigo* was built around that idea. You know, she carries some pretty specialized equipment for a little forty-three footer. I've got three compressors and enough hookah equipment to fill the forepeak. She's even got an SS-80 scanning sonar, if you know what that is."

"You'd be surprised," she said brightly. "I know exactly what it is. It's echo location, like what porpoise use."

"That's right, only it's not *that* good. I use it to find the breaks in the reef, where the tidal currents move in and out. That's where you get good shells."

"That's also where you get the sharks," she said smiling. "I'll bet you've been chased out of the water a few times," she teased.

"It's an occupational hazard, no doubt about it. But they get used to you, eventually. Really, they don't worry me as much as the sharks that run the fishing boats up there. Those are the predators to worry about."

"You mean the fishermen don't want you poking around in their fishing grounds, is that it?"

"Oh no," I said, putting down my drink. "It goes way beyond anything like that. There's a civil war going on up there. It's been going on for years, right on top of the most spectacular collection of mollusks the world has ever known. No serious shell hunting has gone on up there since the invention of SCUBA. It's just sitting there, and nobody can get at it. You see, the Southern Philippines are Moslem. They've been Moslem since God knows when, and they don't like outsiders. They fought the Spanish when they tried to bring in Christianity back in the 1550s and they're still fighting it. The Moros never wanted to be part of the Philippines, and they still don't. Jill, it's almost impossible to travel in those islands. Even the Filipinos can't do it without getting kidnapped or hijacked. Marcos sent the whole Philippine Navy down there and got nowhere. It's real serious stuff."

"Is that why you stopped? Did they chase you out?"

"I wouldn't put it that way," I said, moving to begin clearing the galley counter. "I left because I couldn't work out the logistics. It's that simple. What with the typhoons and the politics, I was spending all my time ducking and dodging. The typhoons were telling me to go south, to get below their track and that's where the best shells are, so I wanted to do just that. But, the threat of being ambushed on the high seas was telling me to go back up north where it was safe. I felt like I was always running away from where I wanted to be; you get paranoid after a while. I ended up trying to split the difference by working the no man's land zone in the northern half of the Sulu Sea. If you're careful and don't attract any attention, you can get away with it for a while. That's where I got my best specimens; on the reefs off Palawan down near the Balabac Straits."

"But still, the Moros drove you out. That is what you are saying, isn't it?"

"Yes, but not before I got most of what I wanted," I began.

Jill turned her attention back to the opened drawers while I continued. She was closing them, one at a time, scanning their contents before clicking them shut.

"I made four trips down there; five if you count last year's run to Singapore. I figure I'm one lucky S.O.B. to have gotten away with it. Believe me, the Moros are people nobody wants to mess with."

Jill gave me no reply. She seemed on a train of thought that had left me talking to myself. Finally, she looked up, having left one drawer opened. "You know," she paused. "This sounds so familiar to me. I see this type of thing all the time in my business. You're so much like a collector I knew who collected Pre-Columbian art back in California. Like you, he could only go so far collecting what the galleries came up with. And eventually, when he knew enough, he decided to go to the source; kind of like what you've done. He went down to Central America and became a grave robber. I'm sure he didn't call himself that, but that is what he did. He dug up grave sites and got killed for it. I remember how stunned I was when I heard about it.

"Jill, that's the most morbid thing I've ever heard!"

"No, please let me finish," she begged. "Let me explain. It was a tragedy I think I could have prevented if I knew then what I know now. You see, after he died, nothing changed at the gallery. We still had a supplier of authentic Pre-Columbian artifacts. I asked myself why my friend died. What had he done that was so different from what our supplier was doing? They both robbed graves."

She was up on her feet now, coming across the salon to make her point at close range.

"The difference was our supplier had consent and my friend didn't. My friend died because he was a grave robber. He was hunting artifacts. Our supplier had everybody believing he was an archaeologist. He was searching for a link with the past. He honored the Indians' ancestors when he dug their graves. My friend desecrated them and died."

"Jill, I'm not out there digging up the dead," I said. "I'm a vagabond malacologist. The worst thing I do is throw mollusks out of their homes. I don't see what this has to do with me."

"Consent! You never had the Moros' consent, Kim. That's why you could never work out the 'logistics.' Your search for shells is really not so different from what my friend was doing."

"Does that mean they'll kill me if I don't become an archaeologist?"

"Come on," she laughed. "Don't make a joke out of this. I think I know how you can get their consent."

"Unless you know the Sultan of Sulu," I laughed, "I'd be willing to bet you don't."

"Kim, I'll bet you are the one person who could pull it off! Don't you see? If you mix what you know about shells with a little old fashioned archaeology, I'll bet they'd beg you to come in. You know, if you played it right, I'll bet the Sultan would throw in an escort."

"Jill, do you know what you're talking about? Those guys are fighting a civil war up there!"

She walked back to the opened drawer of shells.

"I'm sure you know what this is," she said, picking up a bleached out three-inch shell.

"Sure," I answered. "It's an old dye murex."

"Kim, I know you'll think this is a little far out, but I think this could be your key to getting their consent."

"Look, that shell did not come from the Philippines. You're not even close. You get those in the Eastern Mediterranean and off North Africa."

"Did you know they've found mounds of murexes all along the coast of India and even Sri Lanka?"

"Jill, those had to be a different variety of murex. There is no way a Mediterranean snail could be found in those areas. The habitat is totally different down there, and the shells would show it. They wouldn't look at all the same."

"Of course you're right, but it's not the species that should interest you. It's the mounds. That's where the archaeology comes in. Somebody at some distant point in time put a big effort into harvesting murexes. Ancient history tells us who they were and why they hunted little snails."

"Anybody who ever started a shell collection could tell you about dye murexes. Everyone knows about Tyrian purple dye and the ancient Greeks and Romans. It's no secret. It's also no secret why the mounds are there. They say it took a quarter of a million murexes to make a pound of the dye. I'd say that makes a pretty good sized mound."

"Kim, you're missing the connection. Archaeologists use the mounds to piece together the history of the people who did the collecting; in this case I think it's the Phoenicians, not the Greeks or Romans."

"What difference does it make?"

"It makes a big difference if you're trying to determine the boundaries of the Phoenician trading empire in the first millennium before Christ. It's academic, but those mounds are archaeological markers. They keep turning up further and further away from where archaeologists draw the line. Today it's Sri Lanka, but who says it can't be the Malay Peninsula or Indonesia or even the Sulu Archipelago?"

"And you think I can use this to get consent from the Moros?"

"That's where I would begin if I were trying to do it."

"You mean I should announce something like a one-man archaeological expedition? Go out there looking for murex mounds? Jill, it's preposterous."

"It's not near as crazy as it sounds. Not to the ears of a Muslim who lives as far away from Mecca as the Moros. I'll bet they'd buy it if you put it to them right. You see, the Phoenicians are a recognized link to Muslim prehistory. Before Mohammed, who were the Moslems? A lot of people say they were the Phoenicians."

"So, if I said I was looking for murex mounds, the Moros would leave me alone? It's that simple?"

"If you said you were looking for murex mounds, and explained it right, I think it would go right to their essence. You would be searching for a link with their past, and they would be honored by your search. Kim, that's how archaeologists have been doing it since they stopped robbing graves and became archaeologists."

Her case made, she sat back to watch me wipe the galley counter clean. I took my time, wondering how she had taken me from the ridiculous to the sublime, all in the time I took to put the galley right after a couple of not so simple cocktails.

"When you put it that way," I said tossing the sponge into the sink, "it sounds so reasonable it kind of scares me." I moved across the salon to make my point at the same close range she had used. "Jill, if it weren't so bloody dangerous up there your idea might be worth trying. But I don't think I'd want to gamble my life on it, not for a handful of shells."

"Well," she replied, "like I said, it's academic. Most of what I like to talk about is. Listen, Kim, I don't want you to think I'm suggesting you drop everything and go up there and try it. You don't need to anyway. You've probably got everything you were looking for right here."

As her words left her lips, she motioned toward the drawers, trying to direct my attention away from her face, back to the subject at hand. But I let the gesture go unnoticed, deliberately failing to be persuaded away from the look of her china blue eyes and the intent I chose to put on what she had just said.

"You're right," I said in my most solemn tone. "I've got everything I've been looking for right here. Now I just wonder what it will take to keep it."

She took my question in perfect silence, letting its wistful tone ring a hush through the salon. It lay thick in the air for so long I could hear its echo in my mind, and when I finally turned to retreat back to the galley she stopped me cold.

"Don't worry," she laughed. "I wouldn't dare ask for another Singapore Sling."

I turned to see her face lit up in playful delight. She stood and came toward me, her smiling eyes shining wet in the afterglow of her laughter. Her arms opened and we drew together, slowly making contact until her eyes closed and a pair of small tears glistened above her cheeks. They sparkled, then slipped down her face, drawing me still closer until my eyes shut, and I felt the glowing warmth of her soft embrace.

"My flight leaves at noon," she whispered. "Do you think I'll make it?"

CHAPTER SEVEN

We started ashore at first light, unrested and spent, both needing a second wind just to take us into daylight. I rowed, and Jill sat, quiet as the morning calm, her eyes closed while her body swung to the pull and recovery of my every stroke. She let it drain the expression from her face and became withdrawn. I rowed, wondering how she would make it through the day if she started like this: unable to keep her eyes opened for the sunrise, unable to notice the morning light unfolding the color spectrum, and missing the sudden burst of refracted hues that made the morning glow. I wondered how could she keep her eyes closed to the best second wind a tired sailor knows? Did she know nothing about maritime twilight? I wanted to tell her how it works so she could use it like I do, but I couldn't. She was beyond my reach, swaying to the strain of my strokes, rocked numb by the rhythm of the creaking oar locks.

We made shore with a lurch that brought her back to life, but just barely. She slowly opened her eyes and clambered out of the skiff, not saying a word and not looking back. While I dragged the dingy up above the high waterline, she disappeared into the pavilion. She had missed finding a second wind in the morning light, and I wondered what misery this day would bring her if she missed her next chance. She had too many miles to make to let them pass unnoticed. I know how one second wind can lead to another and that a good sailor can ride them all day and all night if he knows where to find them. I wanted to tell her where to start looking, but she had her eyes closed when I found her.

She was sitting in the pavilion with the same expressionless face I had seen out in the dingy. Neither the sunrise nor the feel of firm land at her feet was bringing her around. If anything, she seemed more stuck in the mood now that she had found a quiet place to sit. I crossed the courtyard and headed for the Norton, knowing I had all the time in the world to make it ready for the trip into town. I did everything to waste time; from folding up the tarp, through checking the oil and gas levels, right on to the final wipe down of the seats. When it was all done, I rolled the bike out into the open air and went to deliver the rude awakening with a crash helmet under each arm.

She wasn't sitting where I had left her, so she didn't get the kind of call to arms I had planned. Instead, I found her standing behind the bar, holding a jacket and handbag, looking as fresh as any new day I could remember. Her transformation seemed remarkable considering the way she was when I had left her. Somewhere, behind the blind mask of that blank look, she had found what looked like a second wind. When I asked how she had managed it she laughed, "It's all in the Buddha's smile. I thought you knew."

I kicked the Norton alive and waited as Jill wedged her dress tight to her legs and slid forward in the seat. She had no inhibitions now. Her arms wrapped around me and she drew herself in, pressing a hug on my back that begged a most stirring welcome to the morning she had just discovered. I let the clutch go and she held on, just like that, all the way down to Clifford Pier.

It was about seven o'clock when Jill took notice of the time and became anxious. We had found on-street parking in the banking district, and we were just about to cross Shenton Way when she caught sight of the clock above the concourse building. Without a word, she gave my arm a tug and we broke into a quickstep that took us all the way through the concourse, back to the concrete steps where the big water taxis smoke and thunder about. Then Jill spotted a sampan lying against the seawall in the far stalls, and with another tug she set our tack to the far staircase. I tried to slow her with a last minute bon voyage sendoff, but she walked right through it, insisting I stay with her for the ride out to the *Nighthawk* and the opportunity to meet her brother. After the evening we'd put in, she could hardly be denied. So, with time short and my arm firmly clamped at her side, she led the way down to the sampan where we boarded without ever breaking stride. In seconds, we were running full tilt, directly into the rising sun making an easterly course across the inner harbor.

I had my eyes fixed on *Nighthawk* the moment she came out from under the sun's glare. She looked different than I remembered. She seemed bigger and more powerful than the hulking hundred-foot cargo boat I had seen the other day. Backlit, she was all schooner; her three great masts festooned in baggy wrinkle, with ratlines on the shrouds, and netting in her martingales. Every detail in her rigging made sense, and in light of her purpose, she was much more a sailing machine that I had originally thought. She was, after all, a proper working motor-sailor: battered and bleeding rust, but beautifully rigged for long haul junkets and well laid out for tramping the odd bit of freight to the far corners of the world. The more I saw, the more I liked the concept, and by the time we drove up into her shadows, I was itching to get the tour Jill had offered.

As we swung in for the final approach on the boarding ladder I had turned my focus to *Nighthawk*'s hull lines and in a preoccupation only a sailor can understand, I missed seeing the silent exchange going on between Jill and the guy standing at the rail. They got my attention, however, just after the boatman shut down his motor to glide in on the ladder.

"Christ, Jill!" his voice called out. "Do you know what time it is? How are you going to get to Chiang Mai if you miss your flight? You know you've got to be there an hour before take-off?"

Jill was half way up the ladder before I understood what was happening. The voice was obviously that of her brother, and Jill was more than ready for the confrontation. She swept him back away from the entry gate as she boarded, and I was left in the sampan staring up into blank space while the two of them hashed it out in private. I flashed the boatman my raised palm as if to ask him to stand by while I held on. Then, expecting an introduction and permission to board, I quickly gathered up the handbag Jill had left behind and stood by waiting for their immediate return.

Time passed and I tried to remember if there was an old maxim that says the bigger the boat, the longer the wait for permission to board. Well, I figured twenty seconds would do, and when it went to more than a minute, I started to get edgy. A minute later, I decided I'd spent enough time standing on protocol, so I reached up to grasp the ladder with both my hands, and in that act, I swung Jill's bag directly in front of my face. It spun there, hanging just beneath my chin, blocking my view to the ladder, and stopping my first step. That's when I noticed the muddied sandal lying deep in her bag, and it stopped me like a kick in the stomach.

I couldn't move for a moment. I just stood there, slack jawed, lost in a chaos of conflicting impulses while my mind locked on to the "Made in Italy" stamp on the sandal's sole. I knew exactly what I was looking at. I'd seen the same muddied sandal only two days ago. I'd held it. I'd even carried it. But now I couldn't believe it.

I heard my name called, and I looked up to see Jill walking to the rail.

"That was my brother," she called down in an exasperated voice. "He thinks I'll miss my flight if we don't end it here. Kim, I'm sorry to have dragged you all the way out here for this. You've been so nice. I'll make it up to you somehow."

I quickly turned my palm back to the Chinese boatman, motioning him to stay put while I climbed the ladder. There was so much I needed to say, and so many questions that needed answers, but for some reason, when I arrived to face her, all I could get out was a whispered, " ... don't sweat it."

She put a kiss on my lips and smiled. "I knew you'd understand," she said, mimicking my whisper. "I'll call you the minute I get back. Then we'll take that sail we talked about."

She took the bag from my hand and I started down the ladder, too tongue-tied to muster even a simple "good-bye." It was as if my mind had slipped into rewind and disconnected my tongue. All I could do was to pull back and fade. I watched myself climb down the ladder hardly believing the irony in my own words. "Don't sweat it!" What a thing to say! And yet, Jill loved it. In fact, she was as happy as I'd seen her, laughing and waving as we pulled away, dragging it out until we disappeared into the fleet. Her laugh and the gleam in her china blue eyes gave me every reason to forget what I had seen. And for a moment, there was no muddied sandal, and there were no smugglers' footprints behind the dry-docked boat; there was only her smile and a second wind that came on way too strong to last.

By the time I rolled into the marina, there wasn't so much as a breath of breeze left in the air. Stale scents of spilled beer hung over the place like a fog that wouldn't lift. I parked and crossed the courtyard, sidestepping tipped over plastic glasses and empty bottles that had totally escaped my notice only an hour earlier. Nothing had changed while I was away, but everything seemed different now that the morning light had so much glaring heat in it. It stole my second wind and made me look at things I didn't want to see. Jill had lied when she said she'd never been to the marina before last night. For whatever reason, regardless of her connection to any smuggling that may have taken place, she had lied, and it changed the way I saw things. Even the cool of a midmorning breeze couldn't change the disappointment that had come over me. Scattered chairs and piles of waste blocked my path and made me tired. It was a "day-after" morning back at French's, and I wished I were sleeping it off like everybody else.

I switched on the autopilot that drives me when things get like this, and before another thought crossed my mind I was out in the current, making my last leg home. I rowed without thinking, letting my oars cut a path they knew by habit. And they held course, right up until the last part, when without the slightest hesitation, they veered to answer a beckoning gesture I think I would have shrugged off if I'd had my wits about me. I guess it was the arched eyebrows that did it. Without them it was just a raised coffee cup hanging from an outstretched finger. But with his eyebrows arched, suggesting nothing but the most sordid curiosity, and then that hangdog look that forgave my response before I could even manage one, Bert had me on a line and was reeling me in like a tired fish.

"Dare I ask how your evening went?" he began before I arrived. "You know, you two took off before the party even started? You missed the whole thing! Man, you walked out on Teresa's hot pot. Now that's big trouble!"

I was still on inertial guidance and way too tired to trade quips or react to the needle Bert was trying to work on me. He got nothing for his efforts. I shipped my oars and slapped a bowline on his sternpost without acknowledging any of what he had said. It was my turn to be a hard case, and it would take more than a few one-liners to disarm me. Bert watched me climb the rail and get seated in the cockpit before he started up again.

"Barnaby, is that a hangover I'm looking at, or are you just getting too old to pull an all-nighter?"

"Both," I said while slumping for effect. "I wish I'd never gotten out of bed."

"Well ..." he said, backing his way down into the galley to fill my cup. "That's life in the fast track, my man. Maybe it's time you start taking your vitamins again," he hollered. "God knows you'll need them the next time you get lucky."

I let that one go too.

There was white steam rising from the cup Bert brought up for me. He set it down on the cockpit seat and climbed the ladder to join me under the sun awning. My hand had reached out to shortstop the transfer but he cut me off, lifting my cup until I looked him in the eyes.

"Did you say something, Kim?" he asked.

"No," I said, holding my hand out impatiently.

"Come on, sure you did, just as I came out of the galley."

"Oh," I mumbled. "I guess I said there wouldn't be a next time. Something like that."

He handed me the cup.

"So, you two didn't hit it off. That's too bad," he said while getting settled. "That's just the way it goes; you know? But I think we've been through this before, right? Remember the girl in Auckland?

He watched me bury my face in the white steam and got impatient while I toyed with the cup.

"She's not your type, you know. The last thing you need is some pushy broad calling your shots."

"You don't know what you're talking about!" I shot back. "She's terrific! And that girl you mentioned just needed a ride. There was nothing going on there."

"Well, good morning, Mr. Barnaby!" he said, mocking a toast with his coffee cup. "I thought I'd never get through to you."

"Well you did," I snapped. "And you're all wrong about Jill. She's not pushy. If anything, she's ... just a very informed person. You know, always a step ahead. Anyway, what makes you say she's pushy? I don't think you even met her!"

"Hey, I'm sorry," he countered. "I thought she blew you off. Go easy, Kim!"

"Look, nobody blew anybody off. She had to fly up to Thailand on business, that's all."

Bert's jaw fell and he sat back. "Oh, Christ," he said under his breath, "That's great."

I took it all in and lapsed from indignation into outright hostility. "Okay, what's eating you, man?" I said in something just short of a shout. "You call me over here like you just woke up. Then you hand me coffee that's been boiling long enough to melt a hole in your boat!"

I blew a cloud of white steam across the cockpit.

"I wouldn't be surprised if this coffee's been boiling away down there since you saw me row ashore at sun up. I could see it in your face when you called me over. You've been waiting all morning to tell me something. So, let's have it, Bert! What the hell's eating you?"

"If you'll calm down, I'll tell you," he whispered. "Just calm down, Barnaby." He paused and we exchanged glowering looks, then he started up again.

"Kim, I don't know how you're going to take what I have to say. And maybe I'm way out of line to say it, but it's something you need to hear, especially now, now that you're involved with that girl."

"This better be good, Bert," I growled. "Because if you are about to lay some horse shit on me about ..."

"Now, come on Kim, give me a break," he shot back. "Look. Up until yesterday I've been lying around Clifford Pier with a broken motor. It's taken a month of screwing around to get that damn thing to work."

"Don't tell me you're looking for sympathy," I snapped.

"No, it's nothing like that. Look, you know what it's like when the boat's all ripped up and there's oily bits of motor lying all over the place? You know, like when you can't find a place to sit down 'cause there are tools sitting everywhere you want to sit? Well, that's what I've been doing for the past month. When I wasn't jamming myself into spaces too small to fit a wrench, I was standing around in the cabin wishing I could sit down and forget the whole thing."

"So what?"

"Well, it took forever, and I guess I got to know the anchorage. You know? I'd take a break every now and then and just stand down there, looking out the ports, checkin' out the other boats. And I got to know a lot about what was happening aboard those yachts. Call it snooping if you like, but the more I saw, the more I watched. It became a form of recreation for me."

"Would you get to the point?" I said breaking in.

"Sure, I'll get to the point," he barked in a cracking voice. "The point is, I spent a hell of a lot of time watching that big schooner, the one your girlfriend's living on, and I don't like it at all. Barnaby, those people are bad news, and that boat gives off bad vibrations like a hot reactor."

"So, you call me over here to tell me you don't like black schooners. Is that it, Bert?"

"That's right, and I got more I want you to hear, Kim," he continued. "You know, that boat's been down at Clifford Pier for a little more than a month, and in all that time only two people have gone ashore. I swear, there are at least twenty crew members on that boat and only two ever go ashore. Your girlfriend and the skipper, that's it. Oh yeah, there's the driver of their skiff, but he only drops them off at the pier. I've never seen him set foot ashore."

"Bert, they don't let me off the rig either. That's the way it's done on commercial vessels. The *Nighthawk*'s a working boat. There's nothing unusual about denying shore leave. It's done all the time."

"I know what you're saying," he went on, "but this is different. Besides, there's more. Do you remember a few days ago, when you brought over that shell?

Well, after you left, I swear, I just about fell out of the cockpit. I mean I couldn't believe it when you and that Chinese swung around to make a pick-up over at that schooner. It's never happened before. When the Chinese drivers run around that boat they get waved off. It's like they don't like anybody getting too close or something. I mean they do it aggressively. That's why it really surprised me to see you over there. Nobody gets that close. Then, when I saw the girl get aboard, I didn't know what to think. I mean their skiff was still hanging off the stern! Man, they broke a pattern I'd been watching for an entire month!"

"And who's to say their outboard motor wasn't broken? Damn it Bert! She even told me she'd never taken a water taxi before. That's how we got to talking. She didn't know what the fee was!"

"Kim, they ran the skipper ashore right after you two landed. There was nothing wrong with their outboard!"

I sighed and gathered myself for a new tack. "Bert, I'm wondering if there's something wrong with *you*. You know, it sounds a lot like you went stir crazy down there with your motor all torn up. I think maybe you should stay up here at French's for a while. It'll do you some good. You know it's not healthy to carry around so much suspicion."

"Barnaby, it was curiosity up until last night; now it's suspicion! Why do you think I called you over here?

Man, they went after you and they got you. And don't ask me why; I don't know. But believe me, there's nothing wrong with me, it's you I'm worried about!"

"You're serious, aren't you? You've really got a case on them, don't you?"

"Suppose you tell me what they're doing here in Singapore? I'd really like to know. They've got more crew than they know what to do with, and I've never seen any of them do anything. You'd think if they were commercial, like you say, they'd keep those guys busy in port. God knows what it costs to keep a crew like that for a month."

"They run charters, Bert. My guess is that they're waiting for licensing or something. And who knows, they could be under contract right now. I've seen crews lie around for months waiting on one thing or another. That's the way it goes."

"Kim, it's not charters! There wouldn't be an empty berth on that boat right now. It's loaded to the gills as it is. No, whatever it is they are doing, they're not waiting for more people to arrive. And besides, where are the windsurfers and Hobie Cats? If they're running tourists around, you'd expect to see the decks cluttered with stuff like that, and I haven't seen any of that sort of thing."

"There're other kinds of charters, Bert. What about scientific research, mapping, salvage, not to mention tramping freight? It goes on and on. A boat like *Night-hawk* can do a lot more than shuffle tourists around."

"Well go ahead, tell me what you think they're doing! Maybe I'll get off their case if you can tell me. Kim, you're the only one they've let get close. So go ahead! Tell me what they're doing in Singapore."

"I don't really know. Jill never talked about it, and I never asked. Look, it's her brother who runs the boat. Jill's just out for a visit. I doubt she knows."

"Didn't you just say she was very well informed? Now, come on, Barnaby."

"Okay. If you want my best guess, I'd say it has something to do with salvage. Everything you've been telling me seems to point that way. If they're as secretive as you say, and they've actually quarantined themselves, I'll bet they're negotiating for salvage rights to some wreck. It's a cutthroat business you know, out here especially."

"Barnaby, that's a bunch of bullshit and you know it! That big schooner's either running guns or smuggling drugs, take your pick!"

"I don't see how you could say that!"

"Barnaby, I've had my binoculars on that boat for a month!"

"And I just got off it!"

"Well then explain to me what kind of salvage boat carries a parabolic ear so large you could take a bath in it, and don't tell me you missed seeing that thing. They leave it right on deck. And did you notice that little torpedo they've got tucked away in the stern? I'm pretty sure that's another listening device."

"Bert, I think you're getting in over your head."

"No, they use equipment like that to find each other at sea, for deliveries and payoffs. God knows what other kinds of electronics they've got aboard. I'll bet you got a look at some of them, didn't you?"

"No, I didn't really get aboard. But I did notice that big plastic dome you're calling a parabolic ear. I got close enough to know what it is and you're wrong again, Bert. That thing is nothing more than a crude telephone booth. Divers use it to talk to the surface while they're working. It's nothing more than a microphone and a speaker. They lower it down, then fill it with air. When a diver wants to talk to the surface, he just ducks under the dome, takes out his mouthpiece, and speaks. There's nothing tricky about it. And as for that torpedo, I know what that is without even seeing it. That's part of a proton magnetometer. Every boat that works salvage has got one."

"Okay, forget it! Forget the whole thing. I won't tell you what happened before you rowed ashore last night. You'd probably come up with some bullshit explanation for that one too. Jesus Christ man, you just don't want to believe it, do you? That girl must have really dialed your number."

"Look, let's keep Jill out of this, okay?"

"How can I keep her out of it? She's as much a part of it as any of them. Christ, if it weren't for her, I wouldn't give a damn about what's going on over there. They can all face the firing squad if that's what they want, but don't you go joining them, Kim. You know the risks they're running."

"Who's said anything about joining them? Besides, I'm telling you, Jill's not involved! She's just visiting her brother, that's all."

"Kim, when she rolled in here last night with those French guys, you know I didn't recognize her? I didn't have the faintest idea who she was. And even when all of them came over to ask about you, I still didn't put it together. Man, I didn't figure it out until I saw the two of you leaving in your skiff."

"So, what happened? You said something happened before I came ashore, what was it?"

"Well, that's it! That's when I figured out what was going on. That's when it became obvious that they were trying to recruit you. First the water taxi, now this. Don't you see?"

"I'm still not clear on the 'they' part. And this business about drugs and guns is total speculation. Come on Bert, give me a break! I've found a girl who has more on the ball than any person I've ever met. She likes me, I like her. Can't we leave it at that?"

"Kim, ask yourself who those French guys are. Are they sailors like you and me? You know they don't know the first thing about boats. Look at the mess they've made out of that thing over there. For every step forward, they turn around and take two backwards. I'm convinced they have no intention of ever floating that thing. It's nothing but a crash pad."

"Well, let's shoot the sons of bitches! They're probably plotting to topple the government! Yeah, I'll bet they're KGB. Never mind the fact that they're French. Let's string them up for high crimes and misdemeanors"

"Cut it out, Kim! You know what I'm getting at. Those guys cruise Bencoolen Street for a living. They're not like us. They hang out with the backpackers down in those cheap hotels. It's their business, I tell you. They recruit mules to fly drugs across borders."

"So they're into drugs too! It's not just everybody on the *Nighthawk*, it's Jacques and Dominique too."

"Kim, I've seen them doing it. They find some down and out German kid who's backpacked his way across India and on down to Bali. By the time the kid comes back through Singapore, he's tapped out and looking for a quick ride home. That's what they're looking for. They give the kid a ticket home with a layover in Bangkok. All the kid has to do is pick up a little something extra up in Thailand."

"It's always Thailand, is it?"

"Sure, the stuff comes out of the Golden Triangle. You know, up North around where Burma, Laos, and Thailand come together. You must have heard of the hill tribes. They're the real mules. They're the ones who carry the stuff out of the mountains, down to Chiang Rai Province. After that, it gets spread around, but a lot of it ends up in Bangkok waiting for couriers, and that's where the French guys come in. From their end of it, it's perfectly safe. All they do is screen the applicants and send them up to Thailand. I tell you, that boat's never coming out of dry dock, Kim. They'll be here forever."

My hand reached down for the steaming coffee cup I'd set aside earlier. It had cooled and there was no smoke left to conceal another masquerade at indignation. I drank the cold stuff as though it was hotter than it really was and shifted my focus to the far shoreline.

"That place, Chiang Rai," I said while looking away. "Is it anywhere near a place called Chiang Mai?"

Bert spoke to the back of my head. "The airport is in Chiang Mai, Kim; so is the train station. From there, it's another eighty miles by bus. Chiang Rai is just a dusty little outpost in the foothills."

I eased around to face him, mumbling as I turned, "I could have guessed you'd say that."

"Don't tell me that's where your girlfriend is headed. Kim, is she on her way to Chiang Mai right now?"

"It looks that way."

"I knew it! Now aren't you happy I stopped you?"

"No!" I snapped. "And what do you mean 'stopped me'? Bert, I've been listening to you jump from conclusion to conclusion all morning long, and on the things I know about, you've been off the mark every time."

"Come on Barnaby! Do you really believe that or do you just want to believe it?"

"I'm not sure what I think. But I'll tell you, when she gets back in town, I'll get the answers to end all your speculation. That much I know. And another thing, Bert ... I'll want your apology."

"Kim, I really wonder if she'll be coming back. If she's going as far as Chiang Mai, she'll be up to her neck in informants and double crossers. No outsider walks into that 'company store' and walks out with anything but a nightmare. I tell you, its 'set-up city' for any Westerner who tries to get involved that close to their distribution center. Even the military is involved. She'll be stopped and searched over and over again until they decide whether they want to nail her or not. Kim, if it's Chiang Rai, I wouldn't count on seeing her again. The Thai jails are loaded with wide-eyed innocents who walked into that trap, and you know they never get out! They give a life sentence for drug related crimes up there and they make it stick."

"It won't happen to Jill. I can guarantee that."

"Kim, how can you say that after everything we've been talking about? You can't guarantee anything."

"I can if I go up there."

"Aw, come on, Barnaby. You don't want to do that! Just let her go!"

I rose to my feet and began untying the line I'd put around the sternpost.

"Kim," he went on. "This is exactly what I didn't want to happen. Can't you just take yourself out of this thing and let her go?"

His anguished voice began dropping away as he watched me lower myself down to my skiff. "Aw hell," he groaned. "I doubt you'll even find her if you do go. It's a big country up there, and unless you've already got a Thai visa, she'll have at least a twenty-four-hour jump on you. And you know something, Kim? That would give her enough time to set up another mark, just like you."

I let go of the rail and quietly dropped into my place at the oar locks. And in a moment the current pushed me back enough to let me set my blades, but I just sat, watching the far shore redefine the northern skyline. When I'd had enough of it, I rowed back up to Bert's boat for a final word.

"Bert," I called. "Have you ever seen the Buddha's smile?" He shot me a look that didn't understand a word of what I'd said. "What did you say?" he asked.

"I said have you ever seen the Buddha's smile?"

"No," he said, shaking his head.

I rowed a few strokes to get away. Then I called out, "Well, neither have I."

CHAPTER EIGHT

*I never forget a landfall, especially if
I've had to work for it. Landfalls are the
postcards a sailor sends himself. They come
from out of the blue. No two are ever the same,
but they all say the same thing, "Having
a wonderful time, wish you were here."*

On my fourth day in Thailand I knew I'd missed the landfall. I had that hollow feeling churning away in my gut. The same one a sailor gets when he finds out he's overshot his target and logged the last hundred miles going in the wrong direction. Somehow I knew I'd misread the stars and sailed right by it. I was dead tired and disoriented, slouched in the rack of plastic chairs that run down the center of the Chiang Mai Arcade bus station. Overhead, a flock of slow moving ceiling fans hung down from the second story, barely pushing enough air to hover above the scene. I had my bag at my feet and a monk in sandals at my side.

I sat there, knowing the window of opportunity had just slammed in my face. My bus trip to Chiang Rai had been just as fruitless as the time I'd spent in Chiang Mai. By now Jill was either up to her neck in some outlandish intrigue or under lock and key in some well-hidden hellhole. I had no way of knowing. In fact, I had no way of knowing anything; I was way out of my element and totally out of step.

The idea had been simple. I'd fly up, case the place, and ride to the rescue. It wouldn't be a problem for a beachcomber of my caliber. Finding a Westerner in Southeast Asia never is. There just aren't that many of them living there, and the ones who are can't really assimilate, even if they want to. They all default to the rank of expat or tourist, and whether they like it or not, they're as easy to spot as shaved monks in saffron. Jill was no different. If anything, she'd be easier to find.

I remember how confident I was when I first arrived. Chiang Mai looked like any other Asian city from the airport. It didn't matter that I was a day behind. I figured I'd find her in one of the hotels, or failing that, I'd catch up with her out on the city streets. Business or pleasure, she would eat, sleep, and shop like any other Western woman.

How foolish it all seems now. I remember twisting about in the back of the motorized trishaw that took me into town. Every face had to be examined, every shop window, every street corner. My eyes couldn't stop. And then later that evening, walking the pitch-black streets down to the night market, knowing she'd be there and wondering what I'd say when I looked into those china blue eyes. I was filled with anticipation that first day. I could smell the landfall.

It all changed the next day. Somewhere out on the streets, between a hundred Buddhist shrines and twice that many souvenir shops and hotel reception desks, I lost the scent. It turned out nobody in this backpacker's Mecca had ever heard of Jill Schaefer, and since I had no photo to show, absolutely nothing developed.

Even when I changed tactics and moved in on the art galleries and antique stores, I still got nowhere. Sure, they'd had plenty of people come through; the town was full of junketing tourists and rucksack packing hippies, but there wasn't one blue eyed buyer from San Francisco in the lot. All I could do was collect referrals and move on. In the end I even called on the police and immigration offices, but of course, I came away with nothing. By the end of the day I had walked a marathon and sucked up enough carbon monoxide to make my lips turn blue.

Chiang Rai was a slightly different story, but one that ended the same way. In fact, it started and ended right here in the Chiang Mai Arcade Bus Station. It was a twenty-four-hour loop that left me right back where I'd started, no wiser and a lot more confused. I sat beneath the flock of ceiling fans, wondering where I'd gone wrong.

Maybe I'd come too far inland to use a sailor's skills. Maybe simply being four hundred miles away from the sea was enough to warp my sense of direction. That might explain why I'd gone so many days without plotting a proper course.

The fans turned above me, and my thoughts changed. No, it wasn't my sense of direction that had me crisscrossing and circling. There was too much logic in the patterns for that. No, it was something even more fundamental than direction: something so basic it could disqualify navigational thinking all together.

For there to be a North, I thought, there has to be a South, and the same can be said for East and West. It can't get more basic than that. But before there is a direction, there has to be a place. Because without a sense of place, there is no beginning, and without a place to start, there is no datum for directional logic.

I sat with that thought and got dizzy wondering where that kind of thinking could lead. I know there are ways to get where you're going without a compass; you follow what you see. When a sign tells you to turn left, you turn left, and when it says right, you go right.

Direction has very little to do with place. But when signs turn on themselves, and directions lead to as many dead ends as there are directions, what then? What happens when you can't follow what you see because you don't understand what you're looking at?

All around me there were signs I couldn't read. There were red ones carefully stenciled on the ticket vendor's windows, and there were black ones high up on banners that hung from the second story balcony. There were wriggling words that went on and on, some running twenty characters with swirls and curls thrown in like birthday cake writing. It's such a cheerful looking script, you'd expect to find favorite words you could memorize and learn, but it doesn't work that way. Letters boil over with stylized twists and turns that defy description and you hardly ever see the same combination twice. And short words don't exist because they bury them inside the big ones. It's as though each written word has been designed to mystify the atmosphere before it gives up a meaning, and when lined up to say something, they're deliberately contrived to look more like hieroglyphics than words.

The fans kept turning, and eventually I found a refuge in the floor at my feet. There were no signs to puzzle over down there. There was only my gear to look at, and that's all I wanted to see. I wanted to block the barrage of distractions that seemed to be overtaking me, but of course, it wasn't possible. The man at my side quietly shifted in his seat, and a flash of saffron began to color my thoughts.

How could I make sense of any of the things I'd seen with that saffron robe so close? There can't be a bigger distraction than that wrinkled cloth. It cloaks the nature of everything up here. And the closer it gets, the more it affects you. I'd see them gliding in the early morning light, making excursions on the same sidewalks I'd traveled. They go about in full view, with nothing to show but the gaunt bodies of men who dare a total commitment. Wandering with a purpose known only to them, they assault every notion of twentieth century life and make a paradox out of the mundane. Without so much as a single button to link them to modern times, they wrap a supernatural aura around the people who wear them, and they are at once in tune.

I could walk the same sidewalks and sit in the same seats; I could even nudge my elbow to make contact with that cloth, but it didn't matter. The gulf between us was as big as any ocean I know. He was in tune, and I was not.

The whole thing degenerated in a mood of self-determined disqualification. That man in the robe had put an impossible perspective on everything, and without saying a word, he was witnessing my default. I reached down to fetch a map out of the rucksack that lay at my feet. Then I spread it in my lap and waited. I wondered if maps meant anything to a man in saffron. Did he use these things to plot his path, or did he do it some other way? When his head turned, I waited. Did he understand those wriggling lines the way I did? Did he know the red ones are the good ones and the black ones are better, even though they are slower? His stare was fixed on the paper now. He was navigating, and I couldn't help myself.

"Tell me," I said. "Where does Buddha smile?"

His head hardly moved, but I could see his eyes react, so I kept still. I waited while his eyes toyed with the map, and eventually his left hand began to unfurl itself from the folds in his robe. And just as I thought he was going to recognize my question, he rose to his feet and began to gather his garment. I shot him a look that was supposed to haunt his soul if he turned away and his eyes lit up. "Buddha smiles in Sukhothai," he whispered. Then he stretched to point to a place near the middle of my map. His face shone, then he turned and walked away.

I watched him leave, then I quickly turned back to the map. His finger had touched a point near the middle, but it had happened too quickly for me to record the exact point. I ran my eye down the contour lines to the end of the foothills. The place he had picked was in the central plains, down where the rivers merge and the roads run straight. It was a small place on the map, only a dot with a name, and most likely a simple place, judging by the size of the letters. Without thinking, I gathered my gear and walked to the nearest ticket window. The signs I couldn't read, the compass I couldn't follow, none of that mattered now. It was all behind me. I slid my map beneath the glass partition and jabbed my finger at the pace in the middle. A half an hour later I was headed south, looking for nothing more than a smile.

That's how I came to find Sukhothai, or better still, that's how it found me. I had no idea such a place existed, and even now, I measure every landfall by what I saw down there. It came from out of the blue, as sure as any shrouded mountain peak or shimmering shoreline, and it drew me in with a siren's song as pure as any you'll hear at sea. From the moment my bus left Chiang Mai and through hours of winding upland jungle, I could hear that whisper in my ear. It settled my mind, and until the sun went down, it was all I could think about.

Sometime after dark, after the roads had straightened and the last foothill was miles behind us, my bus slowed to swing through a dimly lit roundabout, and I got my first look at Sukhothai. There are no outskirts to this place, and if it weren't for that pretentious little circle of dirt, you could yawn and miss the entire town. In fact, I had barely enough time to rub my eyes when the bus stopped and the doors swung open on a shadowy slab of concrete where night vendors and townspeople idled the night away. It's the same all over Asia. There is always a place where collapsible tables and clothes trolleys share the night sky with anyone who happens to pass by. This one was smaller than most and remarkable only in that it was so organized. In fact, the town, all four blocks of it, was so well kept it looked a lot like one of the modern roadside villages you find in Singapore; too clean to have a past, or too ashamed to show it

I wandered off to find a place to stay, more aware of what was missing than what was there, and if it weren't for the young man who stopped me at the hotel's steps, I could have missed the whole thing.

"Sukhothai?" he said watching me approach. "You go Sukhothai?"

I dropped my gear at the doorway to address him. "Sukhothai!" I said with a thud.

We watched each other, then he started up again. "Sukhothai? You go Sukhothai?"

This time I had my hands free. "Sukhothai!" I said, pointing to the ground at our feet. "I am Sukhothai!"

He smiled like I'd just told a joke. "It is best in the morning," he laughed. "I come before sun up, if you like."

"Wait a minute," I said, looking hard. "Who are you, anyway?"

"My name is Junn," he said smiling into a laughing voice. "I am Sukhothai!"

It was the perfect echo of what I had said and he stood there with a giddy smile waiting to see how I'd react.

"Look, Junn, it's too late to be playing games," I said. "You come tomorrow. We'll talk then."

He reached to take my hand with the tips of his fingers. "Six hours," he said with a touch. "Before the first light." Then he pressed his palms together beneath his chin, bowing just the way I'd seen them do in Chiang Mai. "Sawadee krub," he whispered as though speaking to his hands, and with that, he simply turned and walked away.

I didn't know what to make of the exchange. I'd played him off like a simple hotel tout, but now I wasn't sure. Maybe it was the way he let me go, the bow, and those words; I was still thinking it over while filling out the hotel's registration card. It was the usual form, with lines to fill: name, address, and so on. I scribbled in the blanks without regard for any of the Thai script, and when I was finished I looked it over. The passport number and the rest, it all looked reasonable at a glance, so I don't know why I thought to turn it over, but when I did, I didn't get past the first line: "Lung Fa Hotel, Nikhorn Kasem Road, New Sukhothai, Thailand."

It was the word "*new*" that caught my eye and my reaction was instant. I thought of that giddy smile I'd just left out on the steps and the rest was obvious. Somehow I'd missed Sukhothai and ended up in a place called New Sukhothai. I worried for a moment, wondering if I'd left the bus too early. Maybe Sukhothai was the next stop down the road, or maybe it was one of those tiny places we'd blown through in the dark. I thought about pulling out my map but stopped. It was the way he let me go that did it. My default had brought me this far, and I was a fool to complicate things. So I let the whole thing slide, knowing I'd be on those steps long before the sun came up.

Junn came as he said he would, though I think we were both surprised to see each other at that hour. It was just getting bright, and his battered pick-up was still covered by the morning mist. We exchanged nods as he rolled in, then simultaneous greetings as we pulled away. Then, almost immediately, we crossed a river and Junn stopped while half a dozen field workers climbed aboard. They carried long handled scythes and machetes, and each had his lunch in a string bag. Junn turned to offer a one-word explanation. "Sukhothai," was all he said, and we set off again, climbing in short turns till the land leveled off above the river.

Once up on the flats, Junn straightened in his seat, and with both arms stiff above the wheel, he began a clipped monologue that seemed to come out of nowhere. "Muang Kao," he began with a sigh. "Muang Kao, the place called Sukhothai, was the first capital of Thailand. It was founded in the year 1238 by King Sri Indradiya. Before then, the Khmers ruled our land from Angkor. In 1287 the Thai kings of Chiang Mai and Sukhothai made an alliance to defend our land from Kublai Khan. There was peace for more than one hundred years. Then the capital moved to Ayutthaya. The most famous king of Sukhothai was King Ramkamhaeng. He gave us the Thai alphabet and brought in many artists to celebrate Lord Buddha. Sukhothai is the spiritual center of Thai Buddhism."

He stopped talking as quickly as he'd started, waiting, I assumed, for a question that would launch the next barrage. I had no words ready. My thoughts had raced ahead to where I could almost see the image of the place he was talking about. A holy sanctuary, I thought: a 750-year-old monastery where saffron robes glide through smoky clouds of incense, and elephants carry kings. I could almost see it.

The quiet lasted another few minutes as the road ran by, and the sun put morning light on the landscape. It's flat for miles around here, and you'll not see any farmers along the roadside. There are no squatters' shacks or torn-up fields either. It's an empty place; really nothing but a wide stretch of rambling ground cover with clumps of stunted trees. Everything's been left alone, and what's left is the plain hush of thick country air on a wide-open skyline. That's all there is around here.

Junn drove and the field workers' blades flicked quick rays of light into the cab. His face had gone solemn in the silence, and behind him the workers sat crouched in the back draft, their heads bowed in a huddle of straw hats and shouldered scythes. It's quiet around here, and you get the feeling it's been that way for years. I looked back to the road and slipped further into the undercurrent, locked to the notion that we had passed into consecrated land.

It was straight to the fringe of consciousness from that moment on. Up ahead, just above the treetops, and perfectly silhouetted, there appeared a cluster of sculpted spires that shot out of the woods like inverted spikes, and in the blink of an eye, they grew in size and number till they filled that part of the skyline. They were elegant shapes: elongated cones with spindled pinnacles and great bulbs that tapered to the finest finish. And, as we came closer, more appeared: repeats and variations, and all so perfectly formed you'd swear they were raised without a human hand in it.

By now I had my head hung out the window like a dog on a Sunday outing. "Can you show me Buddha's smile?" I called in a blur of words. "That's really what I've come to see. Is there a place where I can actually see it? Or is it something you feel more than you see? I mean can I see it? Can you take me to it?"

Junn beamed, nodding his head in delight. "I can take you there," he laughed, "but *you* will have to find it."

He watched me bring my head back inside the window. "But don't worry!" he teased, "It's easy in the morning. That's why we are here. Isn't it?"

"Yes!" I said heading back to the window. "That's why we're here!" I shouted. "But *this* is unbelievable."

I thought back to yesterday, the bus station, and how far my default had taken me. Unbelievable! That's exactly what it was. To come to this place, adrift on a current of ethereal events, it *was* beyond belief. But now, to see it unfold, to feel the hush and then to sense the majesty of this place even before my first glimpse — I was exhilarated, and for the first time in four days I knew I was on course. I could smell a landfall.

We swept into Sukhothai like a bunch of trespassing goofs, blowing past seven-hundred-year-old ramparts and dried up moats like they weren't there. I was back at the window, twisted in the breeze, and completely mesmerized. And Junn — I guess because of what I had said — he'd picked up the pace. Anyway, I had barely time to focus my eyes when we stopped, already deep inside the sanctuary. The field workers were scrambling out of the truck bed, and Junn had that giddy look on his face.

"You will find it here," he began, unlatching the door. "Of course, there are other places," he said with a slam. "But this is where you can see the Buddha calling the earth to witness."

"It's that simple, is it?" I said, swinging out into the open. "I just take a walk and I'll find it? Is that it?"

He nodded quickly as he went off to join the workers behind the truck. "Go," he pleaded before breaking into Thai. "You can't miss it in the morning."

So that was the final siren's song: a boastful challenge to spur me on—as if I needed prodding. My wide eyes alone would have drawn me in, simply to see the bells. Huge brick bells set on neatly stacked slabs with hidden vaults for sacred dust and relics: a cosmic bomb shelter be sure, and yet so delicate they float quietly in the morning light. And if there is a single sound to be heard, it is the voice of the ages that calls you beyond the bells, into a field of ruins where sculpted figures dissolve in heaps of unrecognizable rubble. I can only improvise to see it the way it was. Wars, famine, floods, and droughts, the voices tell it all. And the only eyes that have seen it pass are the closed eyes of a huge standing Buddha. Watching in darkness, he looks out through an upright crypt that's laid open to the fields.

He is the eternal gatekeeper, and I am just another trespasser, walking between everything that has passed and everything that will be.

Of course, there is a center to this place. An inner sanctum, I'd call it now, having left it. But I didn't recognize it then, not while I was in it. After the gate-keeper, there are the watchtowers, eight of them to be exact. They line the perimeter of the largest stone platform: four at the corners, with the others almost filling the middle distances. You can mount the plat-form, but only to walk the inner perimeter, because at the center of it all there is a huge square-based tower. It's elevated to eye level, rising above the heads of a hundred half-emerged marching monks. And, if you've been drawn in this far, you'll join the proces-sion just as I did, wandering behind the watchtowers, oblivious to the process until you've made the circuit and left.

It happens out in the open, after you've come off the platform to walk the line of pillars that takes you away. They run in perfect symmetry, balancing the plane so that a proper course is assured. And when you've walked to the end and you feel you must turn to see what you've left, that's where you'll find him, just like I did.

He's out in the open, too far away to be part of the focus until you see what you've left and what you've done. The walk past the gatekeeper's vigil, the passage behind the watchtowers, and the company of his stone disciples — it's all a setup to bring you into the open — a call to witness. And here in modeled stone he sits, cross legged and naked to the waist, one palm up and the other down, too far from the shrine to be a part of it, and yet, it's all captured in his smile. A subtle firmness at the edges of the mouth, a moment of radiance captured in stone. Here is the center of it all. Here is the invitation to the final incarnation.

I came away after a while, turning now and again for that final view: the postcard panorama that was my prize. I seized it in a last moment's sigh, turning away when I'd had enough.

From then, it was all behind me, and my focus changed with every step. I shortcut my way back to Junn's pickup, cutting across the underbrush that ran adjacent to the roadside. The field workers had spread out into this area, swinging scythes and sweeping debris as they moved along. I passed into their midst, flashing a quick farewell smile that brought nothing but cold stares from all but one of them. He was the last one, the one who had lagged the others to remain closest to the pickup, and when I came to him, he was quick with his smile. It was a salesman's smile, and I was not surprised by what happened next. He let his scythe fall the moment I was closest, giving him time to fetch his string bag. Then, as I watched, he spread his bag and began opening wads of newsprint, spreading and smoothing them to make a place for his wares. When he had a space the size of a large place mat, he knelt to unfold his first sample. It was a broken piece of clay, a piece of a plate perhaps, but one so covered in grime I didn't care to take it from his hand. He laid it on the paper, and in a moment he had others laid out beside it. There were a couple small gray bowls, a tiny base, and then more pieces like the first: creamy green colored pieces, parts of broken plates.

Altogether, the stuff looked about as impressive as a child's bottle cap collection, but as a courtesy I bent to give them a closer inspection. They were all horribly flawed. That's all there was to say. The bowls were bent out of round, and the fragments wore so much splattered glaze I wondered why he had bothered to stop me. I was about to give him my "Thanks, but no thanks" move when I noticed Junn standing above us.

"Did you find it?" he broke in. "Did you get what you came for?"

"Oh, yes!" I said standing. "Yeah, it's more than I can say. Unbelievable! I had no idea there was a place like this!"

"Then we will see more," he offered, gesturing toward the pickup. "There are twenty wats inside the walls and thirty more within a few kilometers."

He was in motion before his lips stopped moving, leaving me with unfinished business as he made for the roadside. I could have just as easily followed, without so much as a single closing word, but I lingered. I stayed while Junn walked, wondering what value the man beneath me could put on those pieces of clay. Was he begging a handout? If so, I needed to know.

"Junn," I called. "Please wait! Come back for a moment, will you? I want to know what's going on here."

"It's against the law!" he called back. "That man cannot sell those things."

I took a last look at that man's pathetic collection of rubble and dug a hand into my pants pocket. Call it a fool's penance if you like, but I could not be denied. I dropped a handful of coins onto the newsprint and left to join Junn.

"What do you mean, 'against the law'?" I said, sliding into the cab. "There can't be a law against begging in Thailand, they'd have to throw all the monks in jail."

"No, that man was not begging," Junn began. "He wanted to sell those things."

"But how could he?" I demanded. "It was nothing but broken pieces and discards. They couldn't have any value, not those pieces."

"They are part of this place," Junn continued. "For that reason they cannot be moved. That man steals when he picks up those things, and there is a law about that. Only archaeologists from the university can remove those pieces. But never mind," he said, pausing to start the motor, "it is still early, and there is so much to see."

We rumbled off and I sat, replaying what I had just heard and reviewing what I had just seen. It was all too familiar.

"Wait a minute!" I said, spinning in my seat. "Those pieces of pottery ... are there archaeologists around here? I mean, are they digging somewhere around here? Junn, stop a minute, will you?"

CHAPTER NINE

We have no instincts out at sea, only intuitions.
A second sight is all we get, and that we hardly see.
We have no instincts out at sea, only intuitions.
The sixth sense never shows itself when there's a self to see.

Her blue eyes shone wet above the veil she wore, and like the others, she was worried by the dust. It was everywhere, falling from the walls of every terraced level they had dug. Down deep it clouded the lights and bothered their work, but at mid-level, say eighteen feet, it looked like something they could manage. They wore hats and wrapped cloths about their faces to be safe.

She was coming up from the depths when I first saw her, masked like the others, but not dressed for serious work. She wore delicate clothes that would have seemed out of place were it not for the man she was with. He was a vision for the *Archaeologist's Journal* — a scholarly looking white-haired rogue in a tailored safari suit, complete with a powder blue surgical mask and a white-topped walking stick. Together they looked like a pair of misplaced medics dodging diggers in an open-cut mine.

They had both noticed Junn when he ducked beneath the oversized roof to come to the top of their ladder, but once he was in position, they quickly forgot about him. I had remained outside the open-air structure, half-hidden by the low-set eaves and still very much unnoticed. They let Junn wait a bit while they talked, then, as they broke for the ladder, they took notice and addressed him with masked faces. A short conversation began at both ends of the ladder, and in a moment Junn's hand flicked in my direction, causing both heads to turn, but only for an instant. They turned as one, necks stretched, but hardly to hold focus before rejoining at the ladder where Junn went on with my would-be tour.

They were tied up with talk when I saw the impulse take her. She disengaged, lowering her line of sight to the shovel-carved wall while Junn and the old man stayed at it. She paused there. Then, as if she'd downshifted, she cranked a slow-motion twist to her neck and brought her eyes around. They lay stone cold above her mask, unstruck, and veiled in vacancy till I couldn't stand it.

"For Christ's sake, Jill!" I called. "Do I need a license to get dirty around here?"

My question fell hard on everybody's ears. Junn's head snapped up, the old man's shot around, and Jill's ... Jill's went back to the wall.

"Jill!" I called, ducking the thatched eaves. "Come on, it's only me. Don't you recognize a ragtag sailor when you see one?"

"My God," she said, spinning away from the wall. "Is that you, Kim? Good God!" she cried, undoing her mask from behind. "What are you doing here?"

That brought me to the ladder, all smiles. "I was going to ask you the same question," I said with a laugh.

"Now wait a bloody minute!" the old man shouted, stopping things cold. "Jill!" he roared. "Do you know what's going on here?"

"Nigel!" she demanded. "Nigel, please! He's a guy I know from Singapore, please ..."

"So, you've invited guests!" he exploded. "Now that tears it! That bloody tears it!"

"Nigel, please," she pleaded, looking me straight in the eyes. "Would you please let me handle this?"

The old man relented without saying another word, and this time it was he who turned to face the wall.

Jill, who had never lowered her eyes, made her way up the ladder, her expression a study in newfound self-control. She came to my side flushed by her quick climb, but in no mood to catch her breath.

"Kim, this is business!" she puffed. "Don't you see? You can't be here."

"Why not?" I said calmly.

"Why not?" she repeated. "Why not! Well, how do you feel when people barge in on your shell hunting? It's not so different you know. Oh, Kim, I'd love to get together back in Singapore, but this is business. I'm working, don't you see?"

"Jill," I said softly, "when MY business gets me shot at, I stop working. Do you understand what I'm saying?"

"No, I don't," she snapped. "I don't know what you're talking about."

"Well then you couldn't possibly remember the gunboats and the sound of those machine guns up at French's, could you?"

"Oh, God," she pleaded. "Kim, what are you doing here?"

"Come on Jill!" I shot back in a muffled burst. "If I told you I'd come to clean your sandals; would that tell you how I know you were there? Or, are you already so stuck in this thing you can't see the hand I'm offering?"

My questions took the sound right out of her voice. She mouthed something totally inaudible, then turned to look for witnesses. Junn was there, but he was still too shaken by the turn of things to know what was happening, so she reeled to pick up on the old man. He was back in the depths, and much too far away to have seen, so she finished her flurry with a quick whirling turn that brought her back to me.

"We've got to talk," she sighed. "You get rid of your guide," she whispered coming to my ear, "and I'll take care of Nigel. And Kim," she said, leaving for the ladder, "I'll never underestimate you again."

She sealed my fate with that one line: a backhanded compliment to be sure, but at that time, in my mind, it was a moment of submission, and I took it with unqualified acceptance. I let Junn go right there, explaining the new arrangements with a full day's pay and not much else. There was nothing I could say. Jill, on the other hand, had a lot to say, staying down in the hole till I started to question the estimate she put on my patience. She spent half an hour "taking care of Nigel" while I paced the perimeter, kicking piles of dust to fool away the time.

It was, most probably, a perfectly innocent maneuver, and considering the blitz I had laid on her, one I fully deserved. But, whether she knew it or not, those thirty minutes completely undermined my efforts to goad her, and when I finally saw her face again, that moment of submission had vanished like a dream.

She came out of the hole like I'd just arrived, pausing near the top of the ladder to cut the distance with a sparkling smile and a twinkling eye. It was a winning look she'd used, a look I measured with a simple straight-faced smile, holding off the spark as best I could. She laughed a bit to smooth her way, and then, as if she'd somehow sensed the slip in time, she hurried round the rungs to play her hand.

"Let's get out of here," she called, ducking the thatched cover with a quick bob. "There's something you've got to see," she said taking my arm in a sudden nuzzling clasp. "You won't believe what they dug up yesterday," she purred.

She led me away with the warm press of soft flesh at my arm, steering our way past the mounds of dug up rubble that lay heaped behind the big roof. "Does any of this look familiar?" she asked as we walked along. "Oh, I'm sure you've seen the process," she cooed, answering her own question. "They take it out here. They sieve it there, and they clean and sort it over there," she said with a sweeping pass of her hand. "And, if I'm not mistaken," she went on, "I'd say that's pretty much the same process you use with your seashells. Am I right?"

"Well, I guess you could say that," I offered. "Except what I do smells like holy Hell. How'd you like to spend a month at sea with a couple thousand dead snails?"

"I'll give that some thought," she laughed. "But really, what you do is not so different. Come look over here," she said with a squeeze. "This is their cleaning and sorting station."

She led me into the shade of a second open-air structure: a much smaller bamboo and thatch cover they used to shelter a line of end-to-end picnic tables. There were marked trays, heavy plastic sacks, and sluice buckets, all laid out to process the morning's haul. "Come look at this," she said, positioning me above the last table. "Would you believe they dug up a cowry shell yesterday? Take a look," she said, carefully handing me the specimen. "This came out near their lowest level, Kim. It's got to be eight hundred years old."

"Does that fascinate you, Jill?" I asked blankly. "Do you always find that old things tell a better story than new things?" I said putting down the shell. "Or is it just a lot easier to smell bullshit when it's fresh?"

"Oh no!" she blurted, sensing confrontation in my tone. "It's quite true! They've unearthed eleven different kilns in that single hole. And the bottom one, the one they're working on now, it was here long before the first stone was cut for Si Satch—."

"Knock it off, Jill! Just put it away!" I demanded. "You know damn well I didn't come up here for that!"

"Kim, please!" she whispered in a calming voice. "Please. If you'll just give me a chance."

"A chance? A chance!!" I exploded. "I'll give you a better chance than the Singapore Navy's likely to give you! Jill, what the hell are you doing up here?"

"It's art business!" she howled. "I told you that! God," she protested, "I'd think YOU of all people would understand. I'm a front-line player, just like YOU!"

"That's your answer?" I pressed. "Jill, that doesn't tell me anything!"

"Look," she said, finding her soft voice again. "You've spent a lot of time hunting shells—you've built your whole life around it—and you're good at it. Kim, you're really good at it! You work typhoon alley year round, you dive with sharks, and you battle pirates who'd take everything you have. Why? Because you are a front-line player, that's why. You go to the source to get what you want, and you do it alone. Why? Because just being another middleman isn't good enough, that's why!"

"Kim, I deal in antiquities; that's *my* life, and believe me, it's no different in this business. You hunt with your intellect, and you go where it takes you."

"So it's the pottery you're after! Is that it? You're up here trying to buy the stuff they pull out of that hole! Is that it?"

"No, that's not it! They don't have anything to sell. And besides, it would be totally disastrous if they were caught. No, this is a dating project; they never expected to uncover any high quality pieces. The good stoneware was always taken away from the kilns."

"So if it's not the pottery, then what is it Jill? What's so damn important that you'd let yourself be shot at?"

"This!" she shouted. "This is why I'm here," she said snatching one of the marked plastic sacks.

"But that's nothing but broken pieces," I said, taking the bag. "And they're all so full of flaws. You can't tell me there's any value in this. Jill, these are just pieces of rejects!"

"It's not the pieces," she whined. "It's the *color*! The green glaze! You only find it up here. It wasn't used anywhere else in Thailand, not even down in Sukhothai, only here!"

"So that makes these pieces unique, is that it?"

"NO, it's nothing like that," she moaned. "Only Nigel values those shards, and only because of the dating techniques he's using—their color has nothing to do with it. But to me, Kim, to someone in the business of antiquities, that color is an icon! It's one of the lost treasures of the Orient. Have you never heard of 'celadon green'?"

"Jill, I wouldn't know celadon green from aquamarine."

"Well surely you've heard of Marco Polo," she said, pausing to sigh. "Genghis Khan? Kublai Khan?"

she went on. "Do you know anything about the Song Dynasty?"

"Jill, you're out of my league."

"I doubt that," she said, taking the bag from my hands, "I really doubt that, Kim."

She set the bag down hard, using the sharp sound of gnashing shards to punctuate her comment. "Look," she said, "I don't know what you know. But the fact that you're here tells me you know a lot more than you're saying. You couldn't have followed me, and I know you weren't on that plane with me; I didn't spend ten minutes up in Chiang Mai. But you are here, and I have to wonder. Kim, you either know a lot more than you're saying, or you're the luckiest God damn shell hunter I've ever run into."

"Jill, you said it yourself. You hunt with your intellect and God knows you've got plenty of that—but me—I go where the wind blows. I mean it, Jill. That's exactly the way it works with me. I may know a thing or two about nautical charts and the night sky, but that's not what got me here. I'm here because *you're* here. That's all there is to it. I'm a sailing vagabond who hunts seashells for a living—no more, no less. I didn't come to steal your prize and I'm not here to crowd you."

She stood motionless in that moment, measuring the nuance of my words with narrowed eyes. "It looks like I underestimated you again, doesn't it?"

she whispered aloud. "You're a rare breed, aren't you? I've got to remember that."

She smiled and turned to the sunlight. "You'll be welcome at the lodge if you care to stay, Kim. Nigel's already given it his okay." Then turning back, "But I'd better warn you of something right now," she grinned. "I'm pretty sure we'll have to double up."

Her eyebrows arched at the sudden whimsy of her suggestion, then, just as quickly, she set off into the sunlight. She'd had the last word, and played it to the hilt; but from my end of it, standing alone at the sorting station, she'd finished on a near-perfect note. So who was I to question? I followed.

Her hand swung out at the sound of my footsteps, touching me blindly as we passed into the space behind the oversized roof. She held my wrist, then slid softly into the fold of my outstretched hand, hardly slowing to take me in stride. "You know," she said, rounding the corner of the thatched cover, "it's all chemistry, Kim. This whole business comes down to nothing but chemistry."

"Ahhh," I toned, coming alongside. "That's what songwriters tell us, but even *they* won't try to define it," I laughed.

"What?" she smiled, turning for the first time. "What did you? Oh!" she cried, breaking into laughter. "But I was talking about ceramics, not you and me!"

We slowed to a standstill as Jill spun a sudden grazing kiss square to my lips. "You're too nice to be a hunter," she said, quietly drawing back. "And much too gallant to be floating around on your own," she said, coming back for another. "So how do we define you, Kim? Devout navigator? Is that what you are?"

"I'd be the last to know," I quipped. "But surely you don't think I'm ready for the monastery, Jill. Not now anyway," I joked, sliding my hand down to her backside. "Not when there are still so many areas left to explore."

She laughed as she danced out from under my playful touch. "I think we'd better get back to chemistry," she beamed. "I might have better luck defining that!"

Her words touched off the first moment of shared laughter since Singapore, and although it was hardly hilarious, we both laughed long and hard, knowing our worst suspicions had touched off the most incisive moment in our relationship. We were, I thought, wholly disarmed by the simple chemistry of our attraction for one another, but, as she soon put it, the business of chemistry went way beyond the spark of desire.

We left the dig site in our dust, shortcutting into the underbrush to get clear of the place, then slowing to a standstill when we came to the banks of a deeply muddied river. Around us, overhanging trees and rampant ground cover hid us like thieves as Jill began with a pointblank question.

"Do you know what iron oxide is, or do you think I should start somewhere else?"

"Jill," I said, shaking my head. "You're talking to a *steel* boat owner! I live and breathe iron oxide! Of course I know what it is. It's *rust!!*"

"Okay," she laughed. "I see it's a touchy subject with you, so let me be as brief as possible. The green color we saw in those shards — the celadon green — it's an iron oxide glaze. When you cook it in a high-fired kiln, you can get brown or black or blue-green depending on the amount of iron oxide you use. Brown and black are the easy colors, but the blue-green requires perfect chemistry and exacting kiln techniques, and that's where the fun begins."

"You see, a true celadon will show its body through the translucence of the glaze. It's a subtle thing, but the color and makeup of the potter's clay has a lot to do with the final effect. In fact, the chemistry of the clay itself is just as important as the glaze. Too much silica and not enough alumina, you get a body that falls apart in the kiln. Too much alumina and not enough silica, you get clay that won't take glaze. It's all very specific, once you get into it."

"Now, look around you, Kim. The river, the foothills, and those rapids down there. You wouldn't think you were standing in a chemist's laboratory, but you are! That's exactly what this place is, or I should say, was. Six hundred and fifty years ago this place was crawling with people who mixed chemicals. Alumina, silica, degenerated granite, lime, potash, iron oxide: we've got names for all of them now. But back then, it was black earth from a dried riverbed, and rice paddy silt. Really, that's what they used! Then, they'd throw some beanstalk ash in the glaze and give it to the potters. It's no wonder they lost over fifty percent in the firing. It was crude chemistry and crude kiln technique that failed them. *But*, in the same kilns and using the same materials, some of their successes were brilliant!"

"Kim, it's one of those classic contradictions ..."

"Wait a minute, will you?" I said, breaking in. "It's time I got a question in, that is, if it's not too technical."

"Sure," she crowed, "Go ahead! The technical side is the most interesting aspect of this."

"Well," I said with some hesitancy, "it occurs to me that your chemistry may overlap into an area I know something about, and it would explain a lot if you could answer this one technical question."

"Go ahead!" she beamed. "I'll bet it has something to do with rust!"

"Well, you're right," I said cautiously. "It has something to do with rust, but really it's more about iron oxide. You see, I was just wondering if there is enough iron oxide in that glaze to set off a proton magnetometer? I mean, if you towed one behind something like a big black schooner. You know what I mean?"

"God!" she howled. "You *do* know how to cut to the quick!"

"I'm just looking for simple answers, Jill. A yes or no would do, unless there's more to it, of course."

"Come on, Kim! You know there's more to it!" she burst. "There's a lot more to it! And there are no simple answers either!" she called, turning to leave. "It's just one big screw up. The whole thing's a blown deal and your being here just makes it harder on me!"

"Now look!" I said, snatching her arm. "I don't know what I have to do to get through to you."

"Can't you see you're scaring the shit out of me?" she howled. "Do you think I like what's going on? Do you think I like being shot at? For Christ's sake, Kim!"

"Okay! You want to know what I think?" I shot back. "I think you're extraordinary! I think you're the most attractive person in Southeast Asia. I think you're caught in something you can't handle alone, and I think you're crazy if you turn me away. That's what I think! I also think you think I know more than I know; if you know what I mean, I think."

She seemed oddly settled by my turn of words, holding fast to an unfocused gaze till a tiny glimmer slowly lit her smile. "This has gone far enough," she whispered. "I think it's time you got the whole story."

"It started a few months ago," she said, drawing a deep breath. "I was back in the States then, working at the gallery and not expecting to hear from my brother for at least another month. He was 'on-site' then and very incommunicado. It's always that way when *Nighthawk*'s working; the radio goes in the safe. Anyway, the call was just the beginning. He said they'd been boarded by the Malaysian Navy and taken up to Lumut. *Nighthawk* was impounded, and her salvage was seized. He wanted me to get the Foundation's lawyers on it straight away."

"The Foundation?"

"Yeah, that's the parent company," she said with a pause. "Kim, this is no smalltime enterprise. *Nighthawk*'s a million-dollar boat. She's got a crew of twenty-five!"

"So, the Foundation is a salvage company?"

"No, it's much more than that. It's a holding company. You know, a company that owns other companies? Well, this one owns two companies, the Jackson Gallery in San Francisco and Bluewater Exploration in the Caymans."

"So, you and your brother work for the same company, right?"

"I got him the job! But really, it's two separate companies. I just happen to be the one person who's active in both sides."

"So, what's this about a seizure? Weren't their papers in order? Is that why they got pulled in?"

"Well, that's what it seemed like in the beginning. But we had the permits. We had everything. And that's why they finally had to release the boat. But they kept the salvage, and with no legal right!"

"So, you're in court trying to get it back. Is that it?'

"I wish it were that simple. Our lawyers are saying the Malays won't admit there was any salvage aboard at the time of seizure. All they'll say is that the permits were incomplete! That's where it begins and ends from their end of it. I mean it's outright theft if you ask me."

"Does that mean there is nothing you can do about it?"

"Oh no, the lawyers are still at it. I mean they'll win, I'm sure. It's just that it's taking so long! And meanwhile, everybody on *Nighthawk* is suffering. Kim, they're down to beans and rice on that boat, and none of them will get paid till the salvage is recovered. That's the way it is!"

"Oh come on Jill, how can that be? You mean the Foundation won't pay the crew? Christ! What kind of company do you work for anyway?"

"Kim, I work for the gallery. The boat is part of Bluewater Exploration."

"What the hell difference does it make? It's all the Foundation isn't it? Jill, I think you've spent too much time around lawyers."

"No! It's not that simple! But it's not that complicated either. Look, I know the point you're making and if it were true, I wouldn't be here. Believe me, I'd never have come out here if it were anything like what you are suggesting."

"Kim, try to follow me and you'll see. The Foundation owns the Jackson Gallery and Bluewater Exploration. Now, at the gallery, we've got two divisions: 'retail sales' is one, and 'research and procurement' is the other. I am 'research and procurement,' okay? Now, on the other side there's Bluewater Exploration, and in spite of the name, it's really nothing but a charter company—I mean like yacht charters, okay? Now, they don't have any serious assets, they're just agents; leasing agents if you will. Now, this is the important part. Among their clients is a company called Bluewater Investors. They are a small, nonprofit, oceanographic research company with only one asset; the *Nighthawk*. The owners make tax deductible contributions to pay for all of *Nighthawk*'s expenses."

"So, why aren't *they* paying the crew, Jill? And don't tell me they don't have the money, not if it's all a big write-off!"

"They DO pay the crew! But in reality, there's only one guy getting paid now — my brother. He's the only permanent crewman left, since the salvage was stolen. You see, all those other guys are contractors for a different company."

"I got it! They work for the outfit that's chartered the *Nighthawk*, right?"

"That's it! And they're the ones who'd claimed the salvage; that is, before the Malays took it."

"So, I'll bet that means the Foundation's lawyers have gone home, and *they've* got their own lawyers on it, right?"

"Oh no! The Foundation's in this for keeps. That's why I'm out here!"

"Well then, it looks like the Foundation's going to pay the crew after all, if simply to buy time till the salvage is recovered, right?"

"They won't! Look, *Nighthawk's* charter agreement always specifies that the non-permanent crew are paid by the chartering group, especially if it's not a research related project. You see, if the Foundation paid those guys, it would look like they were acting for Blue-water Investors, and that would play hell with their tax status. The whole thing would come unglued."

"So, what you're saying is that the crew is going to sit on that boat till the salvage is recovered? Is that what's going to happen?"

"Come on Kim, you know as well as I, they'll sink *Nighthawk* before they'll leave with no pay."

"So, who's going to make the charter group pay their crewmen? I mean if the Foundation won't do it, and Bluewater Exploration can't, who's going to make them do it, the lawyers?"

"No, it's too late for that. I'm the one who's going to do it! And with the full backing of the Foundation too. That's why I'm here!"

"Well, now you've lost me Jill. After everything you've told me, what makes you think *they* still care? They're not even a second party to this thing!"

"Oh, but you're wrong! They're involved because the Jackson Gallery's involved, and that's where 'research and procurement' comes into it. Kim, I set the whole thing up! Those people who chartered *Nighthawk* — they're all *my* clients! They're our best collectors! Don't you see? The Jackson Gallery is the beginning and the end of the whole loop!"

"You better run that by me again. What loop are we talking about?"

"Look, the Jackson Gallery specializes in antiquities, all types and from all markets. But, unlike our competition, we go to the source. I mean, if it's something that can still be had from outside the marketplace, we go after it. That's what *Nighthawk*'s all about."

"But your people don't own *Nighthawk*, isn't that right?"

"Well, strictly speaking, the Foundation doesn't, but if you look at the individuals involved in both, you'll find some pretty familiar faces."

"Okay, now let me see if I've got this. The gallery makes profits for the Foundation. And the Foundation's owners channel tax-deductible contributions to *Nighthawk* through Bluewater Investors. So, in effect, they own and operate a million-dollar boat on tax deductible money!"

"You've got it! But that's only half of it. You see, part of my job is to find work for *Nighthawk*. I mean, what good is owning a million-dollar boat if you can't make money on it? So what I do is set up salvage syndicates. You know, investors who'll pool money to go after a specific salvage site."

"You mean *collectors* don't you?"

"Yes! And that's the beauty of it. Because, you see, when the salvage comes in, the syndicate will market the goods through the Jackson Gallery! You get it? It's all one big loop!"

"Oh, I get it now! It's shrewd. No, it's *artful*! I see exactly the way it works. Every piece fits; each one feeds the other, the perfect loop! But Jill, you've made yourself the go-between, and if that gets you killed, that loop is nothing but a hangman's rope!"

"Oh, come on Kim! I'll admit I've got myself spread a little thin, but the plan we're following is as good today as the day we made it. It's still the only way out!"

"So, is that what you were doing up at French's — taking the only way out? Surely there's a better way to shake that money out of your syndicate! You don't have to get shot, do you?"

"Look, Kim, I've got to finish what I started and that's all there is to it! You've got to understand that, if you're going to stay!"

"Okay! That's enough of that, Jill! You know I said I didn't come up here to crowd you!"

"And I didn't tell you everything because I wanted to run you off!"

"So where does that leave us, Jill?"

"It leaves us sailing in the moonlight! Isn't that what this is all about?"

She moved off the way she had before: suddenly — guiding with a leading question, and giving no time for answers. It was her way — to make the moment and break the moment according to her will. I knew that, but as I watched her walk away, I also knew it was her will that made me follow.

CHAPTER TEN

The lodge sat in a swarm of riverside foliage just downstream from the dig site. It was, and still is, a place so removed and so well hidden I see it best when I close my eyes. Jill had moved off, the way she would, but as I recall, I didn't catch up. At least not until I'd stood in the clearing long enough to watch her walk and then longer still to size up the place.

It was a simple structure by any account: a two-story box on masonry and stilts. But, like all the Thai houses you see, it's the proportions that make them different. This one had a huge pitched roof that over-hung the place like a giant set of wings. It swept long and clear of all the sides, sloping away as if the builders had purposely dared the wind to lift the whole thing with the first good gust. They'd left all the elements right for flight, but somehow the thing had never come off. The explanation, I thought, could only be in the huge breezeway, for it was just as oversized as the roof, and together their proportions were perfectly matched. The opening spanned the full center third of the two-story structure, descending in banks of louvered glass down to a cantilevered entry cover, and then on down to the threshold in wide open air. The effect from the clearing was that the structure had tunneled a two-story viewing gallery right through the thicket, clear out onto the river. I could see shaded chairs lined up in the lower runway and idle hammocks strung in the upper deck.

Jill stood at the threshold, backlit in a shimmering hollow of silhouettes and ceiling fans. She'd waited there while I held back, but as she saw me finally moving in, she left the landing to draw me aside with her soft voice.

"Would you grab my bags, Kim? They're over here," she said, flashing a key from her pocket. "The two big Halliburtons," she laughed. "Nigel calls them my baggage cars!"

She worked the lock, opening a ground level storeroom that had no windows or light. It was a specially fitted place, lined wall-to-wall with shelving that racked to the ceiling.

"I don't think we'll be fooling anybody," I teased while hauling the two bags out of the vault. "The bellhops will see right through this," I quipped.

"Then we'll just have to sneak up the back steps!" she countered, flashing a quick knowing wink.

"Ahhh, then you mean like lovers?" I chimed, "Or do you think we could be thieves?"

"Well, they won't know *that* till it's over," she laughed, "and then they'll just have to guess!"

Her room was on the second level, high in the breezeway with opened shutters and saffron colored sash curtains. Jill hurried about the place, making space while I waited just outside the doorway.

"You know," she said, hustling to clear the mosquito tent that hung above her bed, "nobody was as upset as I was when the shooting started, and nobody had a better right to be either!" she piped, while flicking the netting aside. "We were down to the last detail! Do you know how upsetting that is?"

She sidestepped the bed, carrying on to snatch one of the cases I'd set in the doorway. "Kim, you want to know what happened at French's that night? I'll tell you what happened," she said, thumping the case up onto the mattress. "We lost a treasure! That's what happened. We lost it for the second time running!"

She came back for the second case, dramatically pausing mid-motion to face me in the doorway. "Have you had the chance to know good jade?" she asked in a sudden change of tone. "Have you ever held a good sized piece?" she cooed.

She swung the second case with a two handed whirl, slipping it alongside the other as she carried on. "Now imagine," she said facing away, "imagine what an artist might do if he could capture that essence in a fluent medium—and not just the color, but the feel of the polished stone as well!"

She turned, showing a face so lit in expectation, I stumbled on my words. "I can't. I mean I think you're losing me, Jill. Look, I ... I don't have a background for this kind of thing."

"But you *do*!" she said, spinning to click the latches. "Those shells you collect, they're as close to what I've got in here as anything in the art world!"

"Come on," she beamed while laying the cases open, "you'll see the minute you pick one up!"

The cases were foam-filled, with both sides showing cutouts and contents in perfect opposition. There were rice bowls and dishes and vases and pots, and each in its own shade of green.

"Take one," she said excitedly. "Take any piece you like. Now tap it. Take your finger and tap it with your nail. That's it, right along the lip."

"Now, did you hear that, Kim? When you tap it, it sounds pure. And when you look at the color, it has warmth. Am I right?" she coaxed. "Now feel the texture," she urged. "It's as smooth and cool as a water-worn pebble. Do you notice? Do you feel the pleasure in its touch? It's the same as the artist's own when he handles his finished work. It's the pleasure of balance — in form and weight and texture, all at the same time."

She stood back, fawning with delight and smiling at the way her words had triggered a tremor of caution in my hands.

"'Clever as though molded in metal, yet delicate as jade.' That's how the Chinese describe it. So, what do you say, Kim? Are they as good as sea shells?"

"You'll get no argument from me," I offered plainly. "They're all very nice," I said, carefully slipping the piece back into its slot.

"Then that's all you've got to say?" she asked. "Didn't you feel it?"

"I felt it, Jill. It's just that I wanted you to keep going."

"Oh, you mean the color!" she thrilled. "Well, you see it starts with a pale gray paste—very hard. Here, look," she said, snatching a small bowl out of the case. "After the paste, they used a translucent blue-green glaze—real thick, sometimes twice, and with three firings. Now look hard," she insisted. "You'll see millions of tiny bubbles trapped in the glaze. That's what gives it *dissolve*. Do you see them?" she said, offering me the bowl.

"Yes, it's a very seductive effect," I said, taking the bowl away into the light by the window. "Restrained, like the shape, but alive to the touch. I see the appeal, but we didn't see this out by the river, did we? I mean the color is close, but, those broken pieces, they're not at all like this, are they?"

"I knew it!" she beamed. "You're a *natural*! A born connoisseur!"

I brought the bowl back to her bedside, handling it far more casually than I had before. "You're making fakes, aren't you?" I said abruptly. "You've figured out the chemistry—the way to get from those pieces, to this!"

"Kim, they're not fakes," she laughed while taking the bowl. "We're doing copies! Copies of copies, if you really want to know!"

"Copies of copies?" I echoed. "Aren't fakes the same as copies, Jill?"

"Well, they could be, if we tried to sell them. But they're not for sale, and they never will be!" she charged. "Kim, don't you see? We're making copies of what we lost to the Malays!"

"Copies?" I begged. "You're copying the salvage they took off *Nighthawk*?"

"That's all there is to it."

I stepped back into the light of her window, turning away to rally my thoughts.

"You need *copies* to get the money from your syndicate," I mulled out loud. "So then I'd guess they don't know about the seizure. Jill," I said turning to face her, "you never told them about the Malays?"

"Kim, this is damage control! *Nighthawk* got hit, and whether I like it or not, it's up to me to keep her afloat."

"So, you're buying time with your copies. Okay, that much I understand. But what's this about copies of copies?" I asked. "Why would you need duplicates?"

"We need them to replace what we lost."

"But you already said that, Jill. You're copying what the Malays took off *Nighthawk*."

"Kim, that was before French's!" she exclaimed. "Now we're copying what we lost *down there*!"

"You mean you lost copies you'd already made?"

"Kim, we lost more than half the shipment that night!"

"Then who's got ...?"

"Nobody," she sighed. "The crates were thrown overboard. I mean, when the gunboats showed up, our guys took off!"

"Jeeesus, Jill!"

"I know," she clipped. "We didn't know what hit us."

"But why did you do it that way?" I asked in disbelief. "Didn't anybody tell you what goes on in the Straits? Jill, there are a hundred safe ways to make that crossing."

"I know," she breathed. "But at the time ..."

"You could have put the stuff on a truck and come right across the causeway!" I scoffed. "There's no duty on ceramics. They would have let you right through."

"They would have stopped us," she muttered coldly. "Did you see a country of origin label on that bowl you were holding?"

"I didn't think so," she whispered. "Ahh Kim, it makes me sick to think about it. We were so close."

"Then I guess you thought about diving for it?"

"You mean out in the ship channel? Oh sure," she said, "we thought about it, and there are ways to do it. But considering the current and the lack of visibility in the water, we couldn't manage it without becoming a hazard to navigation, and that would just bring the gunboats back. So ..." she sighed.

"So, you're back up here making copies of copies!" I finished. "That means you're going to try it again, doesn't it?"

"Like I said before. We've got no choice. Nothing has changed."

"Well, I think you're wrong about that," I pressed. "In fact, I know there's at least one difference to consider!"

"Oh please," she groaned. "You're not going to make this thing harder for me, are you?"

"No," I laughed. "I'm offering to make it easier if you'll let me."

"Look," I said, closing the distance between us, "you don't have a problem anymore; at least not with the crossing," I said, closing in. "I can run the stuff across whenever you're ready. You just give me the word."

"The word?" she flushed. "You'd do that?"

"I'd be a fool not to!" I said, taking her by the arms.

"But ..."

"Look Jill, you almost got yourself killed doing something I can do with my eyes closed! Now, do you think I'll stand by while you try it again?"

She closed the gap with a soft longing look and a smile that could warm decency to shame. Then, with the press of her lips and the stir of her body's touch, I came undone, for she held that moment too long into submission. My hands took off with a will of their own, sliding down to her waist to strip her blouse, then on to her skin in a hot-handed fervor. Up, then down, then all around, tracing her contours with hurried intentions and finding such heat in her every soft turn ...

"They're back!" she hissed right out of the blue. "I can hear someone on the steps! Kim, please!"

Her back stiffened as she pushed out of my hold, lurching with fright when her eyes landed on the space above the sash in the breezeway window. Exposed and revealed, her eyes glazed to a sheen, flashing mirrored saffron as I followed her turn.

"Damn!" she called out loud. "Will that old man ever let me grow up?"

"Did you see someone?"

"No, wait!" she whispered, holding a finger to her lips. And in the still of that moment a muffled engine throttled up and the sound of quick rolling tires faded to silence.

"Damn!" she said again. "Why must he live in the past? I mean it's one thing to study, but quite another to live in!"

She looked into my eyes, brooding as she went on. "You know; he's had me in a box since I was fifteen? It's true. He's put me away like one of his finds! I'm dated and preserved, forever in his custody — forever fifteen!"

She turned to retrieve her blouse, showing a shape so taut in form and soft in line, I just couldn't resist the opportunity. "I would have guessed eighteen," I joked.

A quick wincing smile came to her face, and for one split second I thought we might finish what we started, for that unfinished smile had at least some promise, and she might have tossed her blouse to the floor had my attempt touched the right nerve. But, as it was, she looked right through the compliment, letting her smile go flat while her eyes locked hard.

"It bothers you that much then," I offered in a quick change of tone. "So what is he? Another lover?"

"No, it's nothing like that," she said, slipping her arms into her blouse. "Nigel's a fuddy-dud. Straight as Bobby's buttons, and ..."

She let it go while she fussed with her hair, turning quiet with thought as she put herself back in trim. "I owe him everything," she murmured softly. "So much happened at Yassi Ada. Did you ever hear of it, Kim—back in the early sixties? It was the first time that field archaeologists got serious with SCUBA."

"Ahh, so he's your patron saint, is he?"

"Kim, he let me be a part of the team—at fifteen! And it wasn't just a bunch of go-for-broke divers either. Nigel made sure of that. We were pioneering the techniques of an entirely new field for archaeology! He had two full-time photographers, a surveyor, a logistics man, a conservator: the whole complement of technicians, and everybody dove; even the fifteen-year-old draftsman!"

She was back in form now, totally recouped and quick to move with her change in mood. "Come on now," she said, stretching to close the lids on the two big cases. "Let's get these things closed and put away before Nigel blows another gasket! If we get to him soon enough, I'm sure I can smooth things over. Just let's hurry," she begged. "The longer we wait, the harder it's going to be."

She clicked the latches in quick succession, then shooting me her most winsome look, she left for the steps, swinging the door wide to the wind—as if to make my task as painless as the look on her face.

We found Nigel a short time later, bowed at the door of a big brick furnace, and so preoccupied he was unable to rise for our arrival. Jill knew the place to find him, and having wasted no time in our pursuit, it was curious to see her hold back when the moment came; for we idled in the shadows long after our arrival, and now with us all finally so close, she seemed almost stuck in her tracks. Across the way the old man stayed bent at the furnace, poised in a posture that held us at bay. It wasn't until he'd come up out of his stance that Jill finally decided to move.

"He's unpacking the kiln!" she said in a seething whisper. "That's my job, and he knows it," she snapped.

She swept past me, fresh with spite, making a collision course into the open sided shed. But by the time she got to where Nigel stood, he'd pushed his tongs back into the furnace and gone right back into his stance. She stood over him awhile, stewing with her arms folded, watching, and making her presence felt, but hardly taking his notice. Then as if she'd suddenly thought better, she turned in my direction to call me in with an almost frantic wave.

It had all come down so fast: the fracas back at the lodge, the chase, and now the call into the shed. It seemed I'd sparked a contest of wills. And now, with her hand flagging in the shadows, she was asking me to help her finish what I had started — and never mind that it had all happened behind my back. I was part of it now, so what else could I do?

I went in looking for exits, though I'm sure my eyes didn't wander, for before they'd even made the adjustment, I knew I was surrounded. It was the smell that did it. A smell as rich as rain at sea; a wet musty wall of scent that came on with my first step into the shade. It was everywhere around me: in the clay baths and drying trays, the mixing troughs and storage bins; everywhere the shadows fell, there was the smell of earth and land.

Jill stooped and my focus followed. She was down low now, with her hands already gloved and thrust into the rough fired container Nigel had just set aside. Staying down, she lifted her head to see me coming in above her, and then with an expectant pause, she pulled a large round-sided dish into the space between us. She held it there, then rising, she lifted it; then looking for light and finding none, she moved off as sudden as the frown she wore.

She found light in the area they'd set aside for modeling the clay. There, beneath a section of translucent roofing, she paused to turn the dish on her fingertips; then slipping past a pair of half buried kick wheels, she settled before a broad wooden table where books and binders had been laid out among a collection of unfinished works. It was the place furthest from the kiln, a place for final checks and measurements judging by its contents, but more important, it was the place furthest from Nigel, so I followed just the same.

"Is something wrong?" I offered on seeing her look.

"I can't bother him while he's unpacking the kiln," she answered quickly. "He's sure to mess it up if I give him the chance."

"No, no. I mean the dish. Is there something wrong with the dish? You seemed upset back there."

"Oh, you mean this?" she said, turning back to the table. "No, it looks fine, but judge for yourself," she said, sliding one of the binders into view. "Here's our original."

She threw open the cover and peeled through a succession of studio lit 8 by 10s. "We shoot 'em when we find 'em," she said, still paging. "Then we clean 'em up and shoot 'em in the studio. All these shots were done on *Nighthawk*. We catalog everything you know. Here look," she went on. "This is the one we're looking at now."

She ran her finger down the clear plastic sleeve till she came to the reference number and color scale. "We do this with every piece — top view, sides, and bottom. And they're all scaled to the millimeter too. Then we do the write-ups, and in this case we've even made thickness profiles and templates."

"So all that's left is the chemistry."

"That and the kiln work," she added. "Ahh, but don't think it's easy! Kim, between Nigel and me and the pair of potters who work those wheels, there's enough knowledge and technique to copy any piece out there. But, when you're going after *duplicates*— duplicates of something so refined and yet so crudely manufactured ..."

Her voice trailed off as she moved to sort through a pile of Lucite cutouts that lay at the far end of the table.

"Would you believe it took Nigel a year to find his clay deposits? I mean the man's a fanatic!" she whispered. "But you know, he found the source of the raw materials: the clay, the flux, the glazes; everything! And that kiln? Those bricks come right out of the dig over there by the river! Would you believe they're as old as the stuff we're trying to duplicate?"

She flipped the dish, laying it upside down so that the plastic template could be swung. "He's not content to do a simple dating project, not Nigel," she said, studying the fit. "He's a pioneer."

"Jill," I cut in. "We're in Thailand. That clay is Thai clay, and those broken pieces back at the dig site? Aren't you two working in two different directions? I mean, your pieces are Chinese, aren't they?"

"Ahhh," she said looking up and smiling into space, "you do pay attention, don't you?"

She deserved a blank look, and she got it.

"Look," she said, putting down the template. "There are really only two places on the planet where high grade Song ceramics can be accurately duplicated. One is in Southern China, and the other is right here. In China you could go to the Longquan River area and try to do what Nigel has done—you could also try it on Mars for all the luck you'd have up there. No, when the decision was made to make duplicates, there was only one place to do it. Politically, technically, and historically, this is the place; right here on the Yom River! And you know, I'm not the first one to try it either. The Thais tried it seven hundred and fifty years ago! That's what all this archaeology is about!"

"So you're saying those broken pieces back at the dig site are attempts to duplicate the Chinese? Jill, they hardly compare to what you've got in front of you."

"They did the best they could with what they had, but the clay around here just never measured up. It still doesn't. The mineralogy up in those hills just isn't right: not enough pegmatite if you want to get down to it. But never mind. With a little extra care in cleaning, some outside materials, and a touch more phosphorus pentoxide in the glaze ... we've been getting acceptable results."

"So, is that one you've got there acceptable?"

"It's as good as any we've done. The shape and color are spot on. The weight's good, the dissolve is fair, but the signature is still there, so there's still a chance we'll do it again."

"Don't tell me you sign those things!" I laughed.

"No, of course not," she went on. "It's the clay. Or, more accurately, what happens to it when it's fired. Look here," she said, "you only see it on the bottom of the foot ring."

I tipped forward to join her directly above the inverted dish.

"We don't glaze the bottom rim; that's the tradition, so you'll always get a view of the body material. Well ... We can vary the color you see by blending the clays, so you might see burnt-russet foot rings on some pieces and burnt-orange buff on others; then at times we add a brown wash. It depends on the kiln that manufactured the original. Anyway, we've done a good job matching the body-clay types, and when they're fired, we get the colors right. But if you look real close, you'll see a characteristic speckle. It's apart from the color, so you'll see it in all our stuff. It's the impurities of the local clay, and try as we might, we can't seem to vary the effect. Those little black flecks show up the same way in every piece we do!"

I had narrowed my focus as she spoke, but for the life of me, I couldn't see the thing she was talking about. Between the photo and the dish, there was just no discernible difference. Even at pointblank range, with my nose a mere six inches away, I still couldn't see it, but then, I really wasn't given a proper chance ...

"You're not starting up on that again, are you!" his voice boomed from above. "You rubbish their clay, then you rubbish their history! Good God girl, have you no sense of propriety?"

My head snapped up to see the old man's face glowering from across the table.

"PROPRIETY!" Jill called out. "You barge in on me; in the privacy of my own bedroom, and you talk of propriety! Where's your propriety, Nigel?"

"My dear, there are boundaries to what is right, and there are boundaries to what is decent, but I have crossed neither! You'd know that if you weren't up to your neck with green fever!"

He pounded the table and turned to leave.

"Wait!" Jill called. "Don't go! I didn't mean ..."

Her voice trailed off on seeing him veer away from the table. "Will I ever win one?" she whispered. "Or will it always be like this?"

She touched my hand in parting; a reflex, I suppose. A soft squeeze for good luck, and away she went, leaving me as quickly as was proper. And if it were the first time I'd seen her spread thin in a squeeze, I might have watched her go and wondered. But it was all too familiar now; they'd even given me labels: damage control, propriety. They explained her every move.

I stayed at the table, so quelled by her touch that I felt no caution in her absence. In fact, I was into her work from the moment she left: first with the template, then right on to her book. Page after page, shot by shot: top, sides, and bottom; they went on and on, filling the binder with hairsplitting focus and never a break in form. These were the originals, as she had said, and they were, as far as I could tell, the next best thing to having what they'd lost; for they were as comprehensive as modern methods allow and just as tedious too.

I looked up by habit when I'd come to the final photo, and across the way, Jill and Nigel stood squared off in their long overdue heart to heart. Pleas and apologies, accusations and explanations; it was plainly something I had no business in watching, let alone hearing, so I automatically went for another binder, choosing the one they'd left by the templates, if simply to turn away.

"Propriety," I reasoned. "Where was my propriety?" And without further thought, I buried my focus on the matter at hand.

It was another book of well shot photos, bound like the other but not near as formal nor half as absolute, for these were outdoor shots jammed four to a page and much more to my liking.

Encrusted lumps of sea growth and weed, and hairy brown shapes all covered in algae; these are the things I call my own. But there they were, on another man's boat, so strange and familiar I smiled at the thought. "We shoot 'em when we find 'em," I think she'd said. "Then we clean 'em up and shoot 'em again." Well, there they were in perfect order, straight up from the depths and looking so much like something you'd see on my own dirty decks, I had to look hard just to know they weren't mine.

Clusters of shards and moss covered bowls: the items grew far more recognizable as the pages went on, for after the wet shots, which were always too tight, they'd move the pieces up to the cabin top, and with the help of a skyline that put life in the setting, I could see the stuff more as it was. There were rice bowls and dishes against a mountainous backdrop with great ragged ridges that played up the profiles. And there were vases and pots and pinnacled peaks, and a sharp spiking summit for contrast and form. All new shapes, I thought at the time; so where would I find the copies? Their unfinished stuff was right here before me, so when would they show in the book?

I stayed with that thought as I went through the pages, pausing now and then to re-examine the unfinished pieces and wondering about the studio shots too. For they, like the items that sat on the table just never seemed to show up.

All new shapes, I thought once again: the bowls and the dishes, the pots and the vases ...

"Navigating, are you?" a voice whispered from behind. "Or is this just a walk in the woods?"

"Jill," I twitched, for she'd come up in total silence. "I didn't see you!"

"Then you're obviously not a hunter," she quipped while moving in on the binder, and with a quick flip of her wrist, the cover fell shut.

"Kim," she began, "We've got a bit of a problem."

"What do you mean?" I asked, trying to read her expression. "Was I meddling?"

"Probably," she smiled. "But it doesn't matter. You've already seen all those pieces anyway. You've even held a couple of them as I'm sure you already know."

"The Halliburton collection?"

"That's good!" she laughed hurriedly. "I've never thought of them that way. But please, let's not make sport of this. Kim, we've got a real problem with Nigel. He's saying he'll quit the project if you stay!"

"Well that's crazy, Jill! Didn't you tell him I was part of it now? Did you tell him I'm the guy who's going to run the stuff across the Straits?"

"It doesn't matter to him," she answered quickly. "He's absolutely dug in."

"Well then, suppose I have a word with him. Maybe I ..."

"No, you don't understand," she insisted. "He doesn't want to know you for one second!"

"What? Is he so hung up he can't bear the sight of you with another man?"

"No!" she cringed. "I mean, I don't know. Look, Nigel's got himself way out on a limb. I mean, I told you he's a pioneer, right? Well, this time he's pioneered a simple dating project into something so controversial, he's gone and lost his funding. Even his university affiliations are falling apart. Kim, a few months ago he published his preliminaries, and they pulled the plug on him—just like that! Why, when I showed up, the entire project was being mothballed.

"So, that means he'll have a fit if I try to talk to him?"

"Kim, he's on the outs! Don't you get it? He's upset everybody. They want to bury him. And now I've come along with a sidelight project that will fund the dig till his dating methods are backstopped. Don't you see? Even if the slightest whisper gets out that he's involved in making copies, he'll be finished—and not just for now—forever!"

"You can't go on without him?"

"He's vital," she whispered.

"Well then, tell me what it is that's so damn controversial so at least I'll know why I'm leaving. You'll do that, won't you?"

"Oh Kim," she moaned. "Are you sure you want the details?"

"I won't know till I've heard them."

"Okay," she breathed, "if it'll make it any easier ..."

"It's all about magnetism," she began. "You know how a child's magnet will make iron filings line up? Well, picture the iron oxide particles we talked about, the ones we find in our glazes. Now imagine what happens when the glaze gets fired to 1200 plus degrees. The particles swim. They literally come unglued. Now, when the firing is finished, it turns out that it takes the particles quite a while to get set up again. And believe it or not, they align — just like iron filings."

"You mean they realign after they come out of the kiln?"

"That's right. Now remember the rejects we talked about, the misfired and flawed pieces? They're called 'wasters,' and every kiln has a dumping ground for them, usually right alongside the kiln. So," she paused, "when Nigel started to find layer upon layer of thrown-down kilns — he's on the tenth level now — he found the wasters that correspond to each kiln. So, what he's got is a perfect time line, you see; the deepest level being the earliest, right?"

"Now," she smiled. "This part I know you'll like; it's straight up a sailor's alley. When the wasters cool, the particles align to the pull of the big magnet in the sky: the earth's magnetic field. And, as you know, magnetic north and true north are constantly in a predictable variation pattern. So now," she laughed, "can you guess what Nigel's trying to do?"

"He's working backwards, isn't he?' I offered. "He's using the yearly variation difference to document his time line!"

"'Magnetic sequencing' he calls it! Now tell me he's not a pioneer!" she laughed.

"It's exciting, Jill. But why is it so controversial that they'd want to bury the guy?"

"It's not so much his methodology. It's his deductions that have put him in hot water. Kim, he's worked the timeline back to a point where these kilns predate the Chinese ceramic traditions that are their credited source! He's gone on to say that the technology may have, in fact, flowed out of Thailand, not China! Now, that means he's belittled the Chinese, which is not a good idea in the world of ceramics. And he's got the Thais looking like a bunch of thoughtless glory-hounds, which is not so good in the land of smiles. Kim, until the magnetic sequencing technique is backstopped with some other dating methods, Nigel's in real hot water. His official funding has been shut off and his credentials are being stripped away as we speak. So you see, the last thing he needs is to be found working in a kiln that's making copies! It would ruin him."

"Okay, let's just say I don't know him. He doesn't exist! Now does that mean I go away and we forget the whole thing?"

"Of course not," she said softly. "It just means we'll have to work out a plan. I won't be up here forever, you know."

"Well, how long are we talking? Back in Singapore it was three or four days, and we're beyond that already!"

"Kim, Nigel destroyed every piece we left behind! There was nothing left to pick from when I got here. Don't you see?"

"Look," she went on, "right now it's *your* schedule that's important! You're the one who decides how long I'll be here. Kim, without you, there's no crossing the Straits."

"Then you're asking when I'll have *Windigo* ready? Jill, I'm ready whenever. Well, any time before the eighteenth that is, I've got to be back in the Philippines then."

"You mean aboard the drilling rig, don't you?"

I nodded.

"Then you'll travel the seventeenth, and we'll make the transfer on the sixteenth. So, that gives me how many days? Kim, do you know what day it is? I've lost track completely."

"I don't know. It was the day after Christmas when you left, and the next day I landed in Chiang Mai. That was the twenty-seventh, and I was there three nights ... So last night was the thirtieth and that means ..."

"It's New Year's Eve!" she laughed. "Today is the thirty-first!"

She snatched my hand excitedly, and with a gleam and a great playful tug, she launched me to my feet. "Sixteen days?" she said incredulously. "Sixteen days? We'll never make it!" she laughed. "There's not a hope in Hell. Just no way at all!" she said, barely smothering her smile.

"What do you mean?" I let out.

"I mean, if we want to finish what we started," she burst, "we better get started!" And in that same laughing breath she put a quick stunning kiss directly upon my lips.

"Happy New Year," I tossed off lightly. "And just when I thought you'd asked me to leave."

"Don't be silly," she cooed in perfect innocence. "Just, let's get out of here before we have to invite Nigel to the party too!"

There was absolutely no debate on the point she had made; we simply left. And even though I knew I was in retreat, I was more than happy to go along. For the fact was, I was touched by the way she'd managed the scene, and never mind the way her body felt when I slid in for the ride. I was halfway home before we parted, with no mind to complain. And in the end, when it was said and done, she had me lying by her side with nothing left to say.

CHAPTER ELEVEN

The sixteenth fell directly in the middle of the workweek, and as it was the last week before the long Chinese New Year holidays, it turned out to be the perfect time to be out in the Straits. Ocean going traffic had all but vanished that week: what with the shipyard having closed out its inbound schedule, and with a full crew working round-the-clock, it seemed apparent that they were setting up for a massive last minute discharge. In any event, the absence of traffic was only the first timely surprise to affect us that day. The second, and by far the more surprising, was the unexpected state of things down at the boat bases.

There are six marine police boat bases in Singapore, and as you'd guess, they are properly arranged to survey the island's coastal boundaries. Three are on the south side, with good-sized craft to watch the

Singapore Straits, and of course the other three work the north side of the island, up along the narrow waters of the Johor Straits. Now, of those on the north side, one base watches the waters west of the rail and road causeway, while the other two take care of the seventeen-mile strip that I frequent. So it is that I pass the Seletar Base and the Ubin Island Base every time I run the Straits, and there is no doubt that in a full year of running these waters, I've come to know every one of their boats by name and number.

Now, it's not at all unusual to see a boat from one base using the facilities of another base. In fact, this happens all the time. Sometimes a heavy displacement gunboat will come up from the south and lie in the Straits while an Eastern Bloc freighter makes her way to the shipyard. Well, this always means there'll be a lot of activity in the slips down at the Seletar Base, and at the same time, the Ubin Island Base will look nearly empty. There are also times when the ship traffic gets heavy down by the Johor River, and that tends to load up the Ubin Island Base. Either way, there's a fairly regular shuffle that goes on whenever anything is happening out in the Straits, and in a year of casual observation, I've found that I can judge the situation by simply counting boats and taking numbers.

So it was that when Jill arrived, the sails went up on *Windigo,* and in the peace and serenity of a mid-afternoon spin, we got a green light as plain as any I've seen. For not only were the ships nowhere to be seen, but the bases were as settled as I had ever seen them. Both Seletar and Ubin showed all the right numbers, with the resident boats tied right where they should be, and with not one single interloper that would give us a pause. Call it blind luck, or better, home-leave, for with the holidays coming, their boats were called in. And whether they did it as part of a plan, or just for the time we were there, it was a light far better than moonlight, and it stayed with us right into the night — past Ubin, then Seletar, then on up for the transfer. And there, right in the very spot where the Malay peninsula comes closest to French's place, right across the Straits in fact, we took on the crates and made our way home — so simple you'd guess it could never go wrong.

In all I'd guess we spent less than nine hours together. Seventeen miles down and seventeen back; it's really not much of a passage. And yet, in retrospect, those miles were a kind of prelude to everything that followed, and not because I expected to end up back where I started. No, our time may have been short but my prospects were not, if Jill's final words rung true.

"Let's do it again," she'd said when we parted, "only let's not turn back next time."

I spent the next four weeks doing time with Placid Oil and playing with the thought of those words.

They were, I thought, the perfect good bye; so full of promise it didn't matter that I had put thirteen hundred miles between us. She'd tapped the stuff that sends men to sea, and for that I have no defense. Trade wind skies and steady winds, the promise of things to come: "Let's do it again, only let's not turn back" — what more could she say than that?

I did my month hanging on that question, and when at last the supply boat came to take me ashore, it was the fourteenth day of February, and the time was right for leaving. That day of all days, I remember the way it went. Boarding the plane with a gleam in my eye, for what better a day than this? A red-letter day with her waiting to meet me, I could see the way it would go. The airport perhaps, but that was a long shot; no, I suspected she'd be out at French's. And yet, when she wasn't, it wasn't a problem, for I knew she'd have left me a note. That day of all days there wasn't a question. I just knew she would leave me a note.

I woke the next morning with my thoughts in perspective, for nothing had been left to greet my arrival: not a card in the mail nor a note in my cockpit, not even a note of her call. That day of all days had passed in the night, and by dawn it was all but forgotten. The sun rose, the roosters crowed, and *Windigo* lay steady, untouched by a hand. And as for the note, well, it was probably a letter, and what would a day's difference make?

Dawn turned to daylight, and, like a cannon shot, I found myself gunning down the road to Clifford Pier. There was, after all, no reason to hold back, for I'd done all the waiting I could do. Busses became blurs and cars mere flashes as I pressed the Norton down through the city. It was a record run for that time of day though I'm still not sure why I did it, for when I parked at the pier and looked up at the clock tower, I found there was no one around.

It was barely six thirty, and the kiosk owners had not even started to unlatch their armor. A pair of sidewalk sweepers milled about pushing dust through the concourse, but beyond them, the place was empty. I left the Norton to unwind a bit, knowing the stir I'd cause if I rushed out to *Nighthawk*, and not wanting to see Jill undone. So with idle steps and sideways glances, I wandered out to the pier head to get a line on my day.

Out east, the sun had broken above the outer breakwater, and I had to block the skyline to manage even a fleeting view. There were masts and boat-like shapes out there, but given the light and the time of day, they were hardly more than sunspots. Blinding yellow light masked all but the fringes of the inner harbor, and no combination of hand and arm shielding could change it. I stood a moment, then moved back into the concourse, figuring I'd rest my eyes in a patch of broken light over by the queuing area. Over there a line of tied-up water taxis undulated on the surge while a hundred sheets of rushing seawater cascaded in the stairwells. I waited in the shadows, watching the sway and the spill of the sea while the thought of her waking played hard on my mind.

She was packing her bags, with the crew all paid off, as the water rushed back on itself. And then down the steps in a gurgling whoosh, we were sailing away from it all. Over and over the cycle repeated, with those big hulking boats slipping dangerously close. Up with the surge on a bubble of foam, and then falling back as the water receded, we were sailing away from it all. The wind in her hair, and her eyes flashing clear, we were bound for the far horizon.

"Top o' the morning, old buddy!" And a quick heavy hand clapped hard on my shoulder. "Buy ya breakfast?" he roared.

He spun me around with a shift of his grip, then standing before me, he squeezed till I blinked.

"Kim," he said in a far softer voice, "you up for a bite?"

I blinked again to regain my focus, and in finding Bert's face, I went into a grimace.

"Hey, gimme a break, Barnaby. You think I come ashore at this hour every morning?"

"What are you talking about?" I clipped. "I'm down here to visit the schooner. And what are you doing here? Its barely sunup!"

He gave my arm a jovial clap as he finally came off my shoulder. "Come on," he cheered, "let's go get a bite."

I looked beyond to the pier head. "Hey, you came in on a bum boat, didn't you? Hang on, I gotta get that guy!"

I was moving away before the words had left my mouth, breaking to a trot and not slowing down till I'd come to the water's edge.

"They're not here anymore," he called, while watching me go, but his words had no meaning till I heard them again. Softer this time, as if spoken in silence, for the sun had gone clear for my view out into the harbor.

"Buy ya breakfast, old buddy?"

"Where'd they go?" I said, wheeling around. "Are they still on the island? Did you see them take off?"

"They left the anchorage quite a while ago, but I've no way of knowing where they went," he sighed. "Tell ya what though, let's run down to the food stalls now. You can hit Port Clearance right after breakfast. Its right down the road, you know. Anyway, if they're still on the island, those guys will know. And if they're not, they'll know where they've headed. Come on," he urged. "Let's get out of here."

He walked off without waiting. And in that moment, I knew he was holding back. "You saw them leave!" I called. "Was she aboard?"

I broke to a trot. "Come on, I gotta know," I pleaded. "You saw them leave, didn't you?"

He led me along without saying a word, moving on through the concourse and out onto the street as I shadowed his every step.

"Barnaby," he said at last, "you're one hell of a sailor, and nobody would ever doubt your ability to get where you're going. But by God, put you alongside that woman, and you're as lost as a lamb out at sea."

"Are you going to tell me when they left?" I said blankly.

"Look, I don't know if she's aboard. They left at night. But I'll say this: there was a hell of a lot of activity going on over there just before they left. They took on stores like you wouldn't believe — crates and crates of the stuff — like they were stocking for a bloody long haul."

"When?" I plead. "When did all this happen?"

"It was on a Friday: middle of last month, maybe three, four weeks ago. Kim, they've been gone a long time."

I sighed and shook my head in disbelief.

"Want to talk about it?" he said quietly.

"Not just yet," I mused. "Look. I gotta get down to Port Clearance. You don't mind if I leave you here, do you? I'll catch you in the food stalls in about twenty minutes, okay?"

I left Bert mid-stride as I spun to chase down the Norton. "Three or four weeks?" I couldn't wait another minute.

I flew the length of Shenton Way, and in less than five minutes, I was three stories up in the Tanjong Pagar Complex.

"I need a copy of Capt. Schaefer's port clearance. Company records," I offered. "Bluewater Investor's *Nighthawk*. Cleared out a few weeks ago."

The clerk scribbled a bit, then looked up. "You'll have to see the Port Captain if you want a copy," he droned. "I can get the departure time and the next port of call; more than that and you'll need authorization. What company are you with?"

"Never mind," I groused. "Just give me what you can and I'll be on my way."

He ducked back to his files, and in a minute he returned carrying the departure roster. "*Nighthawk*," he pronounced. "Less than 300 gross tons. Your ship sailed on January 18; a Captain Drucker in charge bound for Muara Harbor, Brunei."

"That can't be," I argued. "Are you sure you got the right boat? The captain's name is Schaefer."

"Owner of the vessel?" he responded suddenly.

"... uhh, Bluewater Investors, I think."

"That's your ship."

My heart sunk, my knees went slack, and my feet took hold on the floor. "*The eighteenth*?" my mind screamed. That was *one* day after I left for the rig!

I stood motionless in a rush of self-doubt and unanswered questions. "Brunei?" She never said anything about Brunei. And who's this guy Drucker? Where'd he come from? She never ... A pair of long hairy arms forced a folder of forms between me and the clerk. "Maaf," he barked, and with all the subtlety of a man of the masses, I was unceremoniously wedged away by a dark figured man in a brimless peci.

"Son of a bitch!" I let out wildly, and in the same fire of breath, both the clerk and the man in the hat fell slack-jawed in a startled fluster.

"Maaf," I echoed, and with no thought to their questioning looks, I turned my back and made for the door.

The air was still cool with morning shadows, and hardly a man had broken a sweat. I found Bert parked behind a plate of roti and, without so much as a word, I took my place and sat in silence.

"So," he began. "You gonna tell me where they went?"

"Brunei."

"You gonna do anything about it?"

"Already did," I mumbled. "I quit the rig two days ago."

"What?" he chuckled in disbelief. "You mean you gave up your job? Awww come on Kim, you gotta be joking."

"Don't give me that crap!" I snapped. "There's something gone wrong. God damn it, she never said anything about Brunei!"

Bert lowered his focus to study the plate of yellow dahl that lay between us. He seemed poised to say something, but then chose to let the moment drag. Then, in the fullness of time, he mumbled, "You gonna eat?"

"I don't know what I'm going to do!" I shot back. "I don't know if she's on the boat or still on the island, God damn it!"

"Slow down, Kim. It's too early to get worked up," he cautioned.

"Now," he said in a soothing tone. "Let's put things together. What did they tell you down at Port Clearance? Did they back up my date?"

"The boat left the day after I split for the rig."

"Okay," he thought out loud, "and their outbound port of call was Brunei. Okay. Considering the quantity of stores I saw them load, and knowing like you do, that absolutely nothing goes on in Brunei, I'd say they put in for some of that dirt cheap diesel and they're probably way out of the area by now. Christ, Kim, you should have seen the stores they were loading. They could be anywhere by now."

"A delivery!" I shouted. "That explains it! They've got a delivery skipper! Everyone's been paid, and she's off the hook!"

"So, what does that mean?"

"It means she might still be on the island, God damn it!"

"And how do you figure that?"

"Look," I said, jumping to my feet. "I've got to get back to French's before I miss her completely. She's probably up there right now," I said, backing away. "And you know something?" I laughed. "She could be sick of waiting after a month."

I counted the minutes all the way back to French's, but it didn't change a thing, for I was as wrong at eight thirty as I had been at dawn. She was nowhere in sight, and for the next half hour I sat in the pavilion, pretending to read magazines, as if time alone might make a difference. Somehow, somewhere, I knew I'd have to get a line going, but at that hour, watching my watch was the best I could manage. At nine I debated making a phone call back to her home office in San Francisco. And at nine-ten I gave it up with the idea that time was surely against that line. For not only was the hour too late on the coast, but it was still too early to call.

I was headed back to my boat when I caught sight of the Frenchmen standing beneath the stern of their dry-docked boat. They were, as always, so consumed in conversation that neither paid the slightest attention to my arrival. Jacques and Dominique were a classic pair of eight balls — best left untouched — but for some reason, I felt I had to take a shot.

"You guys seen Jill?" I broke in.

They went back to talking between themselves as if my English had no meaning whatever.

"Come on damn it, it's a simple question!" I fired off.

"You ass *me*?" the big one returned. "You ass *me*?" he spit. "No, Monsieur, you *tell* me! Where is Jill?"

He came forward all puffed with contempt, and were it not that his friend had stopped him with a mere touch to his shoulder, I might have backed up a step. But as it was, I simply stood my ground and waited, for as soon as they turned, they leaped to shoving one another in what looked like a face saving ploy. They shouted and pushed in an arguing way until at last, the smaller of the two seemed to come away with the win.

"Jacques says you owe us some money," he said, breaking into clearly spoken English. "He says you stole from us and he demands you pay us back!"

"Tell Jacques to eat some beans!" I snapped. "I don't know what you're talking about."

The bigger man came forward again, but as before, he reacted quickly when Dominique pushed him back.

"*You* are looking for Jill," the smaller man declared. "*We* are looking for Jill. And the last time *we* saw her, my friend, she was with *you*!"

"You mean at the Christmas party?" I scoffed. "That was months ago. Now don't tell me you guys are still upset about that?"

"Don't flatter yourself, Mister Kim. You know exactly what we are talking about!"

"Sorry guys," I sneered. "Mister Kim is a bit thick today, but I wouldn't push him, if you know what I mean."

"Ahhh, he knows too well!" Jacques roared. "We see you carry her boxes! We know you work together! No! You must pay us."

"FOR WHAT?" I jeered at the top of my lungs. "For almost getting her killed? You two set her up with those tin smugglers, didn't you?" I shouted. "Didn't you?"

They looked at each other in silence.

"You guys are unbelievable!" I went on. "You want *me* to pay you for putting Jill's neck in a noose. You know they hang people on this island. Did you know that?" I shouted.

Dominique came forward. "Monsieur," he said, gathering himself. "Her neck was already there. She asked *us* to set up a boat, so we did. And she paid right from the start, so don't think it was our idea. Half up front and half on completion. That's how she wanted it, and that's how she got it. But," he said, pausing to eye his friend. "But when the deal went to shit, she never paid the rest. And you know, the Malays came back to collect. Many times. We had to pay them to get rid of them. So you see Mister Kim, we want our money, and we know you have it!"

"She never paid me a cent!" I burst. "And why should she?" I yelled, looking right into Jacques's narrowed eyes. "Even an idiot could make that run!"

"Imbecile!" he spit. "She pay you with pussy!!! Now you are zee stupid man!"

The big Frenchman came at me with his arms cocked for a headshot, but as I recall, that wasn't where I first felt pain. The pain came from between my legs, for it was there that Dominique had planted his foot in what had to have been a well-rehearsed maneuver. He kicked hard and by throwing his body, he'd managed to clear the way for his friend's end of the action. I was on my way down, spinning with pain, when Jacques's fist arrived, and although I'd seen it coming from the start, there was nothing I could do about it. My knees collapsed, and I bit the dust in a writhing heap.

I let that mark the end of a misspent morning.

That evening, just as it got dark, the wind rose enough to skew the boats to the set of the tide. Wavelets formed, and for a few minutes all the boats lay off to the wind. It was a quick setting breeze, the kind that sneaks in past sundown then fades to a whisper. The boats swung, then lay back to the tide, and for a short time there were loud teeming sounds of lip smacking claps as the boats slapped back at the sea.

I stayed in bed, immune to the cheer, as if only one sound could bring me to life. A laugh or a sigh, it didn't matter which as long as it meant she had something to say. And yet as I lay there, alone in the dark, there wasn't a sound that even came close; only the sound of some faraway drone, the stillness of night setting in.

I suppose I dropped off while lying there, because the next thing I knew, I was sitting bolt upright with my arms and hands flung out in a balancing brace. And directly above me, up somewhere on deck, there came footsteps and clatter and all kinds of stomping.

"Ta-hell's goin' on!!" I bellowed into the clamor, and in an instant there was quiet again.

"You want to give me a hand?" a voice whispered in. "I'm all alone you know."

"Bert?"

"Come on ol' buddy, up-an-at 'em."

I went on deck to fit my fenders between the two boats while Bert went about snugging lines.

"You really took me by surprise," I opened. "I didn't even hear you coming."

"Yeah, I thought about calling," he said blankly, "But, ahhh … sometimes the radio isn't the way to do it."

"What do you mean?" I flinched.

He moved away to crouch above his stern cleat, and then having doubled a line through the stern chock, he tweaked and pulled till his boat lay right.

"We'll leave it like that," he said wrapping the cleat. "Go ahead and take in the bow."

His tone had gone somber in a soft telling way, and I knew to be quiet as I went to the bow.

"I got a hold of the Port Captain, Kim. He's not a bad guy you know?"

I kneeled to take in the line.

"Look," he sighed. "She's on the crew list. She's gone."

I looked up to see a deep-set face looming above me. "That's it?" I whispered tentatively.

"No. It's just the beginning. The Port Captain had a lot more to say."

I turned to make the final adjustment. "I got an idea what's going on," I said steadily.

He watched me twist a hitch to set the line. Then as I stood to follow him aft, he shook his head as plain as that.

"It's art business," I countered. "She collects for a gallery in San Francisco."

"They're pirates!" he shot back. "They're all convicted felons! Except the girl of course—but she's involved, Kim. They know she's involved."

He stepped down into his cockpit and immediately made for the companionway ladder.

"Who's the *they*?" I followed. "Who *knows* she's involved? The Port Captain?"

"Sit down!" he ordered.

I moved into the only available seat.

"Now," he said, having positioned me across the dinette. "After you left the food stalls, I went down to chat up the Port Captain. He's not all that busy you know. Anyway, I got to him through one of the clerks I know—no big deal."

"What's he know about Jill?" I snapped.

"Barnaby, everybody on that boat—and that's including your girlfriend—everybody on that boat is persona non grata in Malaysia! Did you know that?"

"She told me the boat had problems."

"You bet, ol' buddy! They're not even allowed to drop the hook in Malaysian waters. They're an international disaster, that's what the Port Captain called them, 'an international disaster.'"

"Look, the whole thing's a hustle! They were set up from the start, damn it! *Nighthawk had* clearance to operate in Malaysian waters, but the Navy seized the boat just the same. They hauled them into Lamut, impounded the boat, and stole their salvage! Why, according to Jill, the authorities never even admitted that there was a cargo aboard. They simply took it, then buried the boat in red tape. So, if they *are* convicted felons ..."

"They're pirates," Bert cut in. "He called them, 'cultural pirates' Kim. They were caught stealing a national treasure."

"Oh, that's great! They do the research. They do the funding. They do the exploration. They do the salvage. Then, when it's all finished, and all the risks are behind them, the Malays step in and arrest them. And for what, 'cultural piracy'? You know there can't be such a law!! It's a hustle, that's all it is. And from what I hear, the maritime courts are just about to settle this thing in *Nighthawk's* favor. So go tell that to the Port Captain!"

"Hey, slow down ol' buddy. You're letting this thing get you all worked up."

"Look Bert, if you knew the pressure Jill's been under since this thing blew up, you'd get worked up too. I mean the girl's taking heat from every angle out there. Her home office is pushing her. The lawyers are pushing. She's got a bunch of art investors climbing the walls back in San Francisco and a crew of twenty-five unpaid seamen to take care of out here. Now, you throw in the Malays and the Port Captain and ahhh, and let's not forget the Marine Police — she's taken a shot from them too. Christ, Bert, all she's been trying to do is to get those crewmen paid so that they can go home! Now, is that a crime?"

"Did she tell you that, Barnaby? Is that what she told you?"

"She's a bloody fortress of virtue, God damn it!"

"Did she ever tell you they were *persona non grata* in Malaysia? Did she tell you the boat was under surveillance the minute it sailed into Singapore waters? Did she tell you the Maritime Courts ruled on their case almost a year ago?"

"That's bullshit! The Port Captain's out of his mind!"

Bert's face fell from the force of my accusation. His eyes shifted, his shoulders drooped, and he turned away to settle himself. There was a long pause.

"After I left his office," Bert went on, "I headed for the National Library, over on Stamford Road. You know the place? Well, up on the third floor, they've got microfilm copies of every Straits Times newspaper that's been printed for the past fifty years. You ought to run down there, Kim."

I let out an audible sigh.

"It's all there. Names, dates, and places — the whole shootin' match in black and white. Just check last year's March 5th issue. See for yourself."

"You mean there's no more case to be heard?"

"Kim, it's all over. They're *persona non grata*! They can't come back — *ever*! Hell, if any one of them set foot in Malaysia, they'll be put away for good!"

"But they still have *Nighthawk*! Bert, how did they manage to keep the boat if they were convicted? Surely the Malays would have seized it! Bert, this doesn't make sense at all."

"Look, they got pulled in for conducting an illegal salvage operation. That's what shut them down. Then, before the case was heard, the Malaysian Government passed a cultural piracy law. They got tried on both charges, but because the seizure took place before the piracy law came into effect, they managed to hold on to their boat. It was a technicality the paper said would never happen again. Kim, the article makes it clear. The Malaysian Government has first claim on everything within their so-called 'economic zone.' And anybody who attempts to export an item they deem of historic significance ..."

"They got screwed!"

"No. They got shut down, kicked out, and put out of business. That's what they got. And you know, they were lucky they didn't get worse! Christ, they could have been jailed for years!"

"Outright theft. That's what she called it."

"Well, that may be. But you know what I can't figure? I can't figure why they came back! Christ, Barnaby, Malaysia is hardly a stone's throw from Singapore. And Brunei? Why it's surrounded by East Malaysia! Christ, Barnaby, what the hell were they thinking?"

"They're gone!" I raged. "They're gone, God damn it!! So what-the-hell difference does it make?"

My outburst hung thick while a sudden lingering silence fell between us. It laid there unmoving. And in the stillness, Bert's facial expression drained before my eyes.

"I'm sorry I put you through this," he said quietly. "Suppose we let it go."

I got up to make a parting reply, but somehow the words got stuck in my throat.

"Don't ..." I held back. "Don't sweat. Don't give it a thought," I groaned.

I wasn't happy with the way I left things that night, but given the chance to leave, I had to take it as I could. Jill was gone, that much was certain, and whatever the plan, it was all too apparent that my part had ended the moment those crates came off my boat. And as for telling Bert, well, how could he understand? The question of motives and the letter of law, these had nothing to do with why she was gone! I let go of his lines and watched him kickoff without speaking another word.

I didn't talk again until well into morning. In fact, I did everything I could to avoid making contact with anybody who might stand between me and the question that ruined my sleep. Over and over I'd run down the story, and time and again it came up the same. If I was out, then who was in? That's all that mattered to me.

At ten o'clock I pushed my way through the turnstile on the third floor of the National Library. There are four microfilm viewing stations right at the entry, and you'll find the files just off to the left. I pulled last year's March 5th issue, and from there it was as plain and straight as Bert had told it. *Nighthawk* was indeed the test case, and yes, only a technicality had saved her. But I had not come to question his word, so I flew through the text till my eyes were stopped cold. It was down at the finish; in the place where the article turned to ring out its warning. "The treasure-boat will be released into the custody of her owners and removed from Malaysian waters by her skipper, Captain William D. Drucker. Neither the ship nor her crew will ever sail Malaysian waters again."

"Drucker," I moaned aloud. There was that name again.

I stood to leave in a quick fit of self-doubt, for there was an obvious answer to the question I'd raised. If I was out, then *he* was in, and that's all there was to it. Drucker—not Schaefer—that was his name; so how could he be her brother? I shut down the screen and turned to walk out before thinking of how it could be. A half-brother perhaps, or maybe a marriage; I returned to my seat by the screen.

Was there something she'd said that would give me the answer? I sat long with my head in my hands. Then, with a notion as vague as they come, I went off to the reference files with a thought and a name. Starting in the "A" drawer, I went directly to "Archaeology," and from there I went looking for an author named Nigel. I flipped through the cards, taking titles and numbers whenever an "N" appeared. And although I had five and was working on more, I quit on a whim and moved right to the "M's," for "Marine Archae-ology" seemed a far better thought. There were fewer than ten cards in that category, and yet I didn't need to go past the third. It was a book called *The Byzantine Wreck at Yassi Ada*, and wouldn't you know, it was written by a man named Nigel.

I let go a long sighing breath, knowing I'd heard her speak of that place, and suddenly wishing I hadn't.

"So much happened at Yassi Ada ..." those were her very words; and yet now as I heard them again in my mind, they were more than I wanted to hear. I slapped the file shut with the heel of my hand as if trying to silence my mind.

The *Byzantine Wreck* was one of those blue-bound university texts that have embossed back bindings, unmarked covers, and a cluster of photos at the center crease. The photos, of course, ran in chronological order; beginning with hard-hat sponge divers and moving right along to amphora heaps. There were maps and sketches and lots of underwater shots to detail the technical side of the expedition. All the pictures had an instructive dimension, but none so much as the final shot, for it was that one, and that one alone that told me the way it had been. It was the "yearbook shot" of the expedition team, and there was no mistaking the faces I saw. There was Nigel standing front-and-center, looking every bit the leader. And then, off to the end, as you might guess, there was Jill with a smile as innocent as spring—the fifteen-year-old draftsman—just as she said.

"So much happened at Yassi Ada." You could see it all in her smile, the turn of her lips, the glow in her skin; I jumped right to the titles to check on her name. Then third from the right, I was narrowing my focus when my eyes locked up in the line.

"Son of a bitch," I groaned in a whisper, for they lay side by side on the list. Drucker and Schaefer—paired off and bound—the whole thing turned in the blink of an eye. Family resemblance, a shared last name—the only thing shared was the look on their faces. The turn of her lips, the light in his eyes; I could see the way it had been.

The book fell shut without my lifting a finger. It just happened on its own. And in the same absence, the room faded from view. I was away and shut out, moving for motion and with no sense of purpose. I needed time, but for the life of me, I had no idea what to do with it. I walked a while, leaving the Norton with hardly a thought, for whatever its use, I couldn't give it a purpose. I found North Bridge Road and for no reason whatever, I swung down to the river.

There's always a river for moments like this. They're great for reflective thinking, you know. But with mid-morning traffic and those great blaring busses, the Elgin Bridge was hardly the place for what troubled my mind. I needed time, or better yet, a distraction, for what weighed so heavy was my own sense of loss: no sail in the moonlight, no china blue eyes—and without a distraction it would only get worse. So I headed for Cross Street, down where Chinatown starts, and in a matter of minutes I picked up on the change. The smells and the sights, the old way of life, it's an easy distraction if you give it a chance.

I took to the mood as best I could, watching and stopping when my senses were filled, and looking for action when I felt them unload. Everywhere something would summon a thought, if only I'd focus on what was at hand: the festoon of laundry that blocks out the sun, the old men and children with no place to go, and everywhere shop keeps with lives locked upstairs, in dingy surroundings that never see light. No, I could do better than in a place like this, if only my focus could take to distraction. I tried faces and hands, then finally hit on a truth, a quirk you might call it, but one that's a rule. For Chinese sandals are always too small, and if that's not distracting, then show me I'm wrong.

By Spring Street and Banda, I'd covered the subject, clear through distraction right into a haze and I was thinking about turning to make my way back. Then standing there I stopped, considering my course; I was drawn to a shop window as if swayed by a call. A blue green shape amidst a clutter of gray, it sat off to the side on its own lacquered stand. And there lined beneath it were the usual things: carved ivory tusks and polished jade bracelets — you can see this in windows all over the town. But it was the color that had caught my eye, and without a further thought I walked out of the haze.

Inside, I paused at the door to adjust to the quiet, for with the click of the latch there was only my stillness and the barrier that language always brings to these moments.

"Anybody home?" I ventured, and there came an instant rustle of paper from the far corner of the room. "Ahhh," I chimed brightly while moving in on the sound. And on that cheery note, a young Chinese girl in a blue school uniform shot out the back passage. "Ahhh ... haaa," I finished softly.

I stood now within the place, and all about there were showcases and furnishings, all laid heavy with Asian curios and assorted objects of art. It was also too dimly lit to afford a reasonable examination of anything. So, with blue-green shades still fresh in my mind, I returned to the display window for another go at the bowl. I picked it up and with no compunctions whatever, I was holding it to the sunlight when a voice cut in from behind.

"A fine specimen, wouldn't you say?"

I turned.

"Of course, if you are a collector," he went on in a most proper English accent, "you may already have such a piece."

"No," I said suddenly. "I'm just curious."

He was an elderly man in a mandarin collared shirt, and upon hearing my reply, his reaction came easy.

"Well then," he said softly, "if I may be of service."

"Uh, yes," I began in an unsteady tone. "I think you could help me. That is if you could tell me some things about this bowl I've got. It's a Song piece, isn't it? Celadon, I believe you call it?"

"Yes, but no," he said trailing off slowly. "It is from the Song period," he paused, "but here in Singapore we would try not to call it Celadon. Qing-ci, or if you must, green ware. That piece is a particularly fine example from the South."

"Would you think the Longquan River?" I guessed.

"Indeed," he said in a measured tone. "Fourteenth century, if I am not mistaken."

"Not the thirteenth?" I challenged offhandedly.

"The styles change as you move into the fourteenth century. The older pieces are, as they say, more poetic in form, lighter in weight, and ... restrained. Later they become more exaggerated. That," he said, motioning to the bowl in my hands, "that is fourteenth century export ware."

"Of course," I said clearing my throat. "I wasn't trying to contradict. It's just that I. Well, I've seen some other pieces like this one and well. There's a lot to know, you know?"

"It is genuine, if that is what is on your mind. I'll put my reputation on it."

"No! That's not it, that's not it at all," I objected. "I don't mean to challenge your reputation, far from it. No,

I aim to buy this piece, but you see, I'm not a collector. In fact, I have only recently developed an interest in this sort of thing. And to be perfectly honest, I don't know the first thing about fourteenth century export ware."

"You seem to know something," the old man countered.

"I know this stuff has a special attraction to some people."

"Yes, some people collect the Song to the exclusion of all other periods. And still others only the Longquan pieces. It's a rather peculiar thing."

"Green fever!" I blurted. "They call it green fever, don't they?"

"They might," the old man smiled. "With some people, it can become an obsession—but that's a collector, isn't it?"

"But what is it?" I begged, "and why the fixation on Celadon? Aren't the others as nice?"

"Sir, the Song period was indeed a trying time for China. The Mongols, as you remember, conquered all of China. It was the Song Dynasty they conquered—running dogs I've heard them called. But to some, it was a good time for China. There was movement. Systems were breaking down: the royal court had to be moved south, and there was trade like never before. Artists communicated with artists, and their output flourished. In ceramics, purity of form was the ideal—the principle of pure expression. To collectors, Song stoneware is the high point before porcelain changed everything."

"But why the green?" I interjected. "Why is that glaze so intriguing? Is it a lost recipe, like I've heard?"

"It may be, but I think it is popular because there is so much of it. You see, it came on in the second stage of the Song period; near the end. And by then, there was a huge merchant class who made trade in every corner of the known world."

"That piece you are holding," he said, pointing to the bowl, "that's export ware. Not the highest quality of the time, but a fine piece, and most likely, it was found in an overseas grave. That's where we find it nowadays. You see, green fever, as you are calling it ... it is nothing new. In its day, people loved these pieces so much, they took them to their graves."

"Well, who were these people? Chinese merchants? And what do you mean, 'overseas'?" I pressed. "How far away do they find this stuff?"

"The Song period was a great time for trade. In Hangzhou there were over a million inhabitants. They had canals for moving freight. They had sailing junks that measured over a hundred meters in length. They made trade as far away as East Africa."

"By sea?" I winced. "They crossed the Indian Ocean in the thirteen-hundreds?"

"Yes, they were the first to use the magnetic needle compass, and they were first to put the steering rudder on the center axis of their ships."

"So then, there's green ware in Africa?"

"Coins. Coins in Africa," he went on. "Green ware in Asia, also Indonesia and the Philippines; everywhere there was something to trade for. They would come down from China, sometimes to go through the Straits here in Singapore. Often they would visit Indonesia for aromatic woods and rhinoceros horn. Then, on the way home, they'd move up to the Philippines for bird's nests and pearls. There were outposts wherever trade was good."

"So, it was the Chinese merchants who stayed behind to organize trade? That's whose graves are dug?"

"In the outlying areas, but then, some of the best green ware is found in Japan and Korea. Up there, the Buddhists treasured Longquan ware. They buried it too."

"Green fever," I breathed in quiet detachment. "That's what he called it."

Then, fixed hard to the blue-green shape that had stayed so long in my hands, I found her words in the back of my mind: "... smooth and cool as a water worn pebble," and with that, I let out a sigh.

I could see that moment as if it were stopped on a screen; the cases laid open, her bed within reach, a flutter of saffron blowing right by her side, and those china blue eyes shining wet with desire.

"Clever," I breathed softly, "clever as though ... as though she ..."

"As though molded in metal," his voice filled in.

"What?" I asked as if suddenly brought back. "What did you say?"

"As though molded in metal," he repeated. "The inscription reads: *'Clever as though molded in metal, and yet delicate as jade'* — the Yaozhou Tablet. That is what you are looking for, isn't it?"

CHAPTER TWELVE

The way I've come to see it, I was hot on the path the minute I walked out of that shop; but, if you'd asked me then, I most certainly couldn't have said. I had been dealt all the bad cards, from the beating I took back at French's, to the reality that dawned upon me in the library, and I was slow to put it together. Green fever, ha! Jealousy by another name, it had colored my every thought. And so at that moment, with the bowl wrapped and boxed, and me on my way, there seemed an inescapable finality at hand. Green with dissolve, I had what seemed the loser's prize, a token of remembrance.

By evening I was back aboard my boat, still undone, but settled by a cooling drink and the thought that having loved and lost, I was at least a freer man. For having signed off the rig, all that was left was to stow the boat and bury that bowl. This I did, and by dawn I was slipping my way down the Johor Straits.

In a calendar year there are but two or three weeks when the South China Sea becomes a sailor's sea. Only ten or twenty days when the wind blows steady day and night, and a boat in Hong Kong can sail on the same breeze as one in Singapore. It's a winter phenomenon associated with the west monsoon, but not a monsoon wind at all. It's an interloper, a wind from another sea, allowed passage on the cusp of a fading Asiatic pressure area, and then turned back by the strengthening zone in Australia. The South China Sea is the boundary area between these two pressure areas, and as seasons, or monsoons change, there is a mid-February gap; a gap wherein the Asiatic zone recedes and the developing Australian area can't fill in. What's left is an unmistakable invitation to set sail: the interloper, with air far drier than either monsoon and a sky that's filled with well broken cumulus: a trade wind sky, born in the subtopic Pacific and flown in via the Philippines. It's a northeast wind like no monsoon—steady and free—it was my aim to use it.

I turned east when I came to the open waters of the Singapore Straits. It was a little after seven and the sun was up, shining low yellow-gold above a hundred banks of perfectly regimented cloudlets. Marching men of war on a wind-swept morning sky, could there be a better sky in heaven? My intention, of course, was to set some sail, dodge some ships, and turn back west, knowing I'd need outbound clearance from the port captain's office, and that I'd pay hell without it. But with every tack and every mile, there seemed less reason to fall off the wind and far more to continue. Call it spite, or even malice, but at the time and under the circumstances, there was no way I could waste that day. I made the Horsburgh light by noon and by nightfall I was long gone, well into the southern reaches of the South China Sea.

By the fourth day out I was into the rhythm and getting ready to pick a destination. In truth, I knew I could only bluff the paperwork back in the Philippines. Clearance-wise, Indonesia was out from the word "go," and Borneo not much better. So really, the choice was to either "one-eighty" back to Singapore then and there, or to press on for the Palawan Passage. Either way, I figured I was half way between the two, and the time had come for choosing. I was weighing the cases and getting nowhere when I thought to turn on my radio. Bert had the net that morning and he was just getting into it.

"Any priority traffic or medical emergencies?" he queried. "Nothing heard. Any relays?"

An interval of silence always passes at this point while people listen. "Okay," he broke back in. "Looks like we're all among the living then. So, if you would indulge me, I'll open things up with an odd piece of news that showed up in this morning's *Straits Times*. Now, maybe some of you have already seen it, or maybe it's so far away it doesn't matter. Anyway, I'm going to read it, if simply to warn people away from an area we already know to be off limits."

"It's dated Monday, Sandakan, North Borneo, and the headline reads:

Abandoned Schooner Towed to Sandakan

Two fishermen reported finding an unmanned schooner while fishing in the Sulu Sea. The vessel, Alborak, *appeared to be floating aimlessly and attracted the attention of Pedding Ratman and Kameleh Jarari.*

'We first called out, and when no one appeared we went aboard. There was broken glass and blood on the decks,' said Mr. Jarari. The two men then reported the discovery to the marine police in Sandakan. The deserted vessel was towed into Sandakan Harbor yesterday afternoon.

Alborak *is a registered research vessel out of Cyprus, and it is therefore believed to be the same ship that was recently featured in an article that appeared in the state owned newspaper of Brunei. The article stated that the research vessel was under contract to a group of Middle Eastern academics in association with the Xavier University Museum in Cagayan De Oro,*

Philippines. The collaboration was to study early Arabic trading patterns in the Sulu area by unearthing such evidence as pottery shards, shell mounds, and tools.

Darner Jelong of the Malaysian Marine Police stated, 'An investigation of this incident is underway. We are now in the process of carefully examining the vessel.' He added, 'This may well be another case of high-seas piracy in the Sulu.'

He then urged all fishermen to be extra cautious while in the area."

Bert continued, "Now, we all know we're talking about the Balabac Straits and the Southern Sulu." He paused. "Any questions before we get on to other business?" He paused again.

At this point my mind was in a panic of disbelief — shell mounds? Did I hear him right? Did he say shell mounds?

"Okay," he went on. "Sorry to open on such a sour note. So, if there are no fills necessary, we'll call for check-ins now. Any check-ins, come now."

The radio droned white in meaningless conversation and convention while my mind raced forward. "Sandakan," I howled, "that's the thick of it, God damn it!" I said pounding my fist so hard on the chart table that my pencils flew. "They'd be sitting ducks and she knew it!"

"No," I thought better, "she wouldn't do it. It can't be them. I must be out of my mind."

I was numb to the neck in a fatalistic stupor, and the cabin was filled with her presence. "If you explained it right," she was saying, "it would go right to their essence. You would be searching for a link with their past, and they would be honored by your search, Kim," she whispered, "that's how archaeologists have been doing it since they stopped robbing graves and became archaeologists."

"No," I groaned, "she wouldn't do it. It can't be them."

No, it was all one big coincidence, a misdirect of my own making. It had to be. For surely the academic world was vast, and this type of expedition could evolve on its own. It didn't have to involve the only archaeologist I'd ever met—and as to the boat? There had to be others that could take on the job.

I found the microphone and when an opening came, I signed on. "Bert, this is me, Barnaby. I got a question for you, if you got a minute."

"I got a minute and I got a question for you ol' buddy. Where the hell are you?"

"I'm east; maybe five hundred miles, but more important, I need an answer. Now. Right now. It's important."

"Okay, shoot! What's the question?"

"Okay. The question is: what's *Alborak*?"

"What? You didn't hear? It's the ship. You know, the research boat they towed into Sandakan. What, you didn't get that?"

"No, I got it. I got the whole thing, but that's not the question I'm asking. I want to know, what's *Alborak*? You know, what's the name mean? What is it?"

The radio went silent as he thought. "*Alborak*," he began. "It's Muslim. It's, it's the horse Mohammed rode. You know, it's the horse that took him to the seven heavens. The horse of ascension you could say."

"You got that Barnaby?"

There was no mistaking my course after that. I shot up to the cockpit like I'd come out of a cannon. "Start, you son of a bitch!" I yelled. "Now!" I screamed while turning the key.

The motor rumbled, and in less time than it takes to tie your shoes, I had jammed the throttle, turned on the autopilot, dialed in a course, and sheeted my sails. "Move! Now move, you son of a bitch!"

Windigo heeled hard on the wind. Spray flew and the knot meter clocked to hull speed. We were off and running.

Below, the diesel howled and my microphone tumbled recklessly across the chart table. I went to snatch it.

"Bert," I sputtered, "Bert? Ahh, look," I said clearing my throat. "I got a favor to ask; something I forgot to do before I left. You wouldn't mind sticking around after the net, would you?"

By the time he wound things down, he'd pretty much guessed my predicament with respect to the outbound clearance, for all he wanted to know was where I'd be, and when. And all he let me say was: "KK. Oh-nine hundred. Tomorrow." That was it. No fills necessary. Wudda guy!

Twenty-four hours later I'd made South Hill Rock, the last outlying danger off the city of Kota Kinabalu, the capital of East Malaysia's Sabah State. "KK," as it's called, lay at the western foot of the highest mountain peak in South East Asia, and it is, without question, the prettiest landfall in the South China Sea. Of course, my decision to go there had nothing to do with the scenery; it was purely a question of geography and time. Both Sandakan and KK lie at six degrees north latitude on the island of Borneo, that is to say, they are directly east and west of each other, with KK on the South China Sea side and Sandakan on the Sulu Sea side. Between the two there is 125 miles of mostly impenetrable tropical jungle and a 13,455-foot-high mountain. One can fly between the two cities in a little over an hour, drive between them in eight, or with a good bit of luck, you can sail over the northern top of the island in say, two days. I had planned to fly it.

I made the harbor pretty much on schedule, arriving around nine, but it took a while to find Bert. He wasn't up by the pier head as I expected, so I had to cruise the waterfront for a while. The town lies low on a sliver of flats, a white stagger of modern boxy buildings, racked and stacked thin along the abrupt coastline. Behind it all and quite suddenly, the foothills rise in neat green ridges with ground fog and mist until some twenty-nine miles back, you get the jagged peaks of Mount Kinabalu. Back at the water's edge local fishing boats and lighters go "bow and stern" to a long stretch of sea wall and roadway that might be called Front Street, were it not named after a founding father. It runs the length of the commercial district, boat after boat and car after car, right down to the central fish market where it ends in a waft of smells and odors that could stop your heart.

We made connections on my second pass up Front Street. By then, Bert had managed his way to the bow of one of the tied up skiffs that lay stern to the sea wall. There, bobbing on a slow undulating surge, he snapped his greeting, signaling both hello and success of mission with a quick show of thumb over fist. I closed and he drew an envelope from his shirt pocket—proof positive I was on my way. "You pulled me out of the fire," I crowed. "Great to see you!"

"You hurry along," he called back. "We got a one o'clock flight to make!"

"You mean ...?"

"You don't think I'd come here just to turn around, do you? Now," he shouted, "you drop your hook up in Spangar Bay, you know the place. I got clearance greased. They'll forego the inspection, but we'll have to do a normal check-in with immigration. We got no time," he clipped. "I'll see you up there with a car and driver. Now, move it!" he barked.

To say that Bert had simply come through for me; well, that would understate the whole matter at hand. Sure, there was the long-term bond of friendship between us, and I put a lot of stock in that. But, to take charge as he had, to fly up, and totally deliver, point blank. Well ... it gave me pause.

At one o'clock we boarded a Fokker F 27 for the flight to Sandakan. Bert, staying on top of every detail, chose the seats and took the window. I got the aisle and a dose of strategy. It seemed that Bert figured he was best suited to making the initial contacts; that is, the schmoozing that would gain us access. With success, he would bring me in and together we would make our inquiries. I didn't like it, but I couldn't argue. Time and again I'd seen this man have his way with bureaucrats. Hell, he'd just finessed my outbound clearance, so what could I say? I agreed to stay in the background.

We put down in Sandakan, blew through the terminal, and hailed a taxi. First in, first out, we had it going: Bert in the front seat, me in the back. The driver, a Hong Kong immigrant if I judged the accent, responded in classic kowtow, all smiles and exuberance, promising a city tour in one breath and picking our hotel in the next. Bert rattled some Cantonese and the two bonded like lost brothers at an old home get-together. I couldn't follow, so I did a transcendental fade, right there in the back seat.

Now, maybe it was the fact that I'd not slept in the last thirty-six hours, but the next I knew, we were stopped and Bert was telling me to get out of the car.

"This is where I go to work," he was saying. "You can see the masts? Kim, do you see the masts?"

I raised my eyes to follow.

"Look," he went on. "They're calling this place here a yacht club. The driver says it's a good place to put you off. Now, right over there," he shifted, "that's the Coastal Patrol's dock. You see the three masts beyond that building? That's where they're keeping the schooner. You stick here, old buddy. I'll be back, and hey, don't worry," he said swinging my door open. "We'll get answers!"

As suddenly as that, the door slammed, and I found myself blinking for focus while I reconstructed what I thought I'd heard. The taxi moved hurriedly up to what looked like an unmanned checkpoint shack, paused, then proceeded on into the grounds. I watched it take a position in the dirt lot that fronts the waterside compound. That's when the impact of the moment caught up with me, for there, right behind them and directly above the buildings, three unmistakably raked and dressed masts stood like sentries, glowering down in stone silence.

I gathered myself in a dead run for the waterfront, charging fifty yards of broken roadway, then up onto the entry deck that flanked the shanty styled clubhouse. I was headlong to extinguish the last shred of doubt, for better or worse. Up three long steps, around the structure and out onto the docks, it soon came into view. But then, bow-on and suddenly, and with its name boards in plain view, I would have sworn she was a different boat. *Alborak*!! This was not the boat I remembered. There was something wrong about her, and not just the name. They'd painted the deckhouse an odd looking brown, giving her the look of an old weathered tramp. And if that weren't enough, they'd messed up her rigging, leaving the three topmasts in tatters and tangles that would take days, if not weeks to bring down.

Wild thoughts swarmed in my mind: the boarding party, were they Sulu Separatists bent on kidnappings, or just plain pirates out for a quick kill? Was there fighting, or did it come without warning? Had they stripped the boat or simply plundered it? Who were they, and above all, were there survivors?

There was so much I didn't know and so little to be seen from where I was. The docks I stood on, they were nothing more than a line of simple piles with decking and bracing that butted the sea wall, so there was no vantage apart from the one I had. How I wished I could walk out a bit to study her profile, just a little to get a clue.

"Boat's been here for days," a voice broke in. "But you're the first who came running," he droned. "They'll be thinking 'bout charging admission now."

I turned to face a grinning man in aviator glasses and khakis. "I'd pay to get aboard," I said blankly.

"Well, I'm not the ticket taker," he shrugged, "but I'll tell you, it ain't gonna happen, 'less you're some kind of cop. It's a crime scene over there."

There was a familiar ring in his voice: something Southern, something West Texas and altogether oil patch, judging by his turn of phrase.

"Do I know you?" I asked suddenly. "You ever work the offshore rigs? No, wait ... You fly copters," I said, pointing a finger. "That's where I've seen you.

You used to fly pickup out of Puerto Princessa. That's where I know you!"

The man's smile turned to a beaming grin as he removed his glasses. "You got a good eye," he laughed. "You're one of Bunker's boys, aren't ya?"

"Ex," I corrected. "I gave it up."

"Me too!" he crowed. "Lemme buy you a beer, will ya?"

He clapped my arm with a broad sweeping whack. "Now look son," he went on. "They won't take your money here, so don't try to pay. It's a club, you know — boats and yachts, but ya ain't gonna see any so don't get excited. Why, last time a yacht came here ..." He paused, suddenly breaking the playful cadence he'd built up. "Well, you're lookin' at it, ain't ya?"

We stood eye to eye in that moment and a change came over him. "You knew someone on that boat, that's why you came runnin' ..." He stopped.

He spent the next ten minutes making apologies while we sipped beer together. He was ex-oil patch, now flying for a Chinese timber baron who owned "most every tree in Borneo." Sandakan was his base, but he knew Sabah inside and out. We talked oil and timber until he moved the conversation to regional politics.

"People wonder what's going on around here," he was saying, "what with all the high seas piracy out there in the Sulu. Well, I'll tell you," he said, "I see 'em, most every time I fly the coast. They're out there in their boats, running around, scaring everybody if they're not robbing and killing. So one time I asked my boss what he thinks about all this, and you know what he said? He blamed Marcos."

"Everybody blames Marcos for everything," I added.

"Now, my boss is Chinese," he went on, "and his trade is trees."

"If he's mad at Marcos, he's just like everybody else," I countered.

"No, he's got this thing figured out. Ya see, Marcos owns all the coconuts in the Philippines. I know it sounds stupid, but it's true. If you got coconuts, you sell at the government-controlled price, and you can't export. That's the way it is. The government exports, you don't. You get paid the going rate in pesos, the government gets the international price, and the spread is outrageous."

"Such is life, my friend."

"But ya see, it's what puts this whole thing together. It's why you got them boats out there!"

He was losing me, but I hung in, figuring he'd bought the beer after all, and Bert was nowhere in sight.

"Look, son, here's how it works in a China man's eye."

"A Sulu Moro throws all the coconuts he can in his boat; it's a simple thing. He sets off for Sabah looking for a better price. Well, he gets here and he doesn't want money; he'll trade the first time — things for the folks back home, ya know? Well, now he knows the value of his goods, so the next time he comes ready to do some buying. This time, instead of trading, he buys an old diesel engine, installs it, and becomes a smuggler — hell, he's breaking laws the minute he leaves the Philippines anyway. So now he turns up in Tawau to buy trade goods: radios, sewing machines, bicycles, and the like. He'll run them down the Indonesian coast trading mostly back into copra. Then it's back to Tawau to buy what he's been wanting all along. I told ya, we see 'em every time I fly the coast."

"Smugglers?"

"Yeah, but now he's driving a thirty or forty-foot speed boat with twin outboards so he can outrun anything. He's smuggling cigarettes and making real money. And if that's not enough, he'll pirate his own kind! I'm serious, he'll hit the little guys running coconuts! Sulu pirates! Hell, it's radios and sewing machines, coconuts and cigarettes; it's all moving around out there thanks to Marcos."

I had spent hours, if not days, listening to stories like this one. They are standard fare aboard the rigs. Like Yamashita's gold, Marcos and the coconuts had changed hands so many times, you could get ten different endings to the same set up.

"So. This place Tawau," I said, hoping to move the talk away from politics, "it's something of a smuggler's den, is it?"

"See this Rolex?" he said, flicking his forearm into view. "Two hundred skins, and it's real, by God; genuine item, and still they tell me I could have done better in the Ice Box." He snatched up his drink. "It's a boom town, son. Anything goes."

We'd just finished the first round when I noticed Bert turning his way out onto the docks. He looked undone and drawn, causing me to crash the table when I stood to get his attention. He flagged me once, then twice as he wanted no part at the table. I reckon I got off a word of thanks before joining him, but I'll never know.

"We gotta go!" he hushed while turning me to the steps. "And don't even look back," he rasped. "They got me marked, ol' buddy and you'll be next if we don't get out of here right now!"

"Christ! What happened over there?"

"We're going back to the airport, Kim, and I pray there's a flight."

"What?"

"Look, it all caved in on me," he puffed. "I told them I was with the Embassy; showed 'em the card, it always works. They bought it for a while. Then they wanted to see my passport. Kim, that's the kiss of death in this game. I had to tell them I would bring it from the hotel. Look man, we're out of here! Do you hear me?"

"But!"

"Look, we'll talk in the taxi!" he barked.

We boarded the taxi, both in the back seat this time, with Bert looking pale as I'd ever seen him. He was slumped and still, and not wanting a word of protest. I held my fire, waiting for the color to come back to his face.

"Okay," he sighed. "To begin with, they know the boat is *Nighthawk*."

He shifted to face me as best he could. "Kim, look," he began. "They're in there waiting. They've got the boat, and they know someone will come for it. It's a trap, plain and simple."

"What are you talking about?" I fumed. "There's been a crime committed! People are missing! Jeesus, man!"

"Slow down, Kim! You don't understand this at all."

"Me? You're the one who's missing it, man!"

"Look!" he shouted. "They've got the crew list! Every person aboard that boat is persona non grata, damn it! From their point of view, the crime is the fact that a bunch of convicted criminals entered Malaysian waters in the first place!"

"You mean there's no investigation? No search? No ..."

"It's an immigration matter, with criminal consequences the minute they find a suspect. They're talking CONSPIRACY ol' buddy. You show your face over there, and they'll put you away!"

"I won't accept it, damn it! There was blood on the deck. They said there was blood on the deck!"

"Calm down, will you? You're not thinking," he breathed. "Look, if we can get back to KK, we'll regroup; we'll come up with some other way. Just let's get out of here for now. There's nothing more we can do, okay?"

The taxi rolled on as a sudden, screeching silence enveloped the back seat. We were in retreat at full speed and I without so much as a scrape.

The Sandakan airport rolled into view with us both wearing far-away looks. Silence ruled as unspoken strains rumbled within us. The driver was paid, and Bert led the way into the open-air concourse. Above us a fading of light foretold the coming of darkness. It was after six.

"I'm not going," I blurted as we came to the departure roster.

Bert turned, almost angrily. "Come on, Barnaby. There's a six-thirty flight for Christ sake. Don't mess us up."

"I'm not a team player. You know that."

"If you stay, you won't be a player at all. Now, cut it out!"

"I'm not staying either," I said. "I'm leaving just like you, but I'm not going to KK. Look, I need some space, and a little time. You could help if you'd please kill a couple days on *Windigo.* It would mean everything to me."

"What good will it do? We struck out, ol' buddy. We got nothing more to go on than we had when we got here."

"You're wrong," I corrected. "I know one thing I didn't know. I know they were on a dive site when they were hit."

"How can you say that, Barnaby? You didn't even get near that boat!"

"The phone booth. You remember? You called it a parabolic ear, remember? It's missing. It wasn't on the deckhouse, was it?"

Considering the circumstances, Bert had little to say at this point. We'd moved a good distance on his energy, and we both knew it was ground that had to be covered, but now, with retreat our only option, it was obvious that things would change.

"Don't bother trying to track down the guys who found the schooner," he said, trailing off. "I'm sure they'll turn you in the minute you open your mouth."

We parted on those words.

I found a rack of chairs down by the baggage claim area and sat to think. Another concourse, another crossroad, another path, another decision. Another chair, another floor, another monk in saffron? No, there was no monk, and surely no flash of saffron, but there was, right then and there, a sudden compelling impulse — a dawning perhaps. I picked up my bag and made for the ticket counter.

It was early morning when my flight put down in Tawau, and though I'd lost the night, I felt lucky being back in the hunt. The scent of fresh milled timber hung sweet in the air around me, and I began to smile. *Could it be so easy?* I thought. *Could this be another Sukhothai?* The promise of reckoning lay before me.

The town of Tawau lies at the southeast corner of Sabah, appearing just as you would cross into the wilds of Northern Kalimantan. It's remote to say the least — a small port on the Celebes Sea, just two miles north of the Indonesian border; there might be 25,000 inhabitants. Palm oil farms and timber tracts run deep into a thinly settled interior, while out east, some thirty-five sea miles away, the out-islands of the Sulu Archipelago string an unruly path northeast to Zamboanga and the Muslim heartland. It's a town of smalltime Chinese merchants, Malay field hands, Indonesian transients, and displaced Filipinos, judging by what you see at the water's edge. I'd gone to the waterfront, knowing my path would begin there.

It's shallow all along the shoreline here, with tidal flats and makeshift wooden catwalks that serve as temporary piers. Scores of flat bottomed skiffs lay heavy in the fringing mud, while an even larger, inboard-driven fleet of Philippine kumpits hold ground maybe two hundred yards out. Ashore, a chaotic stretch of two lane road skirts the high water line, almost awash in ripples it's set down so close, with boats and trucks and great hands of bananas all coming and going in a great show of color and sound.

But I had come looking to make a connection: somebody young to get me started. I figured a tout perhaps, a moneychanger, or better still, a young Filipino off one of the kumpits. There were quite a few out there, tending the anchored boats. And if I were to wait, I thought, I might begin on that tack, but then, at that very moment an odd and familiar smell swept through the crowd, and it triggered in me a different direction. I turned my back on the water and headed inland following my nose.

Kretek cigarettes! Gudang Garam, the "clove cigarette king of Indonesia." If it were cigarettes they smuggled, then Gudang Garam would get me there! I wheeled into the Kedai Kopi knowing I had the scent.

I spent less than ten minutes in that little luncheonette. It was all so easy. In five minutes the words "ice box" came flowing off the lips of my newfound friend. And in ten, he'd said it again and we were on our way, out to the street and back to the waterfront. From there, we walked down along the road that parallels the waterfront, and in time, the place and the name came together in meaning. For even at a distance you can see that this place is not just another kampong of thrown up shacks on stilts. The Ice Box, as they call it, has almost no lateral spread to it. That is to say that it takes up as little real property as is possible, and in that aspect it defies the look of a real kampong. Kampongs always grow laterally first. They hug the tide line like mangroves, spreading coastwise till there's no place to go but out, and then they'll only go to waist deep water. This one is different in that it seems to have been regulated by something other than nature, for it heads straight out in one single shot of catwalk planking— one entrance, one exit, the same for some 500 plus people. And the closer you get the more obvious it becomes that it's not a kampong at all. It is no less than a pathetic, water-built refugee camp for un-papered Philippine spit-backs: an unrepentant holding pen they've stuck out in mudville.

I emitted no reaction at the time, but the look of this place is jarring and it's compounded by the desolate faces you see as you make your way down the catwalk. Political refugees? Economic immigrants? Sulu pirates?

Or just a bunch of luckless fishermen? Well, you never know till you find out, so what can you do? You just keep moving, hoping the trip out will be as easy as the one that got you in.

I was led down to one of the better looking shanties, a structure of slatted wood siding and a galvanized roof. Outside, they had extended the eaves to put a bit of shade at the entry. A pair of low benches had been brought up, and now a squad of six dark faced Moros bracketed the doorway from the shadows. I walked gamely between them, gathering myself in the thought that I had made many similar forays while buying sea shells, and that, in its essence, my ploy was not so different than what I had managed back in the Philippines. True, there would be a sticky moment when I moved the order from cigarettes to ceramics, but, as an opening move, the cigarettes were a natural, and I took heart, knowing I could swing a good opening.

Inside, a buzz of mumbled conversations broke out and the room cleared, just like that. I watched maybe eight men get up off the floor and take to the door while my guide settled into the only chair in the room. It was a stark place, a dormitory I'd say, with ashtrays and bed mats laying all about and a half dozen mosquito nets swung back from the rafters. Louvered openings had been cut for ventilation and light, but being high on the walls, they afforded no view. A patchy collage of magazine paste-ups and old yellowed posters dotted the naked frame walls.

I waited in silence at first, mulling my plans with a confidence I can barely relay, for as much as this place did not fit my expectations, it was nevertheless the place I had come to, and there was more than hope in that. Like vision in the absence of light, you look for form in what's around you, and you go on your senses when there's a glimmer of hope. So it was with me, for in form, this was no less than a retracing of steps, and while I did not know where I was heading, my senses told me not to ask.

A crowd had gathered outside the doorway by now, so I made the only move I could.

"Come in," I begged. "Please," I called, sweeping my hand downward as is the custom—over and over. "Tuloy po kayo," I teased, knowing the Northern dialect wouldn't do. "No?" I smiled. "No, no. Permisi, permisi." I corrected. "Silakan masuk, silakan masuk ... Please."

I was playing a pretty standard wrong foot opening here, but you'd be amazed how often it works. "Nama saya: Bar-na-bee, Bar-na-bee," I repeated. "Please. Silakan masuk."

With those words I began a pitch that would lead from cigarettes to seashells, seashells to shark's teeth, shark's teeth to pearls, and right on to Japanese war relics. It took time of course, but before long I got my billfold in the act, and a kind of slow chain-reaction began. They didn't have much, and judging by what I bought — well, you'd call it junk, and it did have me good and worried in the beginning. But oddly enough, as it went on, there came a moment that absolutely eclipsed the plan I was working. Right out of the blue and without so much as a sound, I had what I wanted, and with nothing to show.

It happened fairly late in the process where, having moved through my list, the focus had finally come to ceramics. I told them I was prepared to buy everything from broken pieces to family heirlooms, and that anything that looked like a bowl or plate would do. Of course, what I wanted was something I could recognize, but how was I to do that? Apart from the few pieces I had actually held, I had nothing to go on. Nothing but what she'd given me, that is: a sampling of color, a quick study of shape, and a signature speckle; if I could see it.

So it was that I had no other plan than to examine the underside of whatever I was shown. That's all there was to it. They would bring what they had. I would take it, turn it, raise it to the light to check for speckle, and set it aside. That was the plan. And that is what I was doing when one of the men bent down to pick up one of the set aside pieces. He took it across the room as if to reclaim it, but as I looked up to check, I saw him raise the piece to the high window light and in that moment I suddenly knew all I needed to know. In recreating the manner of my inspection he had positioned the piece directly in front of a yellowed poster that lay in the framing beneath the window. "Land Below the Wind" it read, and behind the script, above a haze of cloud and mist, there loomed a distant view of Mount Kinabalu as I have only seen it once before. High to the light, it was the very picture I'd seen up in Thailand. "We shoot 'em when we find them," I could hear her say those very words. And there it was! Just as I had seen it: the skyline of ridges, the cluster of peaks; why, it was as if she wanted me to know! The wet shots. The Halliburton Collection. Originals. Up from the depths and shot on deck. The mountains echoed her voice.

CHAPTER THIRTEEN

I made a rather abrupt departure, claiming maybe half what I'd paid for in my haste to move on. It didn't matter though. Mount Kinabalu was the witness I needed to see. Then and now, it is the bystander who broke the case.

By late afternoon a solid streak of cloud cover had filled the upland contours behind KK. The trades were in backdraft up there, and the clouds lay trapped and unmoving. I had lost the day between Tawau and here, but as it was, my flight had gone well, and I was happy for that. A taxi took me up to Spangar Bay where I whistled long and hard to get a reply.

"You had me good and worried, ol' buddy. Thought you might not show."

The skiff's bow glided softly into the gravel-like sand at my feet. "I'm back," I said, while hurriedly setting off the dingy with a quick two-handed shove, "and I've got an idea to run at you, my friend. It's big; very big, so let's move it. I think I know where it all happened."

I was anxious to get to my charts, anxious from the second that yellow poster had registered in my mind's eye, and it had been hours.

"So, did you meet someone," Bert began, " ... someone who knew something perhaps?"

He stopped rowing.

"Please," I begged. "I can't say a thing till we're back aboard. I'll need charts and ... Please, just let's keep going. I'll fill you in, but ... Hey, did I say thanks for staying with the boat?"

I rummaged the chart table like a dog hunting bones, hauling one after another out into the light, then tossing them out like so much dirt. It was an Admiralty chart I was after, the ones with etched contour lines and peaks, if you know the type. They cost a ton, but they give you what you want—detail that is—especially when you're reading a coastline by measuring peaks.

"Here it is!" I blurted. "Now. Now we'll see," I crowed.

I slipped the chart out onto the saloon table. I thumped it, smoothed it, and reached for the dividers. "The question is this," I said, spreading the points. "How far can you see? I mean, say you're at sea, and you're making a landfall. How far away could the most distant peak be?"

"On a clear day? Well, I once saw Cedros Island from way out. I think it was eighty miles. Then there's that place off Sumbawa, near Komodo. You know the volcano island? I've seen that one from way the hell out."

"Okay, call it eighty to ninety miles."

"But we're talking special circumstances, Kim. Clear days, high islands; you're not going to get that kind of distance ..."

"How 'bout the highest peak in Southeast Asia?" I clipped. "Say thirteen, fourteen thousand. Would that do?"

I was midway through my count, stepping ten-mile segments with each twist of my wrist.

"There it is!" I called in stopping. Then pounding the spot in a frantic staccato. "So what is that, Bert? Seven? Is that seventy miles?"

Bert met my eyes with a look that merged pity with pain and came up like anger. "It's the Balabac Straits, that's what it is, and you old buddy ... You are out of your mind!"

"No, look at this island," I shot back. "This is the place, I tell you. This. This Mallawalle Island and all this stuff out here. This is where they were working when they got hit!"

Bert placed both palms flat to the table. He lowered his eyes. His face turned down and he began to roll his head, side to side, as if the shame were too much to face.

"Look," I pleaded. "I know what you're thinking."

"Is this your 'BIG' idea, Kim? Is this the big thing you want to run at me?"

He picked his head up, glared, and made a mournful sigh.

"No. No, not at all," I moaned. "I need your opinion. I mean it."

"Look," I went on, "I know you're worried I'll go up there and get killed. I know that's what you're thinking, and you could be right. So, you know what I'm going to do? You know what the 'BIG' thing is? I want YOU to decide it. Decide it for me, Bert. Because I'm not sure myself."

"Well, that settles it then," Bert snapped. "You're not going anywhere!"

"Oh no, no you don't. It's not that easy, my friend. When I said it was big I meant it. No. You're going to have to suffer with me on this one."

"Look, Barnaby! What in hell makes you think you need to go up there? Whatever happened, happened days ago. It's over!! It's done!! Washed away like sand on a beach. Your going up there to do a post-mortem is not only irrelevant, it's suicidal."

"You don't think I know that?" I sputtered. "You don't think I've thought about that? For Christ's sake, Bert! I've spent the last five years dodging that place."

"So, what would possess you to want to go? Is it the hero bit, Kim? Is that what this is all about?"

"No."

"What am I then? The witness you need to validate the act? Well I'm not doing it, old buddy. That's all there is to it!"

"Sit down, God damn it!"

I moved to the galley, turning my back while I dug a pair of bottled beers from the fridge. I fussed with the caps before I began.

"Bert, she's got a mind you wouldn't believe. She challenges you to come to her level — to make the jump. And with every breath, every move, she presses it — God, she presses it. And she knows; she always knows where to set the bar."

"From the very beginning," I said, sliding the bottle into his grip, "I felt she was measuring me: not sizing me up, you know... *measuring*. Bert, I tell you, she has a plan. She has a plan for everything. And I'm part of it. Christ, as sure as I'm sitting here in KK. Harbor, I know I'm part of it."

"How do you know that, Kim? For all you know, she's ..."

"Look, it's hard to explain, but ... I know she's set the bar again. I know I'm here to play a part. Christ!!" I shouted, slamming my fist hard onto the chart. "It's staring me right in the face!!"

Bert lurched back with the blow, tipping his beer as he moved. It covered the chart, setting off a mad dash that rested the moment.

"What does she want you to do?" Bert whispered at length. "Exactly what did she tell you?"

"It doesn't work that way," I murmured. "She doesn't lay it out. Hell, I never know what to do until I've done it."

"You're not making sense, Kim."

"It's like clues, she leaves clues, or I guess I find them—I don't know. It's confusing. They're laid down in nuance. She's got a way of doing it. It's like she can tap my intuition, leave a memo, and waltz away without my even knowing. Christ!" I moaned.

"You mean she's led you here, is that it?"

"Bert, I know everything! Even though she never told me anything. You know what I'm saying? EVERY-THING. And yet, I don't know if it's possible. I mean, can one person do that to another? Can someone plan your thoughts months before you even have them? 'Cause if they can, then I'm on the spot, man. I mean I'm really on the spot."

"Kim, a guy like you should never stop sailing."

"Come on, God damn it."

"No, I mean it. You get too much out of it. If you put it down, even for a little while, you cut yourself off. That's when you get in trouble. That's why you're here."

"Please," I mocked.

"No. What you've described — this clue business — it is nothing short of what we common folk call inspiration. Kim, that's what intuitive communication is. Now, in another man's life it would be a precious moment, a thing of rare beauty. But in yours, it's an addiction — something so consuming you're a slave to it! You take away the ocean and you, you'll find it somewhere else!! It's inevitable, and you know what? I think she knows it."

I was taken aback by his reference to Jill. And never mind what a friend can tell a friend. It felt as if he had turned me inside out.

"Look, ol' buddy," he whispered at length. "I'm here to validate whatever you do. It's right that way. Just one thing though," he went on softly. "Do you have a gun on this boat? Let me see you load it. Right here, right now. 'Cause you're going to need it, Kim. Make no mistake about it. You're going to need it."

On that note, our eyes locked hard on one another — stuck in nearness, and yet moved by the growing distance between us — as if fate would hang in the air while the inevitable speeded ahead. It was the crossroads, and whether the warning was merely a symbolic exchange or whether it had a part to play, I was not to question. I broke out of his gaze with an inertia too compelling to stop.

"You want a gun?" I clipped. "I'll show you a gun!"

I'll not try to describe the rest of that evening, except to say that we parted company in the A.M. hours, just before first light. It was a subdued moment, and one that filled me with misgivings. "Catch you on the radio," he called out tentatively. And before I could manage the thing to say, the throttle went down, the motor rumbled, and I was away.

Looking back, I see how a word of thanks might have played far better, for it was in retrospect that I put sense to what had been said that night. Of course, it was fear that had set me off. The doubts, the cautions, the one-eighties that have always held me back, I was determined to beat them with bravado if nothing else. But as I worked the breeze out to Gaya Heads, it was the focus of his words that set my course, and for that I am indebted.

That morning the sun drew a bead from behind Kinabalu. Shadows stretched, and the skyline laid down on the waters before me. North bound and holding close to shore, I put my back to the peaks as if to shut them away, for I didn't need any reminders. There are seventy miles of coastline between KK and the first of the islands that clutter the Balabac Straits: seventy miles to think it over, seventy miles to figure a plan. I looked far to sea that morning, knowing that in twelve hours the sun would go down, and I would enter the Straits in darkness.

By noontime I was midway up the coast and well out of the shadows of Kinabalu. I was at the chart table now, and the thought of ancient junks and sunken ships was playing on my mind. The Balabac is a sailor's nightmare, now and forever. There's current, there're shoals, there're coral reefs and murky water. It's the spillover zone between the Sulu Sea and the South China sea, and as such, it's shallow and treacherous top to bottom. Up north on the extreme Philippine side, the ships-of-old might have used Balabac Island to make their transit, if they were given the chance. There are reefs to avoid up there, but the setup is relatively straightforward, barring bad weather of course. Further south they'd have nothing but trouble. Shoals and coral patches line the midsection of the Straits, making that passage a blind stab at best. And down off Sabah, well, they wouldn't stand a chance. Day or night, North Borneo is a wreck site waiting to happen.

Instinctively I reached across the table and closed my eyes. It takes fifteen seconds to warm up a scanning sonar and a little more to tune it. First, the white screen goes creamy yellow. Then, an electric motor lowers the sounding device. At about fifteen seconds the sweep line appears and you thank God if the gain control works. I didn't have the courage to watch, but at fifteen seconds I did sneak a peek. I hadn't used it in over a year, not even to dust it down, but there it was, and I breathed a sigh that whistled throughout the boat.

I regained focus on the strength of that, figuring the night might not be so bad should I decide to run it with the SS-80 filling the gaps. Day or night, it's the same for sonar. But at night, I thought, under cover of darkness, it might make all the difference. The islands could be approached at night, even a reef can be run. I began to concentrate now, examining the area that lay ahead with a confidence born of hope.

Pictorially, the North Borneo coast ends in a classic dog's jaws formation. Viewed sideways it takes no imagination to see, the mouth being Marudu Bay, and the jaws being the two muzzle-like peninsulas that bound it. It's a snarling, empty mouthed dog with a wolf-like brow and a quick jutting chin. The largest of the outlying islands, Balambangan and Banggi, lie just beyond its reach, with Malawali falling away at the chin.

I brought out my dividers to check the distances, and, just as I had done with Bert, I wiggled off the seventy miles from Mount Kinabalu. The zone, as it showed itself, lay just beyond the dog's jaws, a range that took in the southern half of both Balambangan and Banggi and all the so called North Borneo Dangers, to include Malawali Island and the dozen or so cays that surround it. In scale, it's a ten or twelve-mile sweep that runs maybe forty miles in all.

At this point my eyes slipped shut again and a faraway focus came over my prospects. There were saffron curtains blowing beside me — the cases laid open before us — what had she said while shutting that book? "Navigating, are you?" How I wished she was here to tell me.

I came to wondering how she had managed, even the very beginning, for it had occurred to me that to make a stand up here, to get anchored and to go about work, she would need much more than some far-flung warrant of security. The name change, the university affiliation, these might have helped, but there would still be the problem of renegades amongst the islanders, and for that, she would have had to make a plan. She would enlist them, I thought, or she would avoid them; but regardless, she'd have a plan. I began to look at the islands again, this time looking for shelter. For if night could give me cover, then I too would need a plan.

As coral-fringed islands go, the two in the dog's breath, Balambangan and Banggi, both offer excellent shelter along their respective southeastern shores, with the bay on Balambangan being the favored big boat anchorage. Chart-wise, this one is easy-in, easy-out, and perfectly sheltered. Over on Banggi, the entire southeast shore makes up what they call Mitford Harbor. It is an extremely narrow, mangrove-lined sluice that parallels the shoreline for about five miles. It is well sheltered and all but hidden by an almost continuous line of outlying islets. The approach and the entry, however, are tight, to say the least, with coral patches and underwater outcroppings bracketing your every turn. As I judged it, it would be hairy enough in daylight; but then, it did afford the kind of close quarters anchorage that would swallow a yacht and show no trace.

Try to imagine a large yacht in hiding. Apart from cover, she would want privacy of the highest order, with no village, no mailboat, no local ferry traffic, no passing fishermen, no nothing. Here on Banggi, the chart shows no sign of population within the so-called harbor, but as it is a listed harbor, you would expect some kind of fishing camp at the least, and more probably, a permanent mangrove fishing station with stilt houses, shanties, and any number of engine driven fishing boats. I tried to imagine the *Nighthawk* tucked in and secured up here—a hundred-and-six-foot schooner in a backwater lagoon, out of sight but not alone. She could launch her expedition from here, run tenders to the site, and still stay hidden. Why, she could use the local's boats and never show herself!

I quickly set to plotting my course again, walking off each hour's travel with a twist of the dividers. The way it was going, I ventured, I would pass over the dog's snout at sundown, cross the jaws in twilight, enter the North Borneo Dangers under cover of darkness, and shoot my entry in the dead of night.

I had, in that instant, laid out the perfect timing, and yet as I looked it over, I found myself backing away in thought. Call it a point of no return, for as the final staging came alive on my chart, I had to stop to measure my path.

Navigationally, the odds were horrible. Nobody would try this at night. And tactically? Tactically it was a presumptuous maneuver at best. For if this was the place they had used, wasn't it also the trap that had closed down the entire operation?

My boat drove north on the strength of inertia, never slowing and never veering, though I can't say the same for the captain. My worries were mounting with each passing mile, my convictions shrinking, and the entire pursuit seemed drawn in fiction. I needed something specific, right then and there, something of undeniable consequence that would pull me back and give me direction.

On deck, the afternoon sun was in final decline, and a group of local fishing boats were streaming south. They'd come around from the other side, hurrying along, and staying inshore as we passed. They were the first I'd seen from the other side, and I will not deny the relief I felt when they vanished off my stern. They were low, open-stacked cabin boats, maybe forty feet overall, with soot flying and a rack of tires slung at their sides. I remember wondering how they might look in the dark of night, for apart from their low profile, they were all wearing unpainted wooden cabin structures, and the dark brown would not show well in poor light. It worried me to think they would be hidden, and yet at the very moment that thought came over me, I leaped to a reality that made all the difference.

"Camouflage!" I blurted aloud. "They painted the cabin!" And with that last line, I dove back down to my charts. The dark brown color they'd used on the cabin; a mangrove cover if ever I saw one. The rigging in tatters, they would have strung palm fronds and brought down the rigging! *Alborak!* I laughed in a fit of awareness—a daytime cover as shrewd as any; I was a fool not to have seen it. They could lay in a backwater with a plan like that—work their site and never be seen—enlist the locals with the "Horse of Ascension." It was Jill right down to her toes.

I stood a while in disbelief, shaking my head at the scale of it all. For if she had gone to the lengths I sighted, then how was I to go with less? I would need shelter, just like she; but then, where was I going to hide — Mitford Harbor?

At sunset, I aimed my boat east into the dog's breath. I had come to conclude that while I couldn't follow, I could be led, and on that basis, I had no choice. I swept east into darkness, drawn by the coincidence of nighttime cover and a faraway siren's song.

Once over the top and heading east, you've got fifteen miles to cross the top of Marudu Bay. It's open water between the jaws, but once you make the far end, the North Borneo Dangers and the reefs and islets off southern Banggi merge into one, and there begins the minefield of coral shoals and submerged rocks that characterize the entire northern area. I had decided to drive to the middle ground, hoping to use the outermost shoal to set up my approach. From here, there is a narrow zone of navigable water that runs northeast to Mitford Harbor, and as darkness was upon me now, I figured I should test the look of that place before deciding anything else.

It was just past nine when I came abeam of the islands that front the harbor. I was a mile out, and while I had seen a hint of light from the beginning, a pattern had formed on one of the middle islands, and it told me all I needed to know about Mitford Harbor.

Out in the islands, electric lighting can indicate anything from a simple power plant to a full functioning ice factory. You never know by the look of the light, but in any case, where there's electric light, you'll inevitably find a noisy generator and a pier big enough to handle the fuel boat. I didn't want to see big boats that night, in fact, if the truth be told, I couldn't afford to cross paths with a dugout. I turned off to the east now, deciding to run a course that would clear Banggi without delay.

Out in darkness, an odd smell of brine had sprung up in the evening breeze. Wetter than normal, a sudden sting of heavy salt air blew in around me, and I paused to draw in my senses. Out in darkness, the smell arrives before the sound, but there is rarely a moment to think. I flew out of the cockpit in a single lunge, leaving the wheel to get to the sonar screen as the smell of froth and coral grew ripe. Wet calcified lime, seaweed and slime, atomized and blown, the night air swept in like a shadow behind me, spilling below as I came to the screen and swirling about as I fumbled for light. I was downwind of the reef and it scared me to think that I had waited.

I drove the next hour right from the chart table, using the autopilot's control head to make my turns, while all the time staying glued to the sonar screen. It takes a practiced hand, a good ear, and constant attention to get the kind of resolution you need to navigate by sonar, but it can be done if your boat is set up to do it. The main thing is to wear the headphones and never move from the screen, for between the pings and the sweeps you have to go into a trance to spot the depths, and without the phones, you'll never hold focus. It's a touch between sight and sound, and you have to cut yourself off to get it. The hard part then is to remember to turn the boat.

I made as many miles as I could, weaving here and there as I lost the grip, but getting it back, and all the time hoping that if I could make the northern reefs off Malawali, I could hug that line long enough to set a safe course. It takes three minutes to get night vision after a spell of light, and if I picked the wrong three, I knew I'd find myself back at the screen struggling for bearings and wishing I'd never left. So it was that I had to wait for a near collision with the longest line of coral I could find. Then, and only then, would I have the time to go on deck to reconnect with the night.

I stayed, and in the last minute I caught myself, eyes closed and counting double time—frantic to make a last count to sixty, much as a child would do. "Christ," I growled in a sudden burst. And with that, I broke for the cockpit.

It had been an hour; say six miles judging by feel, but it could have been a thousand for what I found. The night had changed completely, with a rising moon and milky white sea. The clouds had thinned to a wisp-like veil, and everywhere there was moonlight. I turned to see the reef boiling away at my side and in the same instant, I just about went to my knees. For there, not more than a few hundred yards away, a pair of inboard driven fishing boats floated at anchor just behind the break.

I grabbed my binoculars, and with my heart pounding and my ears still singing to sonar pings, I drew a quick bead on the boats. They were at rest and unlit. I scanned in toward the shoreline and there, in behind the boats, a lone patch of defused light rippled and flicked into focus. There were no less than eight stilt shacks back in there, clustered and joined by catwalks. I moved my view down along the shoreline, only to see a more distant cluster and that was enough. I checked my course, looked up ahead, then dove back down to the chart table.

I was frantic to move, but now, with all that moon-light, I felt trapped as never before. I had breaking waves on my right, a huge field of coral on my left, and no idea if I'd been seen. I needed a place to hide, right then and there — or I needed to cut and run. The two ideas collided on the chart table.

Going forward meant finding a place to hide, but where, and then what? I would still be trapped by the moonlight and then totally pinned down by day. No, the better course would be to leave, and yet, did I really want to go back to the sonar screen? Had I not pushed my luck far enough?

I studied the chart for an easier way, and in a mind that was oddly bent on full retreat, I stumbled on a thought that kept me going. The way out was to circle the island, or at least circle it back to the North Borneo Dangers. From there, I'd be back on sonar, but in the end, the time would be the same. I had stepped off the mileage and was double-checking when my eyes caught a detail that I would never have seen. Admiralty charts volunteer soundings well into shallow water, in fact, they are almost worth their price because of it. They give you what you want. But like the others, they'll show you blank space when they don't know the depths, and that is what caught my eye.

Malawali has a convoluted shoreline, all the way around. Chart-wise, it's a three sided triangular jigsaw piece, with numerous mangrove lined indentations and a continuous coral fringe. My dividers had stopped along the southeast coast, out along the fringe where the tidal shallows begin and the soundings stop. There is a small, finger-like indentation there; but in itself, it wasn't the indentation that had caught my eye because there are no depths in there. No, it was much more the combination of "what was there and what was missing" that struck me. For on that southeast coast, you've got contours and steepness, so well etched as to show perfect details of topography, and yet, within those etchings they've left a wholly blank inlet—not dotted, not shaded—blank. Even the markings for mangroves ran out.

What was an almost infinitesimal detail on the chart, now became the substance of my last hope. I had seen this type of omission, and I knew the possibilities at hand.

I made the push east, following the coral fringe and holding a tight distance off. There were no more lights along the shore now, and I gathered myself in wishful speculation. What I'd seen was surely a kerosene flame, and therefore, it was the proximity to Mitford Harbor that put that fishing village on the northwest edge of the island—that and the natural shelter of course. It meant that the southeast side, the weather side, would most probably be clear. The fewer the lights, the fewer the people; that was the best I had—my comforting thought at the time. And right or wrong, it was the one that stuck in my head as I swung to set up the southeast coast.

I had my entire focus on the shoreline now, and with every minute I was growing more fearful—another light and then what? Would I turn? I was in a fretful way, climbing to the cockpit, then back to the sonar, then up to the cockpit, then back. Most sailors rule out night entries altogether, and here I was, setting up a forced entry on an uncharted inlet in the dead of night; if that wasn't enough, I was going to do it dead downwind, right in the heart of Balabac. If ever a man must live his worst dream, this was mine to bear in my own special way.

I let go a headlong charge the moment the inlet appeared, barely backing off the throttle when the swells began, and never once going down to the sonar. I had come to know the bounds of my limits, and I'd be damned to do it different. I took aim at the center, leaned on the throttle, and let her go blindly as she would; for better or worse. I split a line of heaving froth, kicked hard on a breaking crest, and literally dived down the face of the incoming wave. In one great rush of wake and surge, I was cascaded forward, screaming down a sheet of boiling luminescence and then, just as quickly, I was delivered into grace. The swell vanished in a broad pool of up-welling fizz, and I was quick to back down my speed.

Behind the break, rolling wavelets gushed across the coral shallows in lines of six-inch froth. In the moonlight, they swept a continuous path so far into the mouth of the inlet that you could see them striking mangrove roots out along the shores. I pushed forward, watching the depth meter move to twelve, then ten, then nine feet. I backed off here, watching the lines of froth for any signs of depth, as there is often a run-off trench where tides and rains rut out the coral. I need six and a half feet to float my boat, more if I want to feel safe. But as the mouth of the inlet narrowed, and there was nothing but mangrove thicket ahead, I began to see why the depths had gone missing and sweat flowed down my back. There is no stopping a mangrove swamp, it grows and it blends, and they leave you with blanks.

There is a point of no return on every passage, and when you get there, it's never where you want to be. I shot a quick look back to sea, and then went down to the sonar. From this moment on, my path was a matter of blind fortune and outright guess work. There was nothing more to it than that. I drove for depth wherever I saw it, and it was luck that got me through. Nine feet turned into ten. Ten went to twelve, and out of nowhere the bottom dropped and a trench showed up on my screen. Clean as any river, it drew long and steady pings. Twenty feet and counting. Twenty-five. It meant more than depth to me. I threw down the headphones and burst to the cockpit.

A mangrove swamp lives on circulation. Little swamps have little creeks and bigger swamps have trenches. This one broke into the thicket with a vengeance, throwing back the tree line in a blaze of mirrored moonlight. At twenty-five feet and counting, waters flow, roots stand back, and the skies open up in starlight. I cleared my eyes to see a river of silver sheen and highlights, drawing back like a door into darkness.

CHAPTER FOURTEEN

Swallowed whole and still kicking, I lowered my anchor by hand that night, dropping chain in the middle of a backwater pool with barely a splash or sound. I was the sole survivor in a suicide bid, the last one standing in a crowd of one. Around me, a dark curtain of mangrove cover closed off my entry in a perfect fishhook meander. I was surrounded and alone.

It was at this moment that my last doubts gave way to the weight of my safe arrival. And though I had conjured no plan from here—not even a thought of what to do—I was more guided than ever. I went aft to shut down the motor, knowing only that I would need to take a stern line to shore to make this anchorage work. I turned the key and automatically set to unlashing my sailboard. Perhaps I thought it would be quieter that way, and yet I didn't give a thought to what I was doing. In fact, it was only when I found myself wet to the waist and with a rope in my mouth, that the first thought of using the skiff occurred to me. I remember floating belly down between strokes, midway to shore, and thinking what a fool I was to be doing it this way when I ran right into reality. I remember tying the line to a mangrove root, then rushing back with a plan.

I had never windsurfed at night. I had never seen anybody do it, and I wasn't sure if it could be done. And yet, that was the heart of my plan. As night would give me cover, the way of the wind was the only way out, and the time was now or never. I climbed back aboard *Windigo*, snugged up the stern line, and dove below for my charts. There, bathed in red light and dripping, I scanned the chart with a wet point of view, sneering at depths that would stop a boat cold and wondering what speed a windsurfer makes when he's flying blind in the dark of night.

Day or night, Malawali is charted just below the dog's jaws; east and down a bit, looking more like a falling scrap of meat than a coral fringed island. Chartwise, it is the first, and by far the largest of the scraps they call "the Eastern Dangers." Reefs and tiny islets lie scattered out here, some high enough to support palm trees, others awash with the tides. In all I counted ten islets within the zone to the east of me: ten cays and twice as many detached reefs.

I stood under the spell of my chart then, thinking like a sailor and striking off tacks. With the wind blowing just north of east, I figured I could make a dozen miles to weather that night—enough to cover the zone out east, but not to run Malawali. I would strike a path that zigzagged the zone, tacking away to the east-most island before rounding up for home. I had measured the angles to get me there, avoided the reefs, and included the islets, when all of a sudden my mind shut down with a thought that upended my planning. How was I to navigate out there, when all I could do was barely hang on? It's wet and wild the way I do it, and as for time to navigate, well, it's "line of sight" at the best of times and "by-guess and by-golly" the rest. No, the trick would be to work the wind east, doing nothing but looking for light—stars at first, but better an island with kerosene lights and everyone sleeping—the simpler it sounded the better.

I left the chart table to get ready, knowing the breakers were waiting to test me the moment I broke for the open. Speed was the answer, right from the start, and I wondered if I still had the touch. I threw together some last minute gear, pitched in a flask of water, and set to rigging my mast and sail, all the time hearing that rumbling sound, and wishing I had it behind me.

It was a darker night when I set out, the clouds having gathered a bit. My moonlit path lay strewn in shadows, a river of black at my feet. I hootched along in those first minutes, ghosting a bit on the strength of a wisp, then pumping the sail for more. Slowly, I worked it out into the slot, ripple by ripple, until a sudden chattering of wavelets struck wet at my feet and the wind took hold in my sail. Traversing the shoreline to pick up speed, I was working an angle the beach sailors use; weaving to take the waves on the bow, then easing off for more speed. It carried me down, away from the entrance, far into shallows to set up my exit, then out to where the waves crashed heavy and the reef curved back toward shore. I count myself lucky to have managed that water, because in truth I sailed a reckless line out. The wind blew steady and true that night, the reef broke just as it should.

Outside, I tied in my harness and set to finding the groove; that place where speed and windward stability blend. When found, it is a simple dynamic: a place where speed leads to stability, and stability leads to speed — the more you get, the better it gets. By night, however, it's not so simple. You're convinced you're going faster at night; that's just the way your eye perceives it. You tense up, and it makes the whole thing harder.

I picked up my first piece of land about twenty minutes into my southerly tack. In the moonlight, it showed first as a low silhouette on a gray-black horizon, an island no bigger than a good-sized ship. I sighted no lights on that cay, but as there were palm trees with well-defined spaces, I decided to take a close pass. Coconuts are a cash crop when you see them planted this way, but with no beach, and so little real space, I doubted I'd see any life. It was the first of the uninhabited cays; a farmer's plot and nothing more, so I used it to mark my swing north.

After a while I started to get anxious, and for a moment I thought I had spotted light on one of the scrub covered cays that lay to the east of my line. It was a quick flicking brightness that jumped into view, a pulse, then another, then nothing to lead me on. I veered at first, but in the same fleeting moment a faraway flash of convection-like lightning shone in the very same way. No, I thought, I had come too far to go chasing lightning, so I fell back to the line I was on. I counted two more cays on that northerly tack, both too small for a population, so I didn't give them much time.

My next tack brought results from the very start, as I gained a far better view to the east. Over my shoulder now, a faint light shone in steady cadence, flicking yellow-orange with the passing of each rising swell. It was the first real light of the evening, and it filled me with expectation, flashing as it did, then holding true as I gained the miles that took me past two more cays as I closed on that island, for indeed it was a much larger cay than those I'd seen, and the light was growing in size.

All or nothing, I kept thinking. *All or nothing.*

The focus of my every thought lay with those three words, for it was here that I'd been led — this place, of all places. This place knew all about the big schooner. How could they not have noticed? *Alborak*. They knew her name. They knew the faces. They knew the way it ended.

It was two thirty when I laid down my sail to venture further in. I would swim from here, towing the sailboard and rig to make the last pitch, for there were lights and boats and far too many eyes among the structures that lined that shoreline. This was no outpost. The shoreline was a continuous line of stilts and catwalks and moonlit shadows that dissolved into darkness. I needed to get closer, and yet every stroke was in debate. Electric lighting, galvanized roofing, even a large concrete pier lay before me, so what was it I needed to see? I had no answer at the time, and yet there was no way to stop what I'd started.

I moved on to a position at the outskirts of darkness. Here, well beyond the lighted pier, and away from the anchored boats, a large deep-water mooring float lay ready for the taking. It was the kind of buoy the military use when you see them out on station — restricted to say the very least, but I wasn't there to ask. I tied off and immediately set to scanning the waterfront. At three hundred yards, the nearest lights were those on the pier. Behind them, the silhouettes of inland structures blended with a thousand tree-tops and the natural rise in the island's topography. Down a way, a row of high-strung electric lights lit the kampong roofs where the catwalks connected with land. I saw no movement within the lighted areas, not a soul to speak of, and yet there was an undeniable signal. An inexplicable gleam of highly mirrored light radiated from within the clutter at the far end of the pier. Like a beacon, it seemed to concentrate the light from a nearby lamp post, adding intensity and focus that had no place among the oil drums and pallets and turned over crates. A lens, I thought, but more than a mirror; a curved glass perhaps, because of the highlights. Something polished and bright could make that light, but why would they throw it away? The answer came as quick as the question, though I knew I'd missed with my question.

Out here, nothing gets thrown away: ruptured drums, broken pallets, even rusted car springs get turned into knives. They find a use for everything, though I doubt they think of phone booths. A Plexiglas dome could be most anything, but I doubt they'd use it for phone calls.

The impact of confronting hard evidence had a strange effect on my outlook, for it brought a calming mood to my thinking. The missing crewmen, the bloodied decks; it all seemed removed from what I was seeing. Here I had confirmation of my worst fear, and yet, it put no fear in my mind, not a single thought to what may have happened, only a feeling of nearness that stayed with me right through the swim to the pier.

I had left my sailboard to swim it free, making the distance without a splash and all the time fixed on that gleam. Like a candle on the water, the light drew me in, right to a point where it went out of sight as I passed beneath the pilings. I lay in shadows then, oddly waiting beneath the phone booth, as if someone were about to call down. In one of those moments that transcends time, I waited long for nothing—a lapping of water as it slopped in the shadows, the faraway sound of surf on the reef, a rustling sound like leaves in the wind, and me with my heart in my throat. A deafening sound for a man with no plan, I couldn't think of a single move. To stay; and what? To leave; and what? A shower of heartbeats drummed in my head as I drifted clear of the pilings. To have come so far on the strength of a calling, to get confirmation, and then give up? No. Destiny has too many faces to have it end like that.

I turned toward the land to make my way in, figuring guts would have to carry me now, now that I'd lost my way. Like I've heard them say so many times, "You go on guts, or you don't go at all." The line was burning its way within me. Once, twice, the more I pushed it, the closer I got to making the first stroke in. No more heartbeats, no more waiting, I was just about to go, when a sudden flash of dark and shadow crossed in the light above me. There, backlit and framed, a starved dog walked the edge of the pier, his head dipped low to the concrete. He stopped in the light just above me, and in an almost breathless way, he growled a warning call.

If destiny has faces, then cruel fate is its frown, and doom is its growl. I did a slow motion descent to about five feet, gathered myself, then with all the strength I could muster, I sprinted for open water.

At three o'clock I righted my sail for the run back to Malawali. I was tired and thankful for a downwind leg. With twelve miles to make—downwind wouldn't be so bad—an hour or so by my best guess. I reckoned the sun would have caught me out if I'd stayed, though the thought played hard in my mind. The dog, after all, had never barked, and I might have misunderstood.

I ran a dead straight line on that leg back, taking a westerly course that never varied, for I had only to check the line on Polaris to make the most of that run. At ninety degrees on the starboard bow, I had given away the thought of islands, to go on a light I knew. A fitting end, I thought at the time; to leave with a friend as steady as this; it made my case for leaving. I had my eyes on the stars from that moment on, and I almost missed seeing the light.

It started like a pop of phosphorescence, a mere snap of brightness in the space around me, a pulse and nothing more. I recall the look of white in my wake, but thinking nothing of it. A while later it happened again, and I thought of the lightning that I'd seen earlier; a shower up on Kinabalu, not enough to turn. It wasn't till a third stroke lit white in my sail that I thought to look to my left. There, in the convergence of the cloud covered mountains and the blackened shoreline, an instantaneous flick of white light burst low on the near horizon. Once, twice, and again, like a strobe on a dance floor, it pulsed a blinding shock of clearness that froze the moment and framed a view of white-lit cloud bottoms and a demon-like figure in space. For there, within a sudden circling arc of Xenon flashes, a human form cartwheeled in space, whirling a rope and spinning about until all of a sudden, it stopped.

I'll never know whether it stopped before or after I fell. Either way, the lights went out and I had to swim to recover my board. I remember treading water and spinning in darkness, frantic to find the source of that light, and praying for one more flash.

"South!" I choked, "I was looking south, damn it!"

I snapped my head to pick up Polaris, and in the moment it took to get my bearings, a quick beam of light struck in from the south. A softer light, this one flicked with the look of a searchlight, scanning the distance, then shutting down. On, then off, as it swung lighting wave tops and piercing the night, I couldn't decide if it was searching or signaling until at last it turned on itself. Up and down the beam swung now, drawing a line with a measured swing that flashed on the sand and lit in the trees. Over and over the call went out, flashing strokes that burst from the shore, a mere cry away in darkness.

"Billeeee! Billeeee!" Like the far away sound of a seabird's shriek, a voice flew out on the wind. A call and a plea, more sound than words; I wasn't there to question. I snatched up my sail and drove for the light, knowing this call was mine. "Billeeee!" she called from the depths of shadows where her light soon found my sail. "Billeeee!" she screamed as I closed.

I raced to meet her in waist deep water, dumping my sail as her light flicked off, and taking her quick in my arms.

"I thought you'd never come," she trembled. "Why did it take so long?"

She held me fast in a feverish clasp, her breath and pulse at my ear. "Where were you?" she moaned in a weakened voice, "I could have died out here, you know."

She lowered her arms as she went to pull back, running her hand the length of my back as she gathered herself to speak. "I wasn't sure if you ..."

Her voice stopped on a curious note, while her hand fell quick from my side.

"I had no way to know," I turned to say. But before the words had left my mouth, she lurched away to the side.

"Kim?" she cried in disbelief. "Kim?"

Her eyes shone wide in the shadowy moonlight, her china blue hue awash. She struggled for words she couldn't find, then biting her lip, she shook like a leaf. "Is there nowhere I can hide?" she blurted, frantic to steady herself. "Is there nowhere you can't find me?"

Her eyes let go a stream of tears, as we faced each other in silence. Tears and moonlight, after so many miles, who would have guessed my reply? She opened her arms and I took her in, empty for words that could answer.

I was anxious to get away that night, never mind what should have been said. For having judged her strength on the warmth of her hug, I was quick to press for leaving. We had miles to make before we could talk, no matter what was said, and the fact that she had strength to hold — well, daylight was only two hours away and the wind was right for travel.

We made Malawali under cover of darkness, jettisoning the sail to surf the breakers, for they were more than I could manage. Daylight came as we climbed aboard.

"We won't make it out in waves like that," I groaned. "They're just too big right now."

I had boarded ahead of Jill and was offering a hand up, fully expecting a look of worry as I helped her to the rail. After all, she'd spent a horrible week hiding on that island, and the thought of staying even a moment longer would surely cause her fright. And yet as she took my hand to steady her climb, she seized the moment as only she could. "Kim," she whispered, all breathless and drenched. "If that was the moonlit sail you promised, I'm not so sure I'll accept it!"

It was, as always, her winning way, and were my name the one she'd called, my smile would have turned to laughter.

"You look tired," I clipped while turning away. "Let's get into something dry. We'll rest a bit for now."

We went below and I broke out towels, wrapping her shoulders with the first one out, then handing her one for her hair. She sat at once, hunched and bedraggled, and for one very long moment she hid her face in the towel. "We'll be lucky to get out of here," she whispered, solemnly raising her head. "They know this place too well."

"Then we'll leave right now," I snapped. "To hell with the waves. You want to go? I'm game, let's go!"

"No," she shrilled. "Don't be silly, Kim. They're way too big for leaving. No, we'll have to wait. We can't afford a mistake right now."

"Mistake?" I raged. "Mistake? Hell, I got in here in the dead of night! Drove the whole thing blind! Now you think I can't get us out of here? Well, it's a risk I'm willing to take! Now," I said moving for the cockpit. "RIGHT NOW!!"

"Kim!" she cried in a sudden burst that brought her to her feet. "What's happening to us here? I wasn't questioning your way with a boat, and I'm not here doubting your judgment! Please," she begged. "Please sit down."

I'd gone without rest since my night in Tawau, and perhaps it was showing right now. "Jill," I jeered. "Do you have ANY idea what's happened out there? Your boat's been ransacked. There's blood all over the place. Everyone's missing, and if they're not dead yet, they'll probably wish they were. 'Cause if the Moros didn't get 'em, then the military will!! Jill, the lid's come off this thing completely. It's time to cut and run."

I was half way up the companionway steps, ready to start up the engine and go, when Jill put an end to it all. "Aren't you forgetting something?" she asked in an almost flippant tone. "You're here," she announced.

"I'm here," she went on. "Now, doesn't that tell you something?"

"Yeah! It tells me you don't know how lucky you are."

"No. It tells ME, I didn't underestimate you. Don't you see? Kim, it's not over, it's just beginning! We've got a chance to have it all!"

Her eyes were lit in a sparkling sheen, blue to depths that swallow men whole. "Come back," she whispered in her softest voice. "Please ... We'll need all the rest we can get."

She'd struck a chord with the skill of a master, leaving me stalled on the steps.

"Why did you think I was somebody else?" I posed. "Answer me that if you can."

"How do you call an angel?" she countered. "Do you whistle when you want him to come?"

I was in over my head, lost for words from the very start and now too beat to question. She'd won the day, she'd won the minute, and she'd won whatever she wanted.

"Kim," she said while steering me back. "The fact that you're here is what matters. Nothing beyond that matters."

She sat me down with a tender pat.

"You know it's incredible," she said. "The way things happen. The yin and the yang, you know. The light and the dark, the right and the left, and at the core of each is its opposite — the white spot in the dark lobe, the black spot in the white; all together and all in opposition. I mean you're being here. Kim, you are the part of me that never speaks — the closest thing to my heart."

She stood above me in a most gentle way, her hands moving up to her collar. Then taking her time she began to undress, all the time fixed on my eyes. Blue of blues: the blue of truth in a sailor's eye, how many shades are there? Her blouse fell wet as I struggled for answers, only to fall to distraction. We spent the next eight hours together at rest, both having spent our reserves.

To say that I fell hard, well, that would understate the way I slept, for it was for me a time of total detachment. I remember nothing of the passing of time, only the moment of waking. I was alone in the aft cabin, still in the twilight of sleep when a clicking sound from the forward cabin brought me to my senses. An odd sound I thought; metal on metal, with the sound of precision. I just couldn't place it then. I lingered a bit as if nothing had happened, then reaching for Jill and finding her gone, I thought to go forward to see.

She had her back to the passage as I came through and it caused her to spin in her tracks. "Did I wake you?" she asked in a casual turn that stopped me dead in the passage.

She held my rifle in the crook of her arm, barrel down, the way you would. "I thought you only saw these in Africa," she laughed, tipping the gun for effect. "A pre-64, Model 70 if I'm not mistaken. 375 HH Magnum. The biggest bore Winchester ever made. Quite a collector's piece, Kim."

She laid the gun down as she went to the galley. "The wind is down, you know. Would you like coffee?"

My instinct took me directly to the gun as I wondered how she'd found it. I'd always kept it deep in hiding, that is, until the other night with Bert.

"Coffee?" she pressed.

She seemed too fresh for the circumstance, given the shape we were in. "How long you been up?" I asked.

"You left the gun loaded, you know. You even had one in the chamber. I hope you know that's risky."

"Risky? Did I hear YOU say risky?"

"Well, of course. I mean, loaded guns are ... Well, you never leave one in the chamber. That's how accidents happen."

I had to laugh at the irony of it, coming from where she'd been. To be lectured on risk by someone so vulnerable; I had to control my reaction.

"Okay," I joked. "Then let me add one more to the list, if you would ... You can never be too careful around guns, okay? It's amazing how often they go off."

She took the line in stone silence, measuring the intent of my words with a narrowing look in her eyes.

"You think they're all dead, don't you?" she whispered. "You think I got them shot."

"I didn't say that."

"The implication is there."

"Well, what am I supposed to think? There was blood all over the decks."

"Fish blood! It was fish blood! Did anyone bother to test it?"

"You lost your boat!"

"We'll get it back!"

"Jill," I exploded. "What the hell is going on? This is the Balabac, damn it! You're in MALAYSIA!!"

"And you're here to get me out ... Right?"

"That's right, damn it. I'm here to get you out," I sputtered.

"So, what's the problem?" she countered. "Are you SO surprised to be here that you don't know you were called? Kim, I once told you I'd not underestimate you. Well, I don't think I have."

I was so put off by her change in tack, words failed to come to my lips.

"You don't give yourself credit," she went on. "Yours is a calling. Beyond navigation, and way beyond a mere hunter's. Kim, you are the primordial seeker of truth. But like it or not, to you, the truth is not an answer. To you, '*the quest*' is truth. It's the act, Kim—the seeking. To you, the quest is truth."

"Truth?" I echoed. "You're getting a little beyond yourself, aren't you?"

"No, I'm dead serious, Kim. I had to plan a finish."

"What?"

"I mean it was you or Billy," she clipped. "But in the end it was both. I couldn't be sure; you know?"

"No, I don't know! I don't know what you're talking about, Jill!"

"Kim, this is the finish! Don't you see? The portfolio of shots up in Thailand; the ones we shot aboard *Nighthawk*? Kim, you saw the dive site then. You saw the skyline, you saw the salvage, and whether you knew it or not, you were given the truth."

"The truth? You don't know how lucky you are."

"Kim, it's called a blind contingency, and there's more than luck involved."

"I don't care what it's called. You didn't need to test me. You could have told me outright. I'd have come the minute you called."

"I didn't know I would need you!"

"You didn't know? Jill, this is Malaysia!! You can't be here!! None of you can be here. My God!! After what they did to you up in Lamut, this is suicide!"

"Kim, you couldn't know what happened up there. The truth was never told."

"I read the papers, Jill. I went to the library and read all about it."

"You read what they printed! Did it tell how we got the boat back? Did you wonder how we got off so lightly? Lawyers maybe? Kim, they could have thrown away the key and our lawyers would have cheered. The truth is, our gutless wonders never even voiced our case. All they wanted to know was how much money they could get off us. What'll it take, you know? 'You're out of business,' they said to me. We'd forfeit the *Nighthawk*, throw in some money, and maybe, maybe they'd be able to bargain for jail time. Well, I wouldn't stand for that. No way! It was a shakedown right from the start, and I knew there was someone behind it. Someone had it in for us."

"But, you were being held with the crew, right?" I asked.

"No, I came over after the seizure. But before I arrived, I stopped in Hong Kong to meet with a collector I know. Kim, this is a small world I work in. Collectors know one another. It's global, you know? So, my friend tells me of a certain man; a collector from Sandakan of all places, says he's buying everything in sight. So, before I go down the peninsula, I stop in Borneo for a visit with Mr. Lim."

"Kim, this man turned all the keys! And fast! It was like he had been waiting for me. In three weeks he'd cut the deal to get us off. 'A slap on the wrist,' he called it, 'except for immigration.' He had no pull with them."

"He did this out of friendship?"

"No, not at all," she grimaced. "There was a price — a big one you can be sure. First, he wanted our inventory list; the write-ups on the salvage we had taken. Then, he wanted our valuations. With that, he got started, but I knew he'd want more. There had to be more."

"In the end, it was a charter he was after. He wanted the *Nighthawk*: free of course, fully crewed, and virtually open-ended. That was the price we had to pay. THAT'S what got us off."

"You mean ...?"

"Kim, those pieces you called 'The Halliburton Collection' — the ones you saw up in Thailand? Those pieces came from right out there, not a half a mile from here. And the photos — the wet ones you saw in the folio? Those were shot right here. Now why do you think I let you see them? Do you see I had no choice? I couldn't get you directly involved; you would have tried to stop it!"

"You're saying you were up here before you met me. Is that right?"

"Kim, we made the run right after they let us out of Lumut. It was too early of course, but they wanted to get started. Mr. Lim's orders, you know. They put armed guards aboard and told us to go! That was it. So, we fueled in Brunei, took on some guides, and made the run up here. The locals knew the approximate site so we didn't waste much time. But after a week, it was obvious to everybody that we needed some specialized gear, what with the size of the site. So they let us return to Singapore. The guards never left, of course."

"That's why nobody could leave your boat!" I shouted. "You were under house arrest!"

"Kim, this whole thing has been done at gun point. Do you see why I couldn't tell you?"

I had questioned the reality of everything: her lies, her misdirects, her manner of managing questions. It all was explained by that one line, and for me it was a complete revelation. And yet, rather than being brought to the light, it caused me to question the way I'd been thinking.

"You've got to let me make it up to you," I blurted. "I should have known."

"How could you?" she whispered.

"I should have listened better. You were telling me in everything you did and said. I was a fool," I groaned. "Next you're going to tell me Drucker is your half-brother, right?"

"Billy? I thought I already had."

"Oh, Christ," I moaned.

"You mean you thought we were ...?"

"Look," I said, regaining my focus. "You've got to let me do what I'm here to do. Forget how long it took me to get here. I'm sorry. I'm really sorry I didn't figure it out. But now I know. I'm going to get you out of here," I said, taking her to the cockpit. "You've waited long enough."

Up on deck, afternoon shadows covered the mangrove lagoon. It was past four and only the higher foliage was receiving direct light. Around me, jet-black water and a darkening thicket had already closed out the day.

I looked around to judge the wind; saw enough to worry, and in an instant, I stepped over the rail to board my sailboard. I had to know the height of the seas while there was still some light to see.

"What are you doing?" Jill asked as she suddenly appeared above me.

"We're leaving!" I announced with a parting shove. "I've got to check the entrance first, just to be sure you know?"

I was gone before another word, already figuring the time was short, as dusk was about to set in. I would need some light now, a little bit later, and then none at all after that. I figured the timing as anyone would, knowing the moment when twilight dies, and rushing to get there in time.

I paddled out hard, then back with vengeance, bypassing my boat to get to my stern line, then back to begin hauling chain. It was all a maneuver to end up in darkness, just as we made the last wave.

"Crank her up!" I called as I climbed up the lifelines. "We're outta here the minute the anchor comes up!!"

I ran forward expecting all kinds of commotion as Jill picked up on my mood. Could she start the motor? It didn't matter because I had the anchor up in no time flat, and it wouldn't have saved but a minute.

"Okay," I called, running back to the cockpit, "we're going to start the motor and I'm going to need your help. Jill? Jill?"

I was blindly reaching for the starter key, knowing my boat was completely adrift and worried about how she'd start. "Jill?" I called again.

I ducked my head to view down below while still reaching for the keys. "Jill?" I called while fingering blindly. "I need you up on deck!"

Her appearance and the coincidence of the missing keys struck in a single turn of balance, for as she came into view, so did the keys.

"We're not leaving till it's done," she said, showing the key in her hand.

"The anchor's up!" I shouted. "Now gimme the keys, will you?"

"We're not leaving till it's done, okay?"

She put the key in my outstretched hand. "Promise me Kim, or I'm getting off NOW!"

"Look!" I shouted. "We need the light to run the breakers!! It's now or never, damn it!"

"Then promise, damn it!! Or I swear I'll ..."

"DONE!!" I yelled as I twisted the key. "Now get up on deck and help!"

I was beside myself in a wrenching mood: wanting to fight and struggle for the sake of our safety, and yet willing to lose at once. I knew there was more—I knew from the start—the question was where it would end.

I put Jill behind the wheel and quickly went down to start up the SS-80.

"We'll need a minute to warm up the sonar," I called back. "Just idle her out while I get things set. I'll be up and down after that."

"You mean you're not going to drive?"

"I'll be there once I get us lined up. Just turn when I ask you to turn, okay? Stay dead center till then."

I figured she'd handle the early part out, at least till we saw the breakers. At that point I'd get a bearing off the screen, and we'd run the trench with everything we had—of course, with me at the helm. And yet, as I put on the headphones and went to the screen, an odd sensation of speed and vibration suddenly swept into the boat.

"What are you doing?" I called at first, for she'd set the speed too fast. "I can't get a reading when we're moving like this. You'll have to slow down," I shouted.

I had switched the range settings, varied the sector spread, and dithered the volume, all in a fright to catch up. "Slow down!!" I shouted. And yet there was now more noise than before. Had she panicked at the sight of the oncoming waves? Was it time for me to come up? I threw down the headset and burst to the cockpit just as she opened the throttle.

"Hang on!" she called as the bow lifted sharply. "We're gonna get wet on this one!"

I looked up from low on the cockpit sole just as the wash came down. The bow plunged, the cockpit filled, and there was Jill all smiles.

"We've been running this entrance for most of a month!!" she laughed. "You should see it when it really gets rough!"

I will never forget the look in her eye as she fought with the wheel after that, for just as any brave face can smile, this one had fire and demons to burn. She went at the wheel with mad conviction, pushing me off when I came to help, and lunging to spin it with force. Into the crest, then on to the next, she never let up for a second. She took three walls of water by my best count, all on the bow and all with control. I had to wedge myself in to help.

"You don't back down!" I cheered at the finish. "Nicely done!!" I crowed. "Nicely done!" But rather than join in the moment's triumph, she ordered me off in a rage.

"I've got the helm!" she roared "Stand off!"

"Give me a break!!" I snapped.

We found ourselves locked eye to eye, both on trial at once.

"We're not leaving!" she cried.

"Give me the wheel, damn it."

She gave up the helm with guarded indifference, almost as if she'd caught herself out, but more likely it was something she saw. A weakness perhaps, but I'll never know; her eyes never blinked even once.

"We're going back to where you found me," she ordered. "Set a course for that island back there."

"Look!" I exploded. "Do you think I'd leave your crewmen behind? Of course we're going back. Christ! Just give me the right to be at the helm when I sink my boat, damn it. That's all I'm saying here!"

"Then take us back, will you?"

I couldn't understand the drama before me. Her eyes had gone cold as she glared. Of course we were going back. Did she think me a coward at this late date?

I gave the pilot a rough course to go on, then set to plotting our passage. From below now, the chart showed five miles dead to weather—an hour to make the lee.

"I'm not sure how close I can get us," I began. "Maybe as close as here," I said, jabbing a point on the chart. "We'll need an hour to get there. That makes it seven-thirty. Right? Now, we'll need to get them aboard fast, because the moon comes up between ten and eleven. You with me? I want to be past here — on our way out when the moon comes up. Because it will take another three hours to cross the bay and we'll need to be far from land to run in moonlight. Right? So, let's see. That gives us, one, two ... We've got an hour and a half, once we get there. Otherwise, the moon's gonna catch us out. Now! Are these guys in shape to swim? Jill, how many guys are we talking about?"

"We're not leaving till it's done."

"No question about it. How many are we talking about?"

"Zero"

"What do you mean, zero?"

"Zero, Kim. There are zero people on that island and none of them can swim. Is that clear?"

"God damn it, Jill! God damn it!!" I shouted, slamming my hand on the chart. "This is the Balabac, damn it!! You don't hang around up here unless you want trouble. Do you want trouble, Jill? Is that what you want?"

"I want what I left on that island. That's all there is to it, Kim."

"Green Fever, damn it!! That's what this is all about. You've lost your boat, you've lost the crew, and now you're ready to lose it all!! And for what? A bloody grave robber's treasure, damn it! That's what this is all about, isn't it?"

"Wrong!" she scolded. "Wrong on all counts. Number one: I didn't lose the *Nighthawk*. It's under contract to a Philippine university right now, and they have international approvals to do research in the Sulu—all signed and sealed by the Philippine and Malaysian Governments; we'll get the boat back. Two: the crew is alive and safely out of Malaysia; I'm sure of that. And three: we weren't working grave sites, damn it; we were just doing what had to be done."

"Then leave. Right now. Prove me wrong on everything."

"You know I can't, Kim. And you wouldn't be here if I could. We're front line players, you and me—yin and yang, the black and the white. We've both got something to prove. You wouldn't be here if it was just for me. There's more going on than that."

She had stolen my fire with an insight so brazen, the truth took my breath away.

"The sum is greater than its halves," she whispered. "We're here because we're whole."

She knew my shadow in the dead of night, what more can I say than that?

On deck, reality was the fear of being seen, for even though twilight had faded fast, an eerie loom remained. It lit the spray a ghostly white and bloomed fluorescent in the churn of our wake, haunting our every move. We sat apart then, both having taken to the opposite side, as if on watch in a fog. The mood was thick with apprehension when I broke in to speak.

"You did the right thing back there," I said, motioning back to the lagoon. "You got us out like a pro."

She let my words pass clear into silence, choosing to stay with a faraway look that kept her thoughts in shadows.

"That's a compliment," I went on softly. "You know how to get what you want."

She let that one go as well.

"Look," I begged. "I don't know how you know me so well. But I'm flattered to be in your mind. Believe me. It's *my* pleasure to be here, and don't ever think any different."

On that note, she swung around to face me square. "Kim," she began, "things could get a little sticky from here. I mean, there's more going on than you ..."

"Let me guess," I broke in. "You forfeited the fakes, didn't you? You pulled a switch. You knew they were setting a trap from the start, back when they made you persona non-grata. You knew they would seize the boat. So you re-flagged in Cypress, set up an overlapping charter behind their backs, and made them a treasure in fakes. That's what you were doing up in Thailand, wasn't it?"

"Kim, it was the military and Lim, working together. They skimmed most of what they took off us in Lumut, I mean stuff started showing up in Hong Kong less than a week after I turned over our valuations."

"Just the thing you wanted, right?"

"Well, it was a better opening than what the lawyers were offering, that's for sure."

"A stroke of fortune," I countered. "Considering the circumstances, you couldn't have planned it better. But how did you get the crew out of here? Jill, they wouldn't have just let them go ... not the military."

"That's just what they did! And it made good sense when they did it. They were all persona non grata; the whole crew. Plus, they all had criminal sentences pending. If they were killed, there'd be questions from the State Department. If they took them in, there'd be an investigation. But, if they let them go—no questions, no investigation. And ask yourself, who among the crew would want to talk? Wouldn't they be admitting to the same crime that got them expelled?"

"So, they just let them go?"

"Oh, Kim. You'd have to know the set up. They had us working out of the lagoon back there, running native skiffs and pump boats out to the site—all day, every day. *Nighthawk* was pinned down, literally lashed in the mangroves to keep her masts from moving. Security was big. They had us wearing sarongs and head wraps, even though the locals knew what was going on. My God, did they know. They were in our way from the very beginning, wrecking the dive site whenever we turned. Why, they had to bring in a Navy patrol boat just to police the locals! Can you believe that?"

"Sure, I saw their mooring just last night. Did you know they've got your Plexiglas dome laying on the pier over there? I almost went ashore when I saw it."

"Thank God you didn't, Kim. Those are the guys I worry about most. I mean, they would have killed us all once the salvage started surfacing. It was a frenzy only the Navy could stop. And we were real lucky to have them around because you know, in the end, when the site started trailing off? They were the ones who kept the locals from raiding the *Nighthawk*. That would have wrecked the whole thing."

"You mean nobody told you about the Moros? Jill, I think I might have said something. Didn't I?"

"Come on, Kim, you do what you have to do."

"So, in the end, the Navy kept the operation alive?"

"Not really. In the end, they moved the patrol boat out in front of the lagoon entrance as if they were protecting us, but in fact, we knew it was a blockade. They had doubled the guards only a few days earlier, so it was really not a surprise. They moved in at sundown, guns raised, the whole bit; but you know, I wasn't even there. And they never noticed. That's how confident they were throughout the whole thing. For them, the double cross was a tactical coup — the perfect maneuver — and besides, they had planned a pretty good finish. The Sulu pirates would give them all the cover they needed; if only our crewmen were given a head start, to clear the area you might say."

"They put our guys to sea that night, gave them ten seconds to throw some gear in the skiffs, then made them run the breakers."

"But you say you weren't there?"

"Look, we had months to plan this thing. And, we knew they wouldn't kill us. Really, their plan was too tight for that. But whatever the case, we had a boat ready to go up in the Philippines, only hours away when called. That's how I know the crew is okay. Billy had that set up from the start."

"But what about you? You arranged yourself to be left behind?"

"Kim, I was the only one who had no jail time pending. Don't forget, I wasn't aboard when they took *Nighthawk* the first time. Immigration got me on association, nothing more. So, if anybody were to be left behind, it had to be me. I got no argument on that. In fact, I insisted."

"So, you've been hiding on that island ever since they seized the *Nighthawk*? Jill, that's a week. No, it's more! How did you do it?"

"We had time to set up. You see, we drove past the island every trip out to the dive site. We used to skirt the shoreline. So when the opportunity presented itself, we put a man overboard just as we passed. He swam in, checked it out, and later we picked him up on the fly. Snatched him right out of the water, we did. We got away with it all the time because they only used a couple guards out at the site, and those guys never rode in the service launches. We had time to work the place up, and I ended up with most everything I needed: a climber's tent, water, supplies. We did it bit by bit."

"Well, I hope you're not going to tell me we're going back for the tent," I joked.

"No, I'm not going to tell you that," she smiled. "We're going back for the salvage, just like you said."

"So, you switched it then? You actually traded them fakes! Right under their noses!"

"Literally," she laughed. "And you should have seen the way we did it! After every day out, the pump boat would return to the lagoon to lay alongside *Nighthawk* for the night—guarded of course—they never let up on that. So, as nothing got cleaned at the site, our boats weren't big enough for that, we'd start the cleaning process as soon as we got in. We'd take the stuff from the pump boat and put it right into a chemical bath, all right under their noses. Of course, we had other staging-tanks, so during the night the pieces would be fussed with a bit; enough to give us cover. So, as you'd guess, the guards were there watching, but really, they were only interested in the finished pieces. So, whenever we wanted to make a trade, we'd mix a fake in the staging-tanks. They were so determined to guard what we brought out, they never thought to check what we were putting in. It was a classic 'now you see it, now you don't mix-up,' and we got so good at it, we had to bite our tongues to stop from laughing."

"So," I chuckled. "You made the switch and all we have to do is drive up to the island and load the stuff aboard! That shouldn't take much time. Jill, you've thought of everything!"

"That's right, but don't think it's going to be that simple. Kim, we had to plan a way to get the stuff out to the island. We had to hide it very well out there. And then we had to make it easy to retrieve — at night, and with as few people as possible. We couldn't bury it, we couldn't camouflage it, nor could we be seen carrying it, and so we simply dumped them."

"You dumped 'em? You dumped them overboard? With floats, of course."

"No floats, Kim. We couldn't risk the floats being seen."

"Jeeesus, Jill!! Are you saying you want me to dive for that stuff?"

"That was the plan."

"Well," I sputtered. "Well, I'm too breathless to speak. I mean ... Were you thinking my sonar would spot the stuff? Jill, there's no way on earth it will do that. No way! I don't get that kind of definition. Nobody does. I would have thought you knew that!"

"Of course I know that."

"Then how do you expect me to find your stuff? Have you ever made a night dive? I mean, do you know how dark it is down there at night?"

"You're not afraid of night dives, are you?"

"Of course not. It's just that it's hard to know where you are at night. A search is almost impossible."

"I know that too. But what if I could lead you there—a guaranteed hit—and without a wasted moment? Would you be willing to dive?"

"Of course. But without floats marking the spot, I can't think how we're going to do it."

"Trust me, Kim. We planned this part down to the finest detail. You see, we've always known we'd have to give up the *Nighthawk* to make this thing work. So, the question of stashing the salvage was fundamental.

If we couldn't do it, we wouldn't have a plan. So believe me, we thought this one through."

"We used oil drums. You know those 55-gallon drums? Well, we use them for lots of things on *Nighthawk*. They carry lube-oil and diesel, but we also use them for underwater lifting too. They're real handy so we carry a lot of them."

"You packed the stuff in oil drums?"

"That's right. Back in Singapore, we made up some with removable bottoms — screw on bottoms. It wasn't hard to do."

"So, you hid the new stuff in oil drums ..."

"That's right, and when the service launches were loaded to run back and forth to the dive site, we'd always be hauling drums: fresh water for the crew, diesel for the generators and pumps, gas for the outboards, and every once in a while, the occasional load of antiquities. That's how we got it off *Nighthawk*. Then, we just rolled the drums overboard when we skirted the island. It couldn't have been easier because we never slowed down."

"But Jill, that doesn't tell me where they are! Without markers we're lost, damn it."

"Kim, we solved that problem with fishing line; big, heavy test fishing line, and lots of it! Every time we dumped a barrel, we sent a swimmer overboard with it. Our guy would swim directly to the beach spooling fishing line from one of those big hand-line spools you see the locals use. They're as common as coconuts up here. Once in, he'd slip ashore and bury the spool up by the trees. Kim, we've got a thousand-pound monofilament guide line going to every one of our barrels!!"

"So, we dig 'em up and reel 'em in, do we?'

"That's it! But you'll have to dive to air the lift-chutes. You can do that, can't you? They've all got little lift-chutes, rigged and ready to go."

"No question I can do it, but how many are we talking about? This could take some time, you know."

"We got six to do—all off the northern shore but not so far out. If we do each one individually, it's a half hour apiece. We've worked it out. Kim, I'm asking for three hours. If we go at it, we should be on our way out before the moon comes up."

"Barely," I clipped. "We'll just be getting the anchor up."

"Then we'll make the run in moonlight," she countered. "It's a fitting end, don't you think? After all, we've always known we'd end up in moonlight. Did you think it could be any different?"

Her words belied the seriousness of what she was suggesting, for a moonlit run was anything but fitting. But, by seven-thirty she'd moved the conversation beyond tactical planning, and a scramble for gear and setup was under way. It had been decided that the recovery would involve separate efforts, and that Jill would manage the guidelines by herself. She alone would take the skiff into the island. She would dig up the spools and, one by one, reel to a position directly above the target. My job was to get the boat anchored up wind, put out a float line, and swim to meet her at the target. The float line would serve mainly as a safety line due to the current, but once over the barrel, I was to hand it off to Jill who would use it to hold position while I made my descent. The recovery would involve towing the inflated lift harnesses back to *Windigo* where the whole apparatus would be brought aboard. All that being said, the entire process was to be executed with a minimum use of flashlights: a blink to signal ready, a blink to answer back. So it was that the first barrel came aboard in just under an hour.

We streamlined the process by leaving the scuba tank in the skiff so that I did most all of the surface swimming free. That saved a good fifteen minutes on the second barrel. On the third, I let Jill go in without asking for help on the hoist. That got it down to a half hour, but by then we were horribly late. The moon broke the horizon as I hoisted the fourth, and thereafter we didn't need flashlights.

Light rolled in on the back of darkness, a sheen on jet-black waters. We were silhouettes now, and the fear of being seen was real as never before. Away in the distance you could see Jill moving in on the fifth target, her body bent as she pitched along, reeling for all she was worth. Behind her, the scrub covered cay lay dark on the skyline, just as it had when I'd seen it the first time, but now from a different angle. Jill waved and I dove in thinking. Perhaps because it bothered me still, I wondered how she'd planned it all, only to be surprised when I showed up. Had her brother been waiting and failed to come? Perhaps it was moonlight that kept him away.

I swam to meet her above the fifth barrel, where, upon passing the float line, I mentioned the moonlight, only to get a quick smile. She lowered the scuba tank without saying a word, and I had the entire dive to ponder my question. Was she unaware of the danger around here? Or, had she planned a way around that as well?

The fifth barrel rose like all the others, but this time I chose to ride in the dingy rather than swim the way back.

"If it gets any brighter, we'll be needing sunglasses," I began, tossing my mask to her feet. "You ever seen anything like it?"

"It's just your eyes, Kim. After a night dive, the moon always looks that way. Really, it's not that bad."

"Oh yeah?' I laughed. "I think I can read the name off my transom. Do you see it? I swear I can read it from here."

"Come on, stop it Kim. You're just making me nervous."

"Well maybe that's not so bad. I mean it's time we got on the same wavelength don't you think? It's past three hours, Jill. The moon's up, and we're out here bobbing around, plain as dog's balls, damn it!"

"Calm down, will you? This isn't helping."

"So, what do we do, damn it? Do we run this stuff back to the lagoon and hide out for another day? Is that the plan, Jill?"

"No."

"No? Well, why not? We'll be here till midnight getting the sixth. Don't you think that's pushing it? Look around, we've got no choice."

"It's too dangerous to stay."

"TOO DANGEROUS? It's too dangerous not to hide, damn it. We can be seen for miles out here."

"Kim, why do you think I stayed on this island so long? Why do you think I never called Billy? I had a radio. I could have called, but I didn't. It was too dangerous; he'd never make it."

"And yet, when I showed up, you thought I was him. Jill ..."

"Do you remember back in Si Satch, back when I took you to the kiln? Do you remember those templates; the ones we were using to model our stuff? Well where do you think we got those shapes? Kim, they were taken off the Lumut salvage—the stuff the Navy seized. We were making copies, remember?"

"You mean you forfeited copies of the same salvage they seized back in Lumut?"

"You don't think I'd give them anything of value, do you? When they try to sell the fakes, we'll discredit the whole lot."

"Ah, I get it, another perfect loop, right? But they know, don't they? That's why it's too dangerous. They know you made the switch, and I'll bet they know you stashed the salvage too. That's why you couldn't call your brother. They've been searching, haven't they?"

"It doesn't matter, Kim! We've got it, that's what matters! And in another half hour we'll be on our way out of here! We're whole, you and me—together as FATE would have it. Trust a little, will you?"

A while later the sixth and final barrel lay nested and lashed along the starboard rail. I was anxious as ever, and it bothered me to see my decks obliterated by the barrels, for there was no room for the skiff now and towing it meant a loss of speed, just when we needed it most. Jill had tried to calm me, suggesting we cut it loose, but I couldn't bring myself to do it.

I was tired and drained and a hint of resentment was beginning to show. We upped anchor just past midnight, towing the skiff on a sixty-foot line, giving up speed for spite.

We drove off toward the south side of Malawali, flying a headsail to compensate, and yet, all it did was make me nervous. For though it surely gave us a boost, it raised our profile and blocked our view, adding another anxiety to go with the eyes of night. Stars shone in gossiping clusters, the moon a telltale voice, and all around a night of whispers, betraying our every move.

"Look," I began. "We'll get one last look at the lagoon when we pass, so you decide it there, okay? I'm with you either way, but if you say 'go,' it's 'go,' and there'll be no turning back after that.

"Kim, I already said it's 'go.' We've got no choice, remember?"

"Damn it, Jill," I snapped.

"Damn it what?" she shot back.

"THEY'RE SEARCHING, damn it. Why didn't you tell me back in the lagoon? I could have got us out of here!"

"You still can! You got here in the moonlight. You can get us out."

"That was different, damn it. It didn't get light till I was past the harbor entrance. It was dark then.

Everything is different now. Look around, damn it. They're sure to see us in this kind of light."

"You mean Mitford Harbor? Kim, surely we don't have to get that close. We can run the mainland shore if we have to."

"We can't. Downwind, and with a big current ripping along behind us? We'd be on the bricks before we got started. It's nothing but coral down there."

"Now wait! Wait a minute, Kim. We can do this! You said you saw the gunboat last night on Tingabu, didn't you? So they're not in Mitford Harbor, they're down at Tingabu!"

"I saw the mooring. That's all I saw. The gunboat was nowhere in sight."

"Still, that doesn't mean they're in Mitford. Besides, at this hour they'll be sleeping."

"Don't kid yourself, Jill."

"Then what do we do? We can't go back to the lagoon. With the seas down, they'll be making the rounds. Kim?"

"Go down below. Close all the hatches. Lock 'em! Do the ports too. If they're going to stop us, they'll have to board us, and we're not going to make it easy. Button her up like there's no tomorrow. And keep it dark down there!"

On that note, our course was decided. We would push past the lagoon without looking back, and run the south side close. Then, dousing the headsail in the westward lee, we'd take aim for a straight shot in. Direct to Mitford with a bow-on profile; we'd manage that angle as long as we could, showing as little as was humanly possible, right up to our turn for the open. Straight to the door, then out like a fox; the fronting islands would give us cover when our broadside came into view. That was the plan I'd drawn in my mind, but what happened was nothing so fine.

We were tight as a drum when the sail came down, locked and battened and showing no lights. The western side went flawlessly well, even to find the village lights out, when we made the turn to Mitford. Straight in and charging, right up to the door; we had it all going till the harbor lights showed.

"Kim, there's something moving up ahead. You see it block the lights? It's moving away but ... What do you say we get the gun?"

"Forget the gun!" I snapped. "Jill, I want you below from now on, you hear me? If we're boarded, I want you locked in the aft cabin, okay? We'll be out manned and out gunned, so don't even think about fighting them off. This is a run for open water, nothing more."

I left for the chart table to lay out the plan, leaving the cockpit to drive from below, while Jill came along in silence.

"Come here," I called, showing the pilot control head. "I can drive from down here, so there's no need to be in the cockpit, got it? If hell breaks, we'll lock ourselves in and steer with the pilot, okay? I'll have the sonar on," I said, flicking the switch, "so don't worry about the shallows. Nobody has to go on deck, got it?"

That being said, I turned for approval only to watch her eyes grow narrow as she drew in on the chart beside me.

"I'll con from here," she announced, mounting the companionway ladder. "You drive. I'll be lookout," she said, propping herself in the doorway.

"You didn't hear a word I said!"

"I'll have the door ready if we need it," she snapped. "Till then, I'm the lookout, got it? I'm the one who knows their boat, remember? You wouldn't know what to look for."

I thought of the struggle we'd had in the breakers, back when leaving the lagoon. She'd held me off right to the finish, holding her own all the way.

"All right," I relented. "If it comes to that, that's how we'll do it. But for now, I'll set the courses, damn it. Check her line for the harbor entrance!"

Jill stood tall on the ladder's third rung, raising her head while I measured the turn.

"We'll need to get within a half mile," I shouted. "I don't want to show our profile till the last moment, got it?"

"Kim," she called softly. "I think that boat is heading back for the harbor. He's turned back. That's good, don't you think?"

"He didn't see us, did he?"

"I don't think so."

"Then stay sharp while I figure our course down the channel. I'll need just a minute to work out the run."

At a half mile out, a swing to the southwest would put us directly on top of my original line in—too close for comfort in light like this, but, if we were smart in using the outlying islands, if we were able to turn with the harbor lights blocked, we'd be running away with so little exposure. I could see a glimmer of hope.

"He's just going into the harbor now," she called. "I'm losing him behind the islands."

"Good," I shouted. "We'll make our turn at a half mile out." "NO!" she yelled suddenly. "GO NOW!"

"We're not close enough," I called back. "We need ..."

"Get up here!" she howled. "I think I see the gun boat!"

Her words exploded in the air around me, lifting me straight to my feet. Then madly scrambling for a rung on the ladder, I found myself wedged in the doorway.

"Look!" she breathed without giving me ground. "Dead ahead. He's running across the entrance right now. Do you see the look of that cabin? The hulls are blue and the cabins are white. Do you see him back in the harbor?"

I crowded behind her to gain her vantage, pressing myself to her back.

"He's not coming out though, is he?" she blurted. "He's passing behind the island! Kim, do you think he knows we're out here?"

"I think it's time we turned," I whispered, slipping below as I spoke.

We'd come to the place where hope turns to fear, and the writing gets plain on the wall. For if they were up-and-running at this late hour, they had to know we were here.

I threw my hands across the chart, smoothing the crease to examine the harbor, while delaying my urge to turn. A parallel course would keep our distance, and should they appear in the next island gap, at least we'd be holding our own.

"Aren't you going to turn?" she called. "Come on, we're getting too close!"

"Okay!" I shouted. "Just give me a minute!" And with that I picked up the control head. Ten degrees, twenty degrees, thirty degrees: I was counting my way to ninety, rotating the knob with each spoken count when a light went on in my mind. A thought you might call it, but more like a light, for it showed in my face at point blank range, pulsing for my attention.

"I want you down," I ordered. "Close the door but leave the hatch. We won't be locking it yet."

"What do you mean? We don't really know if they saw us."

"SHUT THE DOOR!" I bellowed. "They're using the southern entrance, damn it. They'll be on us before you know it!"

"THEN TURN, DAMN IT! Let's get the hell out of here!"

"Get the door!!"

The door crashed shut in the blink of an eye as Jill rushed down to my side.

"Why aren't we turning?" she demanded. "Is there something wrong with the pilot?"

"We can't out-run them," I clipped. "We do seven, they do ten, so there's really no point in trying. If we run down the channel, they'll take us for sure."

"So, you're going into the harbor? Kim, is that what we're doing? Are we giving up so soon?"

"We're not going into the harbor, damn it! It just looks that way right now"

I leaped up the ladder to get a last bearing, then carried it back to the pilot.

"We're going to converge at the southern entrance—hopefully with us ahead. If we're close enough," I said while dialing the course, "we'll try to bait him into a chase. It's a sucker play as old as time, but it's the only hope we've got. If he'll follow us round the southern tip, we might have a chance in the coral."

"SONAR!" she burst. "You're going to run them aground in the coral. That's great!"

Her eyes shone wet as she drew in on the chart, bringing her face square into the light that glowed from the sonar hood. Then, turning her head to peer in at the scope, she brushed my face with her hair. Like turning the clock on a quick waft of scent, my mind slipped back to the start. Those china blue eyes, the touch of her hand, and the scent of her hair as she stepped to the landing: I was back where it all began, watching her walk to the top of those steps, the boatman's smile when I turned.

"I really think we've got a chance!" she said, drawing back into the light. "Are we going in down here?"

She had her finger on the four-mile shallows that stream off the southern tip of Banggi.

"That's the plan, but don't get your hopes up. I could put us aground before we get started. It's a bloody labyrinth of coral down there."

"So what do I do? Kim, I've got to help somehow."

"You'll be on the lookout while I'm wearing the headphones. But you must come below the minute they're close, got it? You tell me what side they're on — port or starboard — then lock her up tight. I'll do the rest from down here."

Jill went back to con from the steps, leaving me there with the chart. And though I was frantic to plan our approach, my mind kept playing with the thought of her hair, and the smile that boatman wore. Why was it still so clear in my mind, and why had it chosen this moment to surface? It surely was no comfort.

The motor's roar became incessant as the chart dissolved in my mind. Was he laughing at me because I'd been had? Surely he couldn't know. Then why that smile to mock me now, just when I needed to think?

I left the chart table to pick up my bearings, finding myself parked right behind Jill as we both stood there in the hatchway.

"They're still in behind the island," she whispered, pointing to the passing shore.

"Makes you wish we were faster," I murmured.

"I wouldn't change a thing," she said, pressing in close as she spoke. "I feel very safe with you, Kim. I know we're going to make it."

I took her close with a hug from behind, wrapping her tight in a comforting way while my voice betrayed her intentions. "I wish I could say the same thing," I droned, breathing the words in her ear. "You heard me on the radio, didn't you? You knew I was going to Clifford Pier, the morning before we met. You heard me say I was coming down, that's how you picked me out."

"What? You mean? I don't see that it makes any difference," she said, squirming to turn in my arms. "You think I picked you? Well, I could say you picked me, but the fact that we're here is what matters. I didn't have to turn on the radio that morning, we weren't monitoring any frequencies. Kim, you were the voice that spoke that morning. It's your fate as well as mine."

She gathered herself as she locked on my eyes, peering for understanding. "Don't you see the way it works? We're destined, you and me. That's the reason we've got a chance. Don't you see it, Kim?"

Her eyes had turned to indigo, there in the color-less light. Dark as night and closing in, they pried the depths of all my doubts while tempting my good fortune. To bet on fate in a moment of doubt—why had it come to this?

"I'll tell you what I see right now," I said, shifting my eyes to our stern. "I see this thing coming down to the wire and I pray we're not running late."

I climbed the door that blocked the hatchway, making my way to the throttle control for one last push of speed. "We'll carry this course right up to the coral," I shouted. "Stay sharp while I get some bearings!"

Ahead and to port I could see the sizable island I'd passed on my way up the channel. And behind us now, off Banggi's southernmost point, the off-lying island had just showed its gap, clearing a view up the slot.

"They're on us!" I whispered as I slid in behind her, making my way back down. "We'll know soon enough if they follow us in."

Tactically, we needed a subtle beginning to show ourselves ripe for the taking. Sudden turns, the hoisting of sail; none of that would do. We were there to make it easy, right up to the point of convergence.

I went to the chart and with two measured strokes, I plotted the spot where our courses would meet, assuming they took up the chase.

"They're rounding the point off Banggi!" she shouted. "How long till we get to the coral?"

"Let 'em come!" I yelled. "Let 'em drive right upon our stern, God damn it. The closer they get the better!"

Jill seemed charged by my change in manner, so much that she came to stand at my side, just as I went for the headphones.

"I'll have to put these things on," I said, turning to find her eyeing the chart. "Once they're on," I continued, "I'll be completely tied up with the sonar, so we'll need you up in the hatchway."

"I know the drill," she countered softly. "I'll let you know when they're getting close. Go ahead and put them on."

The engine's roar droned suddenly softer, muffled and lost in the din of echoes that pinged and chirped in my ears. Jill was quick with a parting touch, mounting the steps to the rhythm of chimes as I pulled myself into the screen. Bing-ching, bing-ching, bing-ching, the moment of split awareness had passed; I was wedded to my controls, closing ranges, narrowing sectors, only to switch to the opposite quadrant as the picture evolved in my mind. Mastered and lost in the same passing breath, I was driving in total detachment with time when I felt Jill's hand on my shoulder.

"They're coming in on the starboard side," she breathed, lifting the earpiece to speak. "They followed a bit, then turned on their searchlight. I think they mean to ram us, Kim. They know we're not in the cockpit!"

"Searchlight? Did you say searchlight?"

"Yes!" she howled at point blank range, triggering my turn for the coral.

"Lock her up and stay down low," I shouted, clutching the earpiece for focus. "This is it, God damn it. They're fixed on the light and they won't see the water. We got 'em, Jill. Just wait!"

I went to the screen with my ears ringing wild, watching the targets approach. First one, then another, and on to another; the coral heads charged down the screen. Some too deep, some just right; the point was to thread them as close as I could, baiting the gunboat to damage its props, if not to sink her completely. Then came the coral of denser formation: mounds and ridges that pulsed like lightning, streaking the screen with slashes of brightness that burst to full illumination. This was a minefield of different dimensions, a canyon-like maze in coral. What began on a notion of skimming past targets now turned fast to fear. For with every maneuver to manage the coral, I was losing my sense of direction. Walls appeared in every quarter with me not knowing my way; then all of a sudden, a burst of distraction that wrenched my concentration.

"We did it!" she shouted while snatching my headset. "They just hit off our stern!"

Stunned to the point of numbed reaction, I turned to watch Jill burst for the hatchway without being able to block her. Up she went, right into the fray as I sat by in shock.

"NO!" I raged. "GET BACK ..."

The words had barely left my mouth when the first crack of gunfire rang into the cabin—one, then another, and close.

"Get down!" I bellowed reflexively, ducking my head to the table.

It was then I noticed the flashing screen and a new fear jilted my thinking. A line of coral lay dead ahead, blossoming out in every direction; it forced an instant reaction.

I was jamming the pilot and fumbling the headphones when Jill crashed down the steps.

"Get us out! Get us out!" she shrieked. "We can't let 'em hit the drums!"

All at once I drew in my focus, relieved so much by the voice in my ear, I locked on the screen with vengeance. Coral ahead, coral to starboard, I ran us straight for a blind alley gap, only to find the walls closing in when Jill flew by with my gun.

Up the steps with me in a bind, I desperately lunged to grab her leg as I fought to steady our course. Then into the gap and with nothing to show, my eyes raked over the screen in a panic, searching a break to the open. A line to skirt, a trench to run, I broadened the sector in sheer desperation and turned with the first show of space. A softer light than what I'd been seeing, the headphones literally flew off my head as I raged for the cockpit steps.

What happened next remains uncertain, for my eyes were still in the grip of bright light and not at all ready for moonlight.

I broke to the cockpit bellowing wildly, calling Jill's name in a blind moment's panic while thrashing my way to the helm. Dazed, bedazzled, my vision a mess, I reeled for focus in a dizzying turn that put me square in the searchlight's beam as I braced to find my balance. Where yellow had been the color of brightness, now it burst in stunning whiteness, freezing me quickly in its beam. Lost and gripped in the shock of white, I broke away as if hit by a punch, whirling for cover as gunfire let out and dropping for shelter at once. Up in the light now and dead in my face, a vision of horror danced out of a dream while I lay low in a huddle. Gunshots like lightning, my eyes in the glare, I watched my rifle spit fire at the muzzle and then saw Jill career. A slow-motion twist as she stumbled in space, the rifle in flight as she fell. A desperate grab for the lifelines and then nothing; she was over the rail and gone. I stood up in shock, my hands wildly reaching, when suddenly cracked by a blast at my side, the lights went out in my dream.

Downed and unconscious, I lay in the cockpit, dead to the world as Jill slipped away, for the motor and pilot held steady throughout, driving a line to the depths. Hour on hour and mile after mile, the reefs and the islands would slide by in silence as I lay down in a heap. For as fate is the hunter, I could not turn, and in time it was too late to matter. Night passed to daylight and on into morning with nothing but darkness for me. The lights were out, and there it would end had fate not played the last card.

A trickle of sweat lay pooled in the sunlight, gathering size in the crease of my eye, till suddenly drained by a blink and a wince, the sting of salt brought me back. Out of a darkness that should have been certain, my hand rose up in a light so jarring, it brought everything back in a flash. The sight of her falling crashed in like a deathblow, rolling me across the cockpit floor and leaving me flat on my back. Down again in the heat of bright sunlight, the pain of awareness swept into my body, drawing my focus to dampen the hurt before I ventured a look; for if somehow the drums were a thing of delusion, then daylight might show me okay.

But what if it happened just as it did? And what if the drums were there? Was I to wake to a fate that bleak, after everything I had done? The treasure was only an eye blink away, but so was the pain of knowing.

I opened my eyes to a nightmare in daylight, for there at my feet, wedged right by the helm, my rifle lay splattered by blood. Why had she taken the gun up on deck? Were the drums being hit by their fire? And what if they were, did it make any sense? We had them hard on the reef at the time; did she have to have the last word?

I rolled to my side with the thought of her speaking, recalling the ways she'd worked her will whenever I was around. Why had she had such an easy time, and why could I never stop her?

I got to my knees all grimaced and pained, for the truth was plain to be seen. My part was to do what had to be done, I was there for the final rites: to greet the sun in a void on the ocean and bury the relics for good. I rose to my feet and the shock rocked me back, leaving me clutching the throttle for balance as a wave of dizziness passed. A fated moment lay just up ahead if only my strength would hold.

I hauled back the throttle and made for the kill switch, lurching in fits till my hand made contact there just beside the hatchway. From here I could see the drums as I'd left them, three to a side and racked in the gunnels, laying like bombs on the rail. They had to go, no matter the cost, for the course of fate was obvious now, if only my strength would hold.

The engine died as I slumped for a breather, leaving me seated in stillness and pain as my boat drifted on to a standstill. The sea was calm, the clouds barely moving, and all around there was nothing but the ocean, not even the scent of land. I drew my knife from its slot by the doorway, then struggled to get to the rail. Over the coaming and down to my knees, I was crawling along with the knife in my teeth when the skiff crunched hard on the stern. From sixty feet back it had carried its way, dead to the heart of my transom with force, and the sound stopped me cold in my tracks. A gong-like toll straight out of the blue, it struck like a call from the grave. Was I to stop? Was I to go on? Or was I merely to die at the door, a victim of fate and no more?

I took the knife from between my teeth and rose to make the first cut. No, I wouldn't turn back, not even to look, for the sound was only a noise to be reckoned, and my strength was going fast. I took hold of the lashing and got ready to cut, only to see the knife fall away as a voice from the grave broke in.

"Kim?" she called faintly, "Kim?"

No, I wouldn't turn back, not even to look, for the treasure had no hold on me. I was there to do what had to be done even if it took my dying breath. I reached for the knife, not believing my ears, when the sound of her voice struck again.

"Kim?" she called, "Kim? Are you there?"

The skiff lay sideways to the back of my boat, tucked and close to the transom. With barely a ripple to send it on, it had come to rest with its bow pointing out and its sides just under the stern rail. I mouthed her name as my head turned round, daring a fleeting look to be sure, and catching the bow as it dipped.

She rose from behind with her hands on the stern rail, bracing to stand but losing her hold when her eyes caught sight of my face.

"I called and called," she cried from the transom, "but you never answered back."

She rose again, both hands on the rail, with tears streaming down her face. "The skiff ran me down and I just held on. I wasn't about to let go. I got inside and started to pull, but I never could make any distance. I've been back there since the shooting stopped. Dear God, I thought you were dead."

She worked the skiff round the side of the transom; frantic to get to my side as she wept, she pulled herself up into view. "I knew you were hurt when you didn't turn back. My God, I thought you were ..."

"Me?" I choked. "I saw you fall. I saw the shot take you down."

"No," she wept. "The gun kicked me over. I never was hit. I just fell over, that's all."

She hauled the skiff to the mid-ship rail where she scrambled to get to my side. "You're bleeding badly," I heard her say. "We've got to get you below."

I fell to darkness on a wave of cold sweat that rocked me there in her arms. There I swayed to the heave of her breath—adrift on a faraway sea. Taken to darkness, I drifted in time, away to a world of dreams. And had it ended right there in her arms, then the dreams would have sealed my fate. But as it was she brought me back with china blue tears and a plea. "I'll never forgive myself if you die. Please don't leave me like this."

She cradled my head as the tears spilled forth, a cascade of pure remorse. "I know you were trying to dump the stuff. Dear God, what I've done to you, Kim!"

Her eyes slammed shut in a trembling grimace that wracked her body in shame.

"I'm here," I whispered carefully. "I'm here because I had to be—not because of you."

"It's not that way! You know it's not!! Don't believe the things I've said."

"Look at us now, both wearing wounds. Did you think it would be any different?"

The question lay stuck in the distance between us, a matter of no space at all. The yin and the yang; the black and the white; each with a wound at its heart— the spot of white in the lobe of black—the black in the lobe of white. We'd come full circle in understanding, now that we were whole.